Dear Friends,

I was blessed when I fell into music as a young woman. Before then I'd been independent and unconventional, feeling out of step with the world around me. When I found music, I knew I'd found the place where I belonged. But being famous at eighteen isn't easy, and the chaos of fame can be overwhelming. My life has played on a stage for everyone to see: good and bad, every choice lit with a spotlight.

Restless Heart is the story of another woman called to music at a young age. Destiny Hart discovers her path on a dare—a prank draws her to sing before an audience for the first time, and in that moment, Destiny's life is altered. Success is elusive, and years in Nashville, isolated from her family and friends, have taken a toll on Destiny. And that's when Seth walks back into her life. The boy next door, Seth has always been Destiny's friend, but reuniting as adults brings the two of them closer than ever before . . . close enough that now Destiny has to choose: the man who makes her heart sing or the singing career that makes her feel alive.

I wanted to tell a story of a young woman with her life unfolding before her, facing incredible challenges and incredible opportunities, and making good decisions. A story of dreams and love, of family and friendships, of reaching for the stars and keeping your feet on the ground.

Enjoy!

TAKING THE STAGE

The crowd settled down, watching her....
Don't say anything! Just sing!

Good idea! But her fingers were frozen on the guitar strings and her voice seemed to have taken a sudden leave of absence.

A hush had fallen over the crowd.... Oh, this wasn't good....

Destiny dove into the song, gaining strength and confidence when she had the whole room singing along.... And when she was met with more wild cheers, she learned that connecting with her audience on a personal level was crucial. The amazing thing was that she was being completely honest and simply herself....

And they liked her. Incredible ...

AND DON'T MISS WYNONNA JUDD'S
COMING HOME TO MYSELF

Restless Heart

WYNONNA JUDD

WITH LuAnn McLane

A SIGNET BOOK

SIGNET
Published by New American Library, a division of
Penguin Group (USA) Inc., 375 Hudson Street,
New York, New York 10014, USA

Penguin Group (Canada), 90 Eglinton Avenue East, Suite 700, Toronto,
Ontario M4P 2Y3, Canada (a division of Pearson Penguin Canada Inc.)
Penguin Books Ltd., 80 Strand, London WC2R 0RL, England
Penguin Ireland, 25 St. Stephen's Green, Dublin 2,
Ireland (a division of Penguin Books Ltd.)
Penguin Group (Australia), 250 Camberwell Road, Camberwell, Victoria 3124,
Australia (a division of Pearson Australia Group Pty. Ltd.)
Penguin Books India Pvt. Ltd., 11 Community Centre, Panchsheel Park,
New Delhi - 110 017, India
Penguin Group (NZ), 67 Apollo Drive, Rosedale, Auckland 0632,
New Zealand (a division of Pearson New Zealand Ltd.)
Penguin Books (South Africa) (Pty.) Ltd., 24 Sturdee Avenue,
Rosebank, Johannesburg 2196, South Africa

Penguin Books Ltd., Registered Offices:
80 Strand, London WC2R 0RL, England

Published by Signet, an imprint of New American Library, a division of Penguin
Group (USA) Inc. Previously published in a New American Library edition.

First Signet Printing, January 2012
10 9 8 7 6 5 4 3 2 1

ACKNOWLEDGMENTS

'd like to thank Kara Welsh and NAL for publishing another one of my projects. Laura Cifelli for her fantastic editing work. Mel Berger, my WME literary agent, for always making the right things happen, and LuAnn McLane for her immense help in creating such an interesting, talented, driven, and compassionate character—Destiny Hart.

PROLOGUE

Wilmot, Kentucky

"All right, folks, let's give Danny-Kirk Nelson a big ol' round of applause!"

Gamely clapping along with the rest of the audience for yet another singing cowboy, Destiny Hart hoped poor Danny-Kirk had a decent day job, because it didn't seem likely he'd be giving it up for country stardom anytime soon.

What did I do to deserve this torture on a beautiful summer night? she wondered, watching Danny-Kirk keep right on taking bows even after the polite applause had trickled away.

I'm too honest—that's my problem.

She'd had a feeling she should have lied when her

friend Cooper Sparks popped over earlier to ask whether she had any plans tonight.

"Why do you want to know?" she'd asked warily, noting the gleam in his eye and wondering whether he might be up to some kind of mischief, as was often the case.

With a shrug—and a hurt expression—he'd replied, "I thought you might want to hang out with me and Annie and Seth, but if you're busy . . ."

She wasn't. And so here she was, sitting on a folding lawn chair in a muggy field with her three best friends and a few hundred strangers, slapping mosquitoes beneath the orange glow of the waning sunlight as one wannabe after another took the stage.

"And now for our next contestant in the WKCX Kicks Country Kentucky Idol search . . ."

Leaning toward Annie McPhearson on her left, Destiny whispered, "Please tell me Coop's not going to make us stay till the bitter end?"

"—Destiny Hart!"

Destiny Hart . . .

Destiny Hart?

No. No way. Her own name couldn't have just been announced over the PA system . . .

Or could it?

"Annie—"

"It wasn't my idea." Her friend was suddenly awfully busy tugging her strawberry-blond hair—a longtime, telltale nervous habit.

"What wasn't your idea?"

Annie didn't answer.

Seth Caldwell, in the chair beside Annie, shook his head, looking concerned. "Don't do it."

"Do what?"

"Destiny Hart of Wilmot High School, come on down!" the PA boomed.

She swiveled her head to Cooper, sitting on her right with his long legs sprawled in front of him. He blinked at her with his own attempt at brown-eyed Ashton Kutcher innocence, but the slight twitching of his lips gave him away.

"Oh no, Coop. No. Please say you didn't."

"Yeah," he said cheerfully, "I sure did."

"What?" Destiny's usually husky voice rose an octave and she sat up so straight that her lawn chair tilted backward. She teetered for a moment and would have toppled over if Seth hadn't reached past Annie and grabbed her.

"Destiny Hart, are you in the house?" the DJ persisted, peering out over the crowd with one hand above his eyebrows.

Destiny glared at Cooper. "What makes you think I'm going to get up on that stage?"

"I *dare* you." He arched one dark eyebrow and gave her another classic Cooper grin.

Ah, he knew her too well. He'd been daring her—and vice versa—since they were both thirteen and the new kids in school.

She'd been down that road countless times before—making new friends, only to lose them a year later when her father, an air force colonel, was transferred. Finally, though, he'd retired, and Destiny was here to stay; her mother promised that the bonds she made at Wilmot High were going to last awhile—maybe even a lifetime.

So far, she'd been right.

Destiny first met Cooper in the guidance office, waiting for orientation to begin. The secretary was away from her desk, and there was a delicious-looking chocolate bakery cupcake sitting on it.

Catching Destiny eyeing it, Cooper had said, "Dare you to take a bite."

"Game on," was her reply.

Licking the sugary icing from her lips, she'd seen the gleam of admiration in his eyes, and knew she'd made her first friend in Wilmot.

She hadn't backed down when he'd later dared her to cut through the cemetery alone at night; to call their school principal by his first name, Maurice; to try out for the boys' varsity football team—not that she'd stood a chance in hell of making it—and she wasn't about to back down now.

Cooper knew it, and so did she.

"Destiny Hart?" the WKCX DJ boomed.

"She's right here!" Cooper shot to his feet, pointing at her.

She slapped at his finger. "I'm gonna get you for this."

"You gotta admit it's pretty doggone good." That had come from Annie.

She turned to see her friend grinning at her—no, *past* her, at the oh-so-pleased-with-himself Cooper. Traitor.

Only Seth had the decency to show some concern.

"Seriously, Destiny," he said in a low voice, touching her bare arm, "you don't have to get up there and sing."

"Thanks, but I'm not going to give Cooper the satisfaction," she replied, and shot Seth a grateful grin, hoping he couldn't tell that her heart was suddenly beating like crazy—and not just because she'd been summoned to the stage.

It had been four years since she'd been introduced to

Seth, both literal and figurative boy next door. Two years older than her, the high school's star pitcher with a steady stream of girlfriends, he'd treated her like a kid sister from the start.

Now he was at the University of Kentucky on a baseball scholarship, living across the driveway for just another two weeks before he'd have to head back. She knew she wasn't the only girl in town who was going to miss him like crazy—but she was probably the only one who had no intention of letting him know it.

If she did let on that she had feelings for him and he didn't share them—she was pretty sure he didn't—their friendship would never be the same. She'd be a fool to risk it—and Destiny Hart was no fool.

"Break a leg."

Or was she?

Turning away from Seth, she saw Cooper grinning broadly, waiting for her to take the stage on his dare.

"How 'bout I break *your* leg?" she shot back.

Her flip-flops slapped the ground as she stood up and squared her shoulders.

Yeah. I'm definitely a fool.

The audience applauded and she began weaving her way on wobbly knees past lawn chairs, blankets, and coolers, heading for the stage.

Hearing a familiar voice shrieking her name from the crowd, she spotted her sister, Grace, who was sitting with her own group of friends. Just fourteen months older than Destiny, Grace—ever the overprotective big sister—wore a look of alarm. Destiny waved as if this were no big deal.

Seriously . . . it really isn't. It's not like you're some Danny-Kirk Nelson who can't carry a tune.

She'd been raised on bluegrass, gospel, and classic country; music was one of the few things in her childhood that had been consistent. Her mother sang to her and Grace every night, a lovely lilting quality to her voice that carried Destiny through many a rough patch.

She'd been belting out her favorite songs along with the radio since childhood and taught herself how to play the guitar along the way. Gradually, she'd learned to sing in front of others—in the church choir and at barn dances back at Grandma and Grandpappy's farm.

She knew she had a strong voice, so if she kept her act together the joke might actually be on Cooper . . .

But that was a big *if*. Singing in front of a polite congregation was very different from an impromptu performance before a huge crowd gathered at the town square mostly to snicker at the lack of talent.

Arriving at the stage, she took a deep, steadying breath. *Please don't let me make a complete fool of myself.*

Then she ascended the three steps and smiled at WKCX's Rex Miller.

"Well, hello there, Destiny Hart." He bestowed a toothy smile upon her and extended his arm.

"Hello." Destiny grasped Rex's hand and gave him a firm handshake just the way her father taught her. "Nice to meet you."

"Firm grip," Rex commented, with a knowing wink at the crowd. "But I'm not surprised." He glanced down at the clipboard in his other hand. "Says here you're the daughter of retired air force colonel John Hart."

"Yes, sir, and proud of it," she replied, generating an enormous roar of approval from the audience.

"As well you should be," Rex declared with a wave of

his hand, milking more applause. "And you're attending our very own Carrington College in the fall."

That brought another big cheer from the local audience for the hometown girl; most of the contestants had come from other parts of the Bluegrass state.

"Yes, sir, that's the plan."

So far, so good.

She just hoped he wouldn't ask what she was planning to choose as her major. She'd always thought she'd know by now what she wanted to do with her life, but she still had no clue.

"And it says here that you love to cook, crochet, and ride horses?"

What? Destiny jammed her hands into her jeans pockets and looked over at Cooper, who was doubled over with laughter.

"You could say that," she answered with a tight smile. Just last week, she'd scorched a pan trying to boil water; her mother's attempts to teach her to crochet had left the yarn and both their stomachs in knots; and the only horseback ride she had ever taken had been a dare that ended in disaster—thanks, of course, to Cooper.

"And you're going to sing 'America the Beautiful.'"

"I am?"

Rex Miller tapped his clipboard with his pen. "Says so right here. Seems appropriate on a warm summer evening so close to the Fourth of July. Don't you think so, ladies and gentlemen?" His query was answered with cheers and whistles.

"Y-yes," Destiny stammered, grateful that she knew all of the words.

Oh, she was going to get Cooper Sparks big-time for this one. He had better sleep with one eye open. She looked across the lawn at her friends. Annie had her hand over her mouth and Cooper was laughing so hard that he'd toppled out of his lawn chair. But when her gaze landed on Seth, he gave her two thumbs-up of encouragement.

"Are you ready, Destiny Hart?" Rex was asking.

Not on your life.

"As ready as I'll ever be," she answered aloud.

"Great name, by the way. You even sound like a star."

A cold bead of sweat rolled down her back, but she swallowed her panic and smiled.

Of course it was going to be fine. Her inner strength had never failed her before, right?

Right. Well, except for that unfortunate horseback incident. Of course, she shouldn't have jumped the creek, but it had been part of Cooper's dare . . .

Oh, and there was that time when he challenged her to ride that mechanical bull and she flipped over the horns . . .

A long list of I-dare-you-Destiny played through her brain like a slide show: cliff dive, Polar plunge, bungee jump, worm eating (never again), vine swinging, gate crashing . . . the list was endless.

And now this.

"Destiny, are you sure you're ready?" Rex asked.

The slide show in her head shut off and Destiny nodded. "Yes, sir."

A hush fell over the crowd and Destiny began to sing.

ONE

Nashville, Tennessee
Four Years Later

"I have good news and bad news," Ralph Weston said. "Which do you want first?"

Of all the ridiculous questions Destiny Hart had been asked since she moved to Nashville to try to make it in the country music business—and there were many—that had to be her least favorite.

Leaning her guitar case against the dingy white wall in the employee break room, she pasted on a smile and turned to face her boss.

"Go ahead—hit me with the bad news," she answered, just as his cell phone beeped.

"Hang on a second." Ralph flipped open his phone.

Waiting for him to check his text messages, Destiny

held her breath, though she could pretty much guess what he was going to tell her.

Shouldn't you be used to bad news by now? she asked herself wearily. Lately, it was one thing after another, capped off by—

No. Don't even go there.

Every time she thought about what Billy Jackson had done to her, she felt sick inside.

Ralph looked up from his phone at last. "Listen, Destiny, Cindy Sue called a few minutes ago. She's feeling better and she'll be able to perform, so we don't need you to sing tonight after all."

Destiny deflated. "Oh . . . okay."

Yep—she'd been right. Cindy Sue Smith pulled this stunt all the time.

Destiny longed to ask Ralph why he put up with such unprofessional behavior, but she already knew the answer. All Cindy Sue had to do was bat her big brown eyes and flip her blond hair, and she had Ralph—and countless other red-blooded men—eating right out of her hand.

Watching Ralph sneak another peek at his text messages, wearing a goofy grin, Destiny couldn't resist saying, "So she's feeling much better, huh?"

"Yeah, this text here says she's making the effort just for me."

Destiny swallowed a groan. She'd done some crazy things in an effort to catch a break in this business, but flirting with her middle-aged boss was one horse she wasn't willing to ride.

She cleared her throat loudly.

"Sorry, Destiny." Ralph glanced up and had the decency to show a little bit of remorse.

Maybe Destiny couldn't bring herself to flirt, but she had no problem pouncing on Ralph's guilt. "Well, since I came in, do you think I could sing a song or two? You know, to warm up the crowd for Cindy Sue?" she added with a smile that felt more like a wince.

"Mmm . . ." He shoved his hands in his pockets and rocked back on his heels. "Last time we did that Mandy wasn't none too happy 'bout it."

"Oh . . . really? I wonder why. As I recall, I really had the crowd rockin'. You know, for her benefit, of course."

Ralph scratched his salt-and-pepper beard. "Cindy Sue said you had the crowd too wound up for her style of singin'. Said you're too rough around the edges to open for her again."

Trying not to choke on her anger, Destiny managed to say calmly, "Mr. Weston, it's Friday night in Nashville. Getting fired up is what it's all about."

He didn't like being called Mr. Weston, but she'd been brought up to respect her elders. She just couldn't call her boss Ralph or, heaven forbid, Ralphie, as Cindy Sue called him.

"I know you like to get people up on the dance floor a-hootin' and a-hollerin' and that's all well and good, Destiny, but Cindy Sue likes her performance to be all about the music and her voice. You might want to make note of that for future reference."

And you might want to make a note that Cindy Sue is playing you like a fiddle.

Destiny dug deep for a smile. "I will do that. Now, what's the good news?"

"The good news is we need you on the floor tonight, so your trip here wasn't for nothin'." He eyed her Western-cut fringed shirt. "You've got your uniform, I hope?"

"In my locker," Destiny said glumly. While she needed the money—desperately, thanks to Billy Jackson—she wanted cash from the tip jar, not from waiting tables.

"Good." Ralph absently checked his phone once more, then added, "Oh and, Destiny?"

"Yes, sir?"

"You might want to pull back that hair of yours."

"Yes, sir." Destiny touched the light brown curls tumbling over her shoulders.

"Now get your tail on out there." Ralph jerked his thumb over his shoulder. "We're packed."

She started toward her locker, grumbling under her breath, "Well, isn't that just great."

"Excuse me?"

"I . . . uh . . ." She gave him a tight smile. "I said that I just can't wait."

"Remember, Cindy Sue likes sweet tea to wet her whistle while she sings. Make sure you keep her glass full with lots of ice and a slice of lemon, okay?"

"Yes, sir."

With Ralph safely out of earshot, Destiny yanked her locker open. "Make sure you keep her glass full with lots of ice! Blah, blah . . . blah!"

Catching sight of herself in the mirror attached to her locker door, she saw tears threatening to wash away the smoky gray shadow she'd painstakingly applied to bring out the blue for tonight's performance, along with a soft pink gloss on her full lips.

See? You shouldn't have bothered, she told her reflection.

She'd never been big on primping. But tonight she'd gone all out—not just makeup, but perfume, too, and instead of the flats she usually wore to play down her height, she wore her ruby-red designer heels. They'd cost her a week's paycheck and a diet of cheap canned soup for a month, but she'd always thought they were worth it.

Until now.

Never mind her overdue rent, overdrawn checking account, and maxed-out credit cards. As she glanced down at the sexy red shoes peeking out from beneath her boot-cut Levi's, she knew her dogs were gonna be barkin' by the end of her shift.

After carefully angling her guitar case to fit into the locker, she reached for the extra T-shirt and apron she kept there as insurance against the spills and smears that Destiny could never seem to avoid.

Her daddy, who'd taught her to always be prepared, would be proud.

Daddy . . .

Destiny swallowed a wave of homesickness. Even now, four years after leaving Wilmot, she still had her moments when she wondered whether she'd made the right choice in defying her parents' wishes.

They'd never gotten over her decision to come to Nashville instead of going to college—a plan she'd hatched on a whim after winning the Kentucky Idol competition, thanks to Cooper's dare.

How could she expect her parents to understand what it was like to perform? How could they grasp that the crowd's approval, in that brief, shining moment, somehow fulfilled a need that Destiny didn't even know she possessed? Even she hadn't understood the fierce calling.

Sometimes, I still don't.

Especially on nights like these.

She only knew that while her family traveled all over the country, moving from base to base, she had never developed a sense of belonging. Every new school, new air force base meant trying to fit in all over again, needing so much to be liked . . . accepted. Grace had her tumbling and her cheerleading and always found an instant group of friends.

Destiny had to work harder at it. Yes, she'd made good, solid friends when her family finally settled in Wilmot, but graduation was going to take them in separate directions, and that had unnerved her. Everyone else seemed to know where they wanted to go and what they wanted to do.

Everyone but Destiny.

Then she stood up there on that stage and sang "America the Beautiful," and she felt acceptance. It was such a tingling, trembling rush of instant gratification, as if all her life she'd been drifting and had finally found dry land.

She knew right then that, God willing, performing was what she wanted to do for the rest of her life. She simply wanted to sing and make people happy.

Her father had made it quite clear that he wasn't going to fund what he called her crazy whim. In all fairness, most parents would have protested.

But most parents probably would have gotten over it by now.

Not Daddy. Things between them had never been the same again.

She didn't need his money, though—nor his blessing. Not in the beginning.

The Kentucky Idol prize was three thousand dollars

and a chance to compete against forty-nine other state idol winners for a recording contract with a major label.

Destiny honestly had believed she had a shot at the grand prize. But after a grueling competition, the winner was a fresh-faced thirteen-year-old from Utah. Destiny was second runner-up—after a twentysomething New York studmuffin who'd been on Broadway most of his life and knew how to charm the judges.

In the end, the runner-up prize money—combined with what she'd won earlier—was enough to pay the rent on a Nashville apartment for a year. She promised her parents that if she hadn't made strides in the music industry by the time the year was up, she'd move back home and go to college.

Once she'd gotten a good taste of life in Nashville, Destiny knew there was no turning back. She'd decided she had indeed made strides—by her own definition, anyway—and she was here to stay. Her parents had no choice but to live with her decision.

In the tiny employee bathroom, she slipped out of her fringed shirt, tugged the hunter-green tee over her head, and tied on her apron with its Back in the Saddle Bar and Grille logo stitched in bold black letters beneath a cowboy sitting on a bucking bronco.

Ralph might be clueless in other ways, but he knew how to run a restaurant. The restaurant wasn't even located on the famous Honky-Tonk Row, yet tourists, locals, and the occasional celebrity poured in daily for the juicy burgers, hand-cut French fries, and of course, the music.

Legend had it that Tammy Turner, one of country's all-time greats, had been discovered on the stage right here at Back in the Saddle. She still came in from time to time, Ralph claimed, although Destiny had never caught a glimpse of her.

Back at her locker, she hung up her shirt and quickly pulled out her cell phone. Her sister, Grace, had called twice today, leaving messages both times. Destiny had been so busy preparing to go onstage tonight that she hadn't yet called her back.

She'd better do it now, though, before her shift started.

Quickly, she dialed Grace's number, wondering what was up, suddenly missing her sister desperately.

Close enough in age to be peers, Destiny and Grace had been the best of friends throughout their childhood. In a family constantly on the move, all they'd really had was each other. They shared everything from bedrooms to worry about their father whenever he was on active duty to a longing to settle down in one place and never have to move again.

Oddly enough, when that finally happened, the sisters drifted apart. Over the past four years that Grace had been in college and Destiny in Nashville, they'd seen each other only on rare occasions when they both happened to make it back home for the same holiday. Even then, Destiny never stuck around more than a night or two—not because she had anything urgent to rush back to, but because she wanted her family to think she did.

Now that Grace had graduated and was living back in Wilmot, she seemed at loose ends for the first time in her life. Her old friends had scattered, her local job hunt wasn't going well, and her long-distance relationship with her college boyfriend had had more downs than ups.

She'd called a couple of times recently, offering to come visit Destiny in Nashville.

"That would be great," Destiny told her, but kept putting her off about a date, saying she was too busy working on her demo.

Ha. Look how that had turned out, thanks to Billy Jackson and her own gullibility.

Anyway, she wasn't too busy for visitors—she was too ashamed to admit that her dreams were a long way from coming true. She couldn't bear to disappoint her family and friends; it was bad enough having disappointed herself.

Grace answered on the first ring, sounding so grateful for the returned call that Destiny instantly felt guilty.

"How have you been?" Grace asked. "Have you been working on branding yourself, like I told you?"

Destiny sighed. Her sister the business major had urged her to come up with a tagline of sorts—a short description of her music that encapsulated the unique style that set her apart from other artists.

"Not yet. I've been busy."

"I'm sure you have. Have you gotten a record label deal yet?"

"Um . . . not yet."

"I know it'll be any second now."

"I sure hope so." But that would be a miracle, considering that Billy Jackson—and the truckload of demos he had allegedly produced for her—had vanished into thin air.

She quickly changed the subject. "What's new with you, Gracie?"

"Hmmm, let's see. I broke up with Jason."

"You're kidding."

"No, and don't say it was about time. I know he's a jerk."

"I wasn't going to say it." Destiny opened her purse to look for a ponytail band.

"Yeah, but you were thinking it. Apparently everyone was, but that's another story. I guess I was just blinded by his charm."

Cute, blond, and petite, Grace would have no problem replacing Jason, as far as Destiny was concerned.

"How's the job search going?"

"About as well as my love life. Apparently, a marketing degree doesn't hold much weight here in Wilmot."

"Maybe you should move to a bigger city," Destiny suggested, knowing Grace would never take her advice. She was a hometown girl through and through, as eager to put down roots as their mother had been through all the years of air force wandering.

Destiny and Grace had gone to nine different schools before their father retired and moved the family to Wilmot. They'd been so happy not to have to move anymore . . .

And then I did.

She'd never forget her first day in Nashville. Cooper and Annie had come to help move her into her dumpy apartment. She'd refused to let them see that she found the place less than inviting, or that she was on the verge of tears the whole time they were there.

After they'd driven off into the hot August night, the dust settled and an eerie silence crept into the apartment. Unnerved, Destiny climbed out onto her fire escape. In the distance, in some honky-tonk down the street, she could hear someone singing a cover of "Friends in Low Places." Even now, whenever she heard that song, it took her back to that night, and the good hard cry she'd had on the fire escape.

Her own reaction to the move caught her off guard. She'd been so used to moving because of her daddy's military career that it never occurred to her that the move to Nashville would be traumatic. But she'd forgotten one important thing: This time, she'd be totally alone, leaving not just her friends, but her family behind. She was suddenly on her own for the first time in her life, without the support of her parents. They weren't there to hug her hard and wish her well the way they would have if she'd gone off to college.

But now that she'd lived longer here in Nashville than anywhere, including Wilmot, she was starting to feel restless. Maybe she didn't even know how to live in the same place or understand the concept of roots.

"Maybe I should."

"What?" Destiny asked, not because she wasn't following the conversational thread, but because she couldn't believe what Grace had just said.

"Maybe I should move to a bigger city, like you said."

"But . . . I thought you wanted to live back at home with Mom and Daddy."

"I did—until I got here and realized they're barely speaking."

Destiny stopped fumbling in her purse. "What do you mean? Did they have a fight or something?"

"I wish they would. Anything would be better than the stone-cold silent treatment they're giving each other."

"But why?"

"I have no idea. That's just how it is, I guess."

"Is that why you called? Are you worried they're going to . . ."

Split up.

Destiny couldn't even bring herself to say the words. It was unthinkable that could happen to her parents, who had been high school sweethearts and seemed to have an idyllic marriage.

Especially since Daddy's pension had allowed him to retire young, and their children were grown. The world was waiting at their feet; now was the time when they should be making up for years lost while John Hart was on his tours of duty.

"Actually, Destiny, I called because—"

"Destiny!" Ralph shouted.

"Hang on a second," she told Grace. "I'll be right there, Ralph! I'm coming!" Her fingers closed around a rubber band in the bottom of her purse. "Grace," she said hurriedly, "I've got to run."

"Okay, but let me just—"

"Seriously"—she tried to pull her hair up while holding the phone, but it was impossible—"my boss is going to kill me if I don't get . . . out onstage," she lied. More guilt. She couldn't wait to get off the phone.

"All right. But—"

"Destiny! Quit lollygagging, get your apron on, and get out here and start taking orders! We're swamped!"

"Grace—"

"I know. Call me back as soon as you can, though, Des, because there's something—"

"I will. Promise."

She quickly hung up and pulled her hair back into a ponytail. Before long, stubborn curls would escape captivity to tickle her cheeks and neck, but for now they were tamed into submission.

And so am I.

Grace must have heard what Ralph said and figured out that Destiny wasn't performing; she was waiting tables.

I'll explain when I call her back . . .

But what was there to explain?

She tucked away her purse and closed the locker door with a quiet click instead of slamming it shut the way she wanted to. For a moment, she rested her forehead against the cool metal in an effort to get her emotions under control.

"Destiny!"

With a sigh, she pinned on her gold name tag and headed out, knowing that despite her red heels and extra makeup, this Saturday night was shaping up to be just like any other.

Busy but boring.

In other words—dangerous.

Boredom had always made Destiny restless and edgy.

Now, as she entered the crowded bar, she wistfully eyed the still-empty stage in the corner of the room.

"Miss?" A customer waved an empty longneck at her. "We need another round over here."

"Be right there." She chewed the inside of her cheek, wondering where Cindy Sue was.

"Excuse me," called a disgruntled-looking woman from a table filled with disgruntled-looking women. "We need menus!"

"Sure thing, just a sec."

Again, Destiny looked at the vacant stage, then cast a glance around the room.

No Cindy Sue.

No Ralph, either, though he must be lurking nearby.

You'd better get busy, Destiny told herself.

Yet she was fixated on the microphone, sitting there like a silent beacon.

"Excuse me," the woman called again. "Our menus?"

Destiny nodded politely. She meant to head toward the stack of menus over by the hostess stand ... yet somehow, her pretty red shoes seemed to have taken on a life of their own, carrying her toward the stage instead.

What the heck are you doing?

I'm taking charge of my life for a change—that's what.

For a change? Come on, you've been in charge of your life ever since you left home, and look where it's gotten you. Lying to your family about being successful—

"Waitress!"

Tuned in only to the voices in her own head, Destiny kept right on walking and wrestling with her conscience.

Dreams don't come true overnight, and you know it.

Right. That's why you can't sit around waiting for someone else—someone like Billy Jackson—to make things happen. You have to make it happen.

Yeah, but there must be a better way.

Oh, come on, this is a golden opportunity. What can possibly go wrong?

Surely once her voice filled the room everyone would forget about eating and drinking. And Ralph would be grateful that she stepped in for his magnificent little Cindy Sue, who still hadn't graced the stage with her presence. Right?

Maybe in your dreams.

Undaunted by her own better judgment, Destiny moved on toward the stage, pulled by some invisible music magnet. Her heart thumped harder when she reached the first step and suddenly her heels were glued to the floor.

Feeling very alone in the crowded room, she looked again at the mike and the tall oak stool beside it. Then her gaze fell on the guitar propped in the corner. It wasn't hers . . . but it would do.

If only Cooper were here to dare her . . .

"Hey, just what do you think you're doing?" Cindy Sue Smith shoved past her with a loud huff.

Destiny staggered backward and felt herself falling . . .

But instead of hitting the floor she landed on something human.

"Uh, sorry, but this seat is taken," a familiar male voice said low in her ear as a pair of strong arms wrapped around her waist.

Two

For four years, Destiny had managed to pick herself up and get herself past every little mishap life had thrown her way.

But she might have just reached her breaking point.

Seth Caldwell.

In Nashville.

With me in his lap.

At a glance, she concluded that he somehow looked exactly the same, right down to the familiar red baseball cap with a scripted letter W. Then she allowed herself to take in his rugged features at close range and saw that while his warm brown eyes and easy grin remained just as she remembered, Seth had matured from a cute high school boy to a hard-bodied man. His once shaggy brown hair that had given his mother fits was neatly trimmed close to his head from what she could see beneath the cap. Recalling how proud he'd been of the appearance of scraggly facial hair, she noted that Seth's jaw was now shaded with a five-o'clock shadow, giving him a dangerously sexy edge that made her heart race.

She opened her mouth to ask him what he was doing here, but one of the young ballplayers sitting at his table spoke up before she could.

"Well, snap, Coach, why can't something like that happen to me?"

"Face it, Brett," said one of the others, "you're not that great a catcher. Didn't you figure that out back there in the bottom of the eleventh?"

"I keep telling you, the sun was in my eyes, Chase!"

"Look," Seth put in, "I can't help it if I have pretty women falling all over me. Doggone curse follows me everywhere."

He added a long sigh that felt deliciously warm on the back of Destiny's neck, and it was all she could do to suppress a long sigh of her own.

Pretty—Seth had called her pretty.

She was going to stand up any minute now . . . really.

"Guys," he said, his arms still around her, "this is Destiny."

"Sure is," Chase said. "I mean, when someone drops right into your lap like that—"

"No," Destiny protested, hoping her voice wouldn't betray her breathlessness, "that's not what he means. It's my *name*. My *name* is Destiny. Although, really, of all the laps to fall in . . ." She reluctantly pushed herself to her feet. "How come you didn't tell me you were going to be in town?"

"*I* sure would have told her," one of the guys quipped, but his grin faded when Seth gave him a look.

"I was going to look you up later," he told Destiny, "but suddenly there you were in my lap."

"Yeah, I'm nice that way. Saved you the trouble. So . . ." She gestured at the uniformed players gathered around the table. "I didn't even know you were coaching."

Seth toyed with his napkin. "I guess we've been out of touch lately."

"Guess so."

They both knew why. Her parents weren't the only ones who didn't agree with her decision to leave Wilmot for Nashville.

"Why," Seth had asked her on that long-ago summer night before they parted ways for the last time, "can't you just work on your singing skills while you're in college?"

"Because I finally know what I want," Destiny told him.

"What happens when things go wrong? And they will. Things will get really trying and you'll wish you had something to fall back on."

"No, I won't. Not me. I'm not taking the easy way out."

"I didn't mean—"

"You have to make things happen, Seth, not sit back and wait for them to happen."

"Things happen if they're meant to, no matter what."

"I don't believe that. I think you make your own luck and seal your own fate. So I need to go after this full throttle, or not at all. It's how I do things. Don't you get that?"

No, he didn't. Didn't get *her*.

That hurt. So badly that she left town the next morning without stopping over to say good-bye.

In all the years of their friendship, she'd always been able to count on him. Even when no one else seemed to lend moral support, Seth always had—until he turned against her, along with the rest of the world, when she set out to realize her dream.

Then again, maybe she didn't get *him*, either. After all, she didn't see why, after going away to college and getting out into the world, he'd ever want to return to his small-town roots.

Hadn't he once dreamed of becoming a major-league baseball player?

"I changed my mind," he'd said simply, when she'd reminded him.

You mean you gave up before you ever had the chance, she wanted to say. *You were so afraid of failing that you wouldn't even try.*

Oh well. They were obviously two very different people headed in opposite directions.

"I'm teaching American history and political science at Wilmot," he told her now, "and I just took over coaching this summer when Dean Reynolds retired."

"That's great. Are you living with your parents, then?"

"I was, until February. That's when they sold the house and moved to Florida."

She wondered why no one back home had told her any of that.

Probably because you didn't ask.

Once in a while, her sister mentioned Seth in passing, but Destiny wouldn't ask her to elaborate, and Grace wouldn't think to. She considered Seth a brother figure, just as Destiny once had.

"So where are you living now?" Destiny shifted her weight. She'd been right; her feet were killing her already.

"In a crappy rental apartment over by the interstate. But only until I can find a place of my own. I've been house hunting."

"You're going to buy a *house*?"

"No, I said, 'buy a house,' not 'eat a mouse.'"

"That's what *I* said."

"Really? Because you were looking at me like you thought I said I was going to eat a mouse, or do something even more insane."

Oops. "It's not that buying a house is *insane*," she clarified. "It's just that . . ."

Well, it's insane.

"Don't you think," she asked, treading carefully, "you're kind of young to be doing something so . . . permanent?"

"Oh, I don't know about that. Someone once told me that if you know what you want, you should go after it full throttle. And I know what I want."

Ouch. Time to change the subject.

"What on earth are you doing here in Nashville?" she asked Seth.

"We got into a tournament out in Brentwood as a last-minute replacement for another school that had to drop out. We just came from the first game."

"Did you win?"

"Barely. Went into extra innings and lost our first baseman to a knee injury."

"Poor kid."

"Yeah. He might be out for the rest of the season."

"That stinks. But, hey, you guys won. That's what counts, right?"

He raised an eyebrow at her.

"I didn't mean at the expense of one of your players," she said hastily. "Just . . . oh, you know what I mean."

Winning—coming out on top. It was what Destiny had been working toward ever since she'd left Wilmot, and she wouldn't be content until she'd succeeded. Seeing Seth Caldwell not only reminded her of how far she'd come, but of how far she had yet to go.

She cleared her throat, avoiding Seth's probing gaze. "Well, I've got to get to my tables. Looks like I've got some thirsty customers. It was good seeing you, Seth. Guys, good luck with your tournament."

She gave them a thumbs-up and a smile and started to walk away.

"Wait!" Seth reached out and grabbed her hand. "Are you singing later?"

"N-not tonight." Destiny felt heat creep into her cheeks. No one back home knew how hard she'd been struggling to make it onstage—any stage—and she wanted to keep it that way. "I was supposed to, but . . ." She paused and then looked toward the mike, where Cindy Sue was fussing around with her hands on her hips. "Cindy Sue Smith is performing instead."

"Oh, that's too bad." Seth gave her hand a sympathetic squeeze and she attempted a smile in return.

"Well, good luck, Seth. It really was nice seeing you." She tugged her hand from his grasp, quickly turning around before she burst into tears.

"Destiny . . ." he said, but she kept right on walking.

*   *   *

"Hey, Coach, you gonna eat that burger, or what?"

"Huh?" Seth dragged his attention away from Destiny, on the opposite side of the room, whispering in the bartender's ear.

"I asked if you were gonna finish your burger," Chase Miller repeated loudly over the music. "If not, hand that sucker over and let me do it for ya."

He glanced again at Destiny, just in time to see her blow the bartender a kiss.

"Here you go." Seth shoved his plate across the table and reached for his Coke, no longer interested in the juicy bacon cheeseburger.

Chase—who was always hungry and never got much to eat at home, thanks to a stepmother who was a lousy cook—devoured it, then went after Seth's half-eaten fries and polished off the pickle spear. Within seconds the only thing left on the plate was a lonely sprig of parsley. Chase held it up and sniffed it as if he were thinking about eating it.

After tossing it aside, he looked at Seth and said, "That dude might be big, but you can take him."

"Take who?"

"The bartender who's hitting on that hot Destiny babe."

"Now, why would I want to— Wait. Do you really think he's hitting on her or the other way around?" Oops—that question was supposed to stay in his head.

"She was whispering in her ear, so he's got some game. But, Coach, you can take him. We got your back," Brett promised and the rest of the guys nodded.

"Nah, that's none of my business." Seth couldn't help but grin at their loyalty—misguided or not.

"Come on, Coach. You're totally into her. Admit it."

"Guys, we're just old high school friends."

"Yeah, right." Chase snorted.

"It's true. We've always been . . . you know, *buddies*."

"Gimme a break. Girls are not buddies," Brett informed him. "Especially girls who look like her."

Seth glanced in Destiny's direction just as she bent over and put a glass up on the stage. He noticed several other guys checking her out and felt an unexpected flash of . . . what? Jealousy?

Destiny turned around again, and he felt the full impact of the beautiful woman she had become. All knees and elbows in high school, she seemed to have grown into her skin and somehow appeared . . . softer. Sexier.

He'd laughed when she fell into his lap, thinking she may have done it on purpose. Once upon a time, it would have been just like her to pull such a stunt. What he hadn't expected was the pure male reaction to his arms wrapped around her while his nose had been buried in her soft, silky hair. Her sweet floral scent had filled his head and the desire to kiss the delicate curve of her neck had slammed into his brain. If he hadn't been sitting with his team, he might have given in to the urge.

"We're just friends," he repeated, more to himself than to his players.

"No way." Holden extended his palm across the table. "If that's true, then hand it over."

"Hand over what?"

"Your man-card." Holden wiggled his fingers. "Cough it up."

Seth folded his arms across his chest, trying to appear coachlike. Although he was only six or seven years older than these guys, he needed to remind them that he was in charge. "Maybe it takes a real man to be able to be friends with a girl."

"Yeah, and maybe you'll be wearin' a fanny pouch pretty soon."

"Listen, I could take all of you with one hand tied behind my back and that bartender included," he boasted in a tone tough enough to keep his man-card intact, even though they all knew he was kidding. "And don't forget it."

Holden pulled back and raised both hands in the air. "Hey, I believe you, Coach."

"Good." He snuck another peek at Destiny, glad he'd driven his own car to the tournament instead of squeezing onto the team bus. "Listen, you guys head on out to the bus with Coach Tanner and the rest of the team. You've got to get back to the motel and rest up for tomorrow. I'm going to stick around here to ... settle up the bill."

*C*indy Sue needs a slice of lemon in her sweet tea," Ralph urgently informed Destiny. "I thought I told you that."

"There's lemon in it."

"It's a wedge. She needs a slice."

Oh, for the love of ...

"I'll get right on it." She forced the words past a clenched jaw, holding back what she really wanted to say to him.

Your day will come, she promised herself as she returned to the bar yet again.

Dwelling on her disappointment would get her nowhere.

Nothing to do but go about her business just like she always did . . .

Except that tonight it was more difficult to keep her chin up.

She refused to rubberneck in Seth's direction, but couldn't help wondering whether he'd been watching her wait tables.

So what if he was? It's an honest way to make a living.

Still, she was a little self-conscious scooping up tip money now that Seth was a teacher and coach, doing exactly what he'd always wanted to do.

She still couldn't believe that he'd happened to wander in here, of all places—much less that she'd tripped and dropped into his arms.

"Long time no see." Max Walker, the big bear of a bartender, flashed his easy grin.

"Cindy Sue needs another sweet tea, with a slice of lemon, not a wedge. Can you hook me up?"

"You bet, sugar," he said with the affection of a longtime pal.

Destiny and Max had cleaned up and closed the place many a night, singing together while using broom handles as microphones. Max could rock the house or sing a surprisingly tender love song—as long as no one else was listening. Put him in front of an audience, though, and he froze.

It was a crying shame, Destiny thought, that someone like Max was stuck behind the bar, while the stage was occupied by someone like . . .

She winced, listening to Cindy Sue's painfully high-pitched rendition of "How Do I Live Without You."

"God love her," she said with a shake of her head.

"You're much better than she ever thought of being."

Max leaned across the bar and put his big hand on her shoulder. "Don't you give up, you hear me?"

"Never," Destiny said with more conviction than she felt at the moment, and gave Max a grateful smile.

As she carried Cindy Sue's drink back to the stage, she allowed herself to look over at Seth's table. Her heart sank when she saw that he'd been replaced by a boisterous family group.

So he'd left without saying good-bye.

An eye for an eye, she thought wryly. Still, four years was a heck of a long time to wait to get even.

THREE

*P*acing the sidewalk with his phone pressed to his ear, dutifully giving Dean Reynolds a play-by-play recap of the game, Seth wished he'd succeeded in flagging down Destiny before he'd stepped out to answer the call.

He'd tried, but she seemed to be avoiding him. Or maybe he was reading too much into it. After all, the place was busy and her boss had her hopping, waiting on tables and on Cindy Sue Smith.

That, in particular, bothered Seth. Why was that flimsy little blonde up there onstage instead of Destiny? She was nowhere near as talented. Not that he'd heard his old friend sing since the night she'd won the Kentucky Idol contest, but even back then, he'd been blown away by her gutsy performance of "America the Beautiful."

He had wanted to kick Cooper's butt for goading her

into it—at first because he knew Destiny didn't want to do it. Then because she did it—and well.

Her voice was truly amazing, clear as a bell and straight from the heart. He'd been a ballplayer, not a musician, but even he recognized that she had that special something.

If it hadn't been for Cooper and his dare, things might have turned out very differently for her . . .

And for me.

For us.

Yeah. There might have actually been *an "us."*

But Seth had realized that night—probably even before she did—that Destiny was going to move on. Away. Away from Wilmot, and from him.

Sure enough, she'd won the contest and gone on to place in the national competition. Overnight, she discovered a burning desire to make it in Nashville. Seth had tried to convince himself that he wanted only the best for her, but that wasn't quite right. No, he'd simply *wanted* her, had been wanting her all that summer, ever since he'd returned from his sophomore year at college to find that the girl next door had grown up.

He happened to be in between girlfriends at the time—and though there was no shortage of old flames around town, he found himself surprisingly reluctant to reignite them.

He only wanted Destiny. He just couldn't figure out how to make the move that would take their relationship to another level. Slow and steady—that was Seth.

Destiny was just the opposite.

If he'd ever doubted that, she proved it when she left without a backward glance. He'd convinced himself that he was better off without her in his life. It could never work between them. He'd come to realize he was a hometown boy. She didn't want an anchor; she wanted wings.

Well, she got 'em.

But . . .

Something wasn't right. Back home, whenever he ran into her sister, or Annie, or Cooper, they all talked about how well she was doing in Nashville—yet here she was, waiting tables.

Seth couldn't help but wonder if there might be hope after all. Hope for an "us."

When his team had unexpectedly landed in the Nashville tournament, he'd thought maybe it was a sign. He'd hoped to find that she was ready to give up this crazy lifestyle and come back home to Wilmot and her family . . . and perhaps even to *him*.

But he could tell that wasn't going to happen. She might be waiting tables, but she had some fight left in her.

A telltale warning beep in his ear dragged his attention back to the conversation, and he realized his cell battery was on its last bar.

"Listen, Coach," he said abruptly, "my phone's about to die here, so . . ."

"All right, son. Congratulations on the win. You're doing a good job with the kids."

"Thanks to you. You're the one who laid the groundwork," Seth answered as the phone beeped again. "These guys know the fundamentals—just like you taught me."

Back inside the bar and grill, the dinner crowd had thinned. Seth scanned the room, but Destiny was nowhere to be found. Had she left without saying good-bye?

Yeah, well, it wouldn't be the first time.

All right, maybe he hadn't made things easy on her

when she confessed her dreams to him on that long-ago night. But he had his reasons—reasons that weren't all selfish.

Everyone knew show business was tough. Maybe he just wanted to spare her the anguish. Maybe he didn't want to see her suffering, all alone, so far from home. And him.

Yeah, that was unselfish, all right.

I should go, he decided, taking one last look around the room. His gaze fell on the big bartender, who was drying a glass now that business had slowed down.

It couldn't hurt to ask. He walked over to the bar. "Excuse me, but could you tell me where Destiny Hart went? Is she on a break?"

"She only had the dinner shift tonight."

"So she went home?"

"Don't know."

Okay, this was getting him nowhere. Seth extended his hand. "Seth Caldwell. I'm an old high school friend of Destiny's."

"Max Walker." The guy set down the glass and shook Seth's hand firmly but briefly.

"The souvenir shop that Destiny lives above is about two blocks south of here, right?" Seth jammed his thumb over his shoulder and waited.

"Look"—Max vigorously wiped down the bar—"I'm not at liberty to tell you where Destiny lives. If you know her so well, then give her a call."

"Right." Seth couldn't fault the guy for not giving out any personal information. In fact, he was partly relieved that Destiny had this big dude looking out for her—and partly jealous. He fervently hoped they were just co-workers and friends but didn't have the nerve to ask. All he said in parting was, "Thanks."

"Sure, man," Max replied, and there was still an edge in his tone.

Outside, the sultry summer air carried the scent of restaurant food and car exhaust. Music filtered onto the street from various nightspots and the sidewalk was crowded with groups of laughing people out to have a night on the town in Nashville.

Seth flipped open his phone, intending to take Max's advice. He'd gotten Destiny's number—and her address, too—from Annie, a while back . . . a *looooong* while back. Way before he'd ever realized he might actually find himself in Nashville.

The phone went dead, though, as he dialed the second number. "Well, that's just great." He flipped the phone shut and shoved it back into his pocket.

Now what?

Figure it out . . . It's not that hard.

Right. He'd done his homework, getting in touch with her sister, Grace, right before he left Wilmot last night, to make sure he knew where to find Destiny.

"You're going to visit her?" Grace asked in surprise.

"Well, I'm going to be in Nashville anyway, so I thought . . ."

"Are you going to call her and let her know you're coming?"

"No, because I might not have the chance to get there after all, so . . ."

And besides, I might chicken out, he'd thought at the time.

But he hadn't. He'd even used the team's eleventh-inning win as an excuse to treat them to dinner at Back in the Saddle Bar and Grille in hopes of hearing her sing.

So far, so good.

He knew her apartment was only two blocks away. Might as well leave his car in the public lot. It was a nice night for a stroll.

As the sun dipped lower in the sky, neon lights flickered and popped on to create a festive, charged atmosphere.

Seth took it all in, noting that the neighborhood seemed to be a safe one, just as Cooper had assured him back when she'd first moved in.

Actually, what his old pal had said was, "If you're that worried about her, why don't you go down to Nashville and see for yourself?"

"I can't do that."

"Why not?"

"She doesn't want to see me."

"How do you know?"

"*You* told me," he'd reminded Cooper.

"Well, I'm sure she's over it by now—whatever 'it' is. Seeing as neither of you wanted to tell me and Annie what happened, all I can do is guess that you must've done something to piss her off."

"Yeah, or maybe it was the other way around."

Cooper just shook his head. He'd been the one—along with Annie—who helped Destiny load up all her possessions, drive down to Nashville, and move into a one-room apartment.

"I give her two weeks," he proclaimed to Seth. "Three, tops. Then she'll be running back home where she belongs."

But unlike Cooper—and everyone else, it seemed—Seth had known this wasn't just a whim for Destiny.

Seth absently tossed a five-dollar bill into the open

guitar case of a street singer and looked around to get his bearings.

Ah—there it was.

Nessie's Nashville Novelties.

Destiny's apartment was on the second floor of the old brick building, above the souvenir shop. Annie had mentioned that visitors had to walk down a narrow alley to her entrance around back. Seth was about to round the corner when Destiny's voice drifted to him from somewhere overhead, probably through an open window.

"Yeah, right, Mike. I know I was gone for a long time, but your kisses won't make up for the mess you made."

Seth definitely should have called first. No, he shouldn't be here at all. Jealous and embarrassed, he started to turn around.

"Cut it out," Destiny said, her voice more urgent than teasing now. "I don't want your kisses. Just go on and *go*. Hurry!"

Seth frowned, wondering if everything was okay.

"Mike! Come on! You're going to get me in trouble!"

Adrenaline rushing through his veins, Seth rounded the side of the building with his fists cocked, ready to teach this Mike character a thing or two.

*S*ara Hart drifted through the empty house, wishing her daughter Grace would come back from her latest round of job hunting so that she wouldn't feel so alone.

She couldn't help but remember the old days, when they were a bustling family of four—Grace and Destiny, Sara and John. The picture-perfect family she'd always wanted.

You still have them, she reminded herself, settling on

the couch and idly picking up one of Grace's magazines. *Everyone is just busy doing their own thing, that's all. That's how it's supposed to be.*

She opened the magazine, trying not to be startled by photos of cleavage and headlines about sex.

This was no *Good Housekeeping*, that was for darned sure.

She was about toss it aside when a quiz caught her eye: Does Your Relationship with Your Mate Have Sizzle or Fizzle?

Sara decided to take it. It was silly, but what else did she have to do?

She answered all twenty questions honestly, then tallied up her answers and turned to the results page to check her score.

If you answered mostly B's and C's, she read, *your sizzle has definitely fizzled. In fact, if you were a sparkler you'd now be nothing more than a charred stick ready to crumble. But fear not! You can get your groove back! The question is, do you want to—or are you ready to move on?*

Move on?

The thought was shocking . . .

Not, however, so shocking that Sara was ready to swap the magazine for one of her issues of *Good House-keeping* that were stacked neatly on the end table.

She narrowed her eyes in determination and flipped back to the sidebar that had ten ways to get the spark back . . .

Oh my.

By the time she got to number five, Sara was blushing. She doubted she'd ever dare use any of the creative ways to jump-start her man . . . or would she?

Maybe not now . . . but once upon a time . . .

Her husband had been her high school sweetheart. Brash and rough around the edges, John Hart had made Sara's pulse pound from the moment she first spotted him, roaring into the high school parking lot in his souped-up Firebird.

He was the new kid in town, the bad boy with a black leather jacket and an attitude that made all the girls sigh and the boys move out of the way.

The first time Sara saw him close-up, in the hallway at school, he'd given her such a probing once-over that she immediately felt silly in her broomstick skirt and peasant blouse. She had turned her back on him quickly, but remembered feeling his gaze on her as she walked away.

The next time they connected, though, it was for good. John was failing English and needed the credit to graduate; the teacher asked Sara, her prize pupil, to tutor him. It didn't take her long to discover that beneath John's surly attitude was a sharp brain.

Abandoned by his mother and raised by his mad-at-the-world father, John was a classic chip-on-his-shoulder underachiever. They'd been such opposites, she and John—Sara's free-spirited love of poetry, music, and literature in sharp contrast with John's hard-edged lifestyle.

And yet they fell madly in love.

When his trouble-making ways landed him in hot water one too many times, John's father finally kicked him out of the house. Out of nowhere, in a last-ditch effort to change his life and make something of himself—mostly for Sara's sake—he'd signed up for the air force. To everyone's surprise—particularly his own—he'd embraced the military lifestyle. It instilled discipline, gave him direction and a sense of pride in himself and his country. He shed his bad-boy ways and a year later, they were married.

It had been idyllic at first. But as John climbed the ranks in the air force, he became more regimented, squashing his wife's free spirit little by little. Wanting to be the perfect wife, she had allowed it to happen without even realizing it.

After twenty-five years of marriage, Sara knew Colonel John Hart like a book.

And maybe, she decided, it was about high time they started a brand-new chapter.

*C*rouched on the fire escape, hearing heavy footsteps coming around from the alley, Destiny frantically waved at Mike, who angled his furry head at her in doggie confusion from the ground below.

Terrific. Of all the moments for an impromptu visit from her landlord, probably here looking for this month's late rent . . .

Kenny Tabor didn't allow animals in the building, but the furry freeloader who had scratched Destiny's back door on a cold, rainy evening had appeared as forlorn as she'd felt that particular night. Destiny couldn't resist letting him in for just one night.

That was several months ago, and Kenny had yet to figure out that she'd adopted a canine roommate. But apparently, all that was about to change.

"Mike, get over here!" she called in a loud whisper.

Too late. A figure emerged from the shadows and into her back door spotlight. She couldn't see his face, but she immediately knew it wasn't her short-of-stature landlord, Kenny Tabor.

No . . . it happened to be the one and only Seth Caldwell.

So he hadn't left town without saying good-bye.

"Seth!" she called brightly—and immediately regretted it. Did she really want him to see her like this?

Thanks to the evening humidity, her hair had taken on a life of its own the moment she'd removed the ponytail holder. Her face was well scrubbed. She had changed into baggy gray sweatpants and a large white T-shirt that was printed with an *I*, followed by half of a smeared red heart and then *Nashville*—yet another of her downstairs neighbor Nessie's flawed inventory castoffs.

Seth looked up. "Oh . . . hi. Sorry to just show up . . . I, uh, would have called, but my phone died."

"No problem," Destiny assured him, tucking a wayward lock behind her ear as she tried to come up with something clever to say.

Mike beat her to it, emitting a couple of decidedly cranky barks.

"Stop that!"

As usual, he paid no attention to Destiny's command, instead growling in a surprisingly menacing tone for a creature who looked more like a cartoon character than a guard dog.

Destiny descended the metal fire escape steps. "Mike! I mean it! Cut it out!" His spiky hair stood up as if he had just put a paw in an electrical socket and he gave Seth a bring-it-on-baby stare.

"*That's* Mike?" Seth gaped. "He's a *dog*?"

"What did you think he was, an alien?"

Seth took a step toward the fire escape. "No, I thought—"

Teeth bared, Mike launched himself at Seth.

"Mike, no!" Destiny watched helplessly as Mike's short little legs propelled him as high as they possibly could. Upon impact with Seth's thighs, the dog bounced off like a Ping-Pong ball hitting a paddle. His deep bark turned into a high-pitched what-was-I-thinking yelp as he flew backward and hit the ground hard.

"Mike!" Destiny scrambled down the fire escape and knelt beside the pitiful pooch. "Are you okay?"

Mike looked up at her with his bulging I-must-have-some-pug-in-me eyes and gave her a weak but reassuring, "Woof."

Seth crouched beside them. "I'm sorry, fella."

Mike gave him an accusatory glare.

"Guess I shouldn't have come barreling around the corner," Seth told Destiny, "but from what you were saying I thought you were talking to some guy who was giving you a hard time."

"You're kidding." She couldn't deny a flutter of appreciation that Seth had thought he was coming to her rescue.

"Hey, you have to admit that Mike isn't a normal name for a dog. But then again, you never did like *normal*, did you?"

"Normal is *so* overrated."

It was almost like old times, kidding around. Their eyes met and Destiny felt that all-too-familiar pull of attraction.

"Well, at least some things never change," Seth said casually.

"You got that right."

If he only knew.

When Seth's gaze dropped to her mouth, she wondered, for a wild moment, if he was going to kiss her. The idea so unnerved her that she jerked her head back and tumbled from her knees to her butt, nearly landing on poor recovering Mike. He gave a startled bark, and she scooped him into her lap and gave him a pat on his head.

Seth cleared his throat. "So why were you upset with Mike?"

"Because he's not supposed to be here. He showed up as a stray and pets aren't allowed, and I know my daddy raised me not to break the rules, but I was afraid to take Mike to a shelter. He has a face only a mother could love and the thought of . . ." She shook her head. "Anyway, he came along just when I needed him most."

Seth seemed to be contemplating that. "When things like that happen, I sometimes think there's a little divine intervention at work."

He pushed to his feet and then offered a warm, firm grasp to pull her up, still clutching the dog under one arm.

"Let's be friends, okay, little guy?" He had the strong, callused hands of a hard-working athlete, she noticed, watching him scratch Mike behind the ears.

She fully expected her cranky dog to growl again, but he surprised her by nudging Seth's hand for more.

"Guess you won him over."

Seth grinned. "Was there ever any doubt?"

"Not at all."

And Mike's not the only one who's falling for your charm.

Hearing a door squeak open, she turned to see a familiar figure stepping out onto the first-floor doorstep.

"What the heck is goin' on out here?" Nessie Newberry asked in her high-pitched twang.

A mere few years older than Destiny—but infinitely wiser, as far as Destiny was concerned—Nessie was a backwoods Barbie, raised in the hills of Tennessee like her idol Dolly Parton, and darned proud of it. Her figure was the opposite of Dolly's hourglass build, but almost everything else about her was over-the-top. Her teased blond hair was pulled back with a pink polka-dotted scarf knotted at the nape of her neck. Her lips were painted ruby red to match her long fake nails.

"Mike's got himself all worked up as usual," Destiny told Nessie. "I hope he didn't wake you up."

"At this hour? Honey, the kids are with my ex, the night is young—and so am I, although maybe not as young as you are. You, either," Nessie added, shooting a glance at Seth, followed by a pointed one at Destiny. "Aren't you going to introduce me?"

"I was getting around to it. Nessie, I'd like you to meet Seth Caldwell, an old friend from high school. Seth, this is my downstairs neighbor, Nessie Newberry."

Nessie, who was lucky to break five feet tall even in her wedge heels and big hair, tilted her head back and gave Seth her best smile. "Well, hey there, good-lookin'."

"Nice to meet you," Seth responded politely and extended his hand gingerly, probably because of the long fingernails—or perhaps her small stature. But while Nessie looked as if a strong wind would blow her away, she was a force to be reckoned with.

So, for that matter, was Mike. He barked, looking from Seth to Nessie.

"What's the matter, Mikey-boy? You jealous?" Nessie

reached back into the house, then tossed something at the dog.

Mike happily scurried after it.

"What was that?" Destiny asked.

"A toy mouse. Just got a shipment."

Mike pounced on it as if it were alive and a threat to the well-being of all mankind, whipping the fake rodent back and forth, showing it who was the boss. The fuzzy mouse squeaked as if in protest, and went flying into the air. It landed belly up on Seth's outstretched arm with a defeated high-pitched wheeze.

"Oh my," Nessie said weakly. "That must be some bicep."

"Here you go, buddy." Seth tossed the squeaky toy for Mike to chase down again.

"So are you just in town for a visit?" Nessie asked casually but gave Destiny a glance filled with you-go-girl.

"Actually, I was over in Brentwood for a baseball tournament. I coach the Wilmot High School Panthers."

"Well, now, just how fun is that?"

Seth grinned. "Very. Anyway, Destiny's sister had told me where she was working, so—"

"Grace?" The light dawned. No wonder her sister had called earlier. "I thought you just happened to be at Back in the Saddle, Seth. I didn't realize you . . ."

Were looking for me.

"Back in the Saddle," Nessie said. "That reminds me—how did your set go? I hated to miss it, but the shop was open."

"You didn't miss a thing." Destiny felt her cheeks warm up. "Cindy Sue showed up after all and so Ralph let her go ahead and sing."

Nessie pressed her lips together. "Why, if I looked in

that man's ear I'd see daylight clear out the other side," she said fiercely. "If his brain was dynamite, he still couldn't blow his nose."

Destiny laughed. "Thanks, Nessie. You're my number-one fan. Oh, wait—my *only* fan."

"Yeah, well, it might seem like you're on the back side of hard times, but it's not gonna be for long, girlie. I've heard your golden pipes and beautiful songs that come straight from your heart." She tapped a red finger-nail to her chest to demonstrate.

Destiny glanced at Seth, wishing Nessie hadn't said quite so much. "Yeah, well, all I need is a little bitty break."

"You'll get one. Remember, the sun don't shine on the same dog's butt every day." Nessie rubbed her hands together. "Well, I'd better get back to my inventory."

"It was nice to meet you, Nessie."

"Same here, Coach." She turned and gave Destiny a quick hug. "You hang in there, hear me? Talk to you to-morrow."

"Sure thing, Nessie. Oh, and thanks for Mike's mouse. You're the best."

"Don't I know it?" She made kissing noises at Mike, who was trotting back over with the rubber toy in his mouth.

"Off I go," she announced breezily, but when Seth turned his attention to retrieving the mouse from Mike's mouth, Nessie eased up on tiptoe and said in a stage whisper, "Mercy, he sure is hot stuff!"

"We're just friends," Destiny whispered back, hoping Seth couldn't overhear.

"Well, now, see, you gotta work on that! My oh my, I just want to dip that boy up on a chip. And he sure looks at you with big brown adoring eyes."

"Oh, go on with you ..." Destiny scoffed, but her heart hammered at the thought.

Destiny watched her meddlesome but well-meaning friend disappear back inside, then turned to see Seth looking after her as well.

"Whew! That little gal whips around like a hurricane-force wind."

"She sure does."

"Looks like she keeps an eye on things around here."

"You mean, on me?" Destiny nodded. "I couldn't have survived living here without her humor and encouragement, that's for sure."

Seth nodded and rocked back thoughtfully on his heels. "Um, I don't want to put you on the spot, but can I ask you something?"

"Shoot."

"I won't be offended if you say no."

"I'll keep that in mind."

"Our game tomorrow is in the morning, and if we win, we stick around to play again the next day—and the fellas will have to rest up. If we lose, they'll head back on the bus, but ... either way, I have my own car."

"That's nice." Destiny wanted to reach over and shake whatever he was trying to say out of him.

"You're not going to make this any easier on me, are you?" Seth plucked a blade of grass and gave her a grin that did funny things to her stomach.

"Sorry, but ... you kind of lost me." He hadn't really, but she wasn't about to go out on a limb here and assume he was trying to ask her out.

"If you're okay with it, I thought maybe we could have dinner tomorrow night. It would be fun to catch up."

"Of course I'm okay with it. Why wouldn't I be okay

with it?" It was all she could do to keep her voice non-chalant.

"You might have plans or a boyfriend who might not like the idea."

"Well, I'm off tomorrow, so . . ." She shrugged.

"What about the last part?"

"Huh?" Her heart pounded.

"The boyfriend part." Seth arched a brow and pointed to her shirt. "Says right there that you only have half a heart. Where's the other half?"

"There's nobody special in my life . . . you know, right *now*." She didn't bother to tell him that she'd recently dated yet another struggling musician for a few months before he moved on.

Nashville was full of interesting men, but its population was fed by a transient industry. It seemed that all the guys Destiny had dated and the women she'd befriended eventually gave up altogether or found a promising gig elsewhere.

"That bartender of yours wasn't too happy about me coming here," Seth said.

"Max? He's just a friend."

"Well, I'm glad he looks out for you."

"Yeah, Max is a good guy. Protects me just like Mike, here. Listen, if you want to come in right now for a cup of coffee or something . . ."

Or something?

Like tea?

Or me?

"Maybe I will. Just for a little while."

FOUR

As Destiny led the way over the threshold, Seth took in the loft-style apartment. Admiring the high ceilings, hardwood floors, and exposed brick walls that gave it a rustic appeal, he commented, "Nice place."

"You sound surprised."

He was, given Cooper's and Annie's descriptions. But they hadn't visited her here in years, he realized.

"Were you expecting a dump?"

"Maybe not a dump, but not . . ." He trailed off.

"Garage-sale chic—that's what I like to call it." She indicated the mix-and-match decor with a wave of her hand. "Don't mind the mess." Destiny buzzed over to the kitchen area, hurriedly throwing away junk mail scattered on a butcher block.

"You don't have to clean up for me."

"Sure, I do. I don't want you going back home and telling the whole town I'm a total slob."

"Don't worry. I won't tell anyone anything they don't already know about you." He grinned, but she didn't return it. "I'm just kidding, Destiny."

"I know." Something flickered in her eyes, and was gone.

There was a pleasant clutter to the place, he decided, noting the details of her musician's life: guitar case and amp, stacks of CDs beside the stereo.

"So this place needed a lot of work when I moved in," Destiny chattered as she stacked dishes from the sink into the dishwasher. "I scrubbed it from top to bottom, buffed the hardwood floors, and painted the kitchen cabinets . . . By the time I was done, it looked so much better that Kenny wanted to increase the rent when my year lease was up."

"Kenny's your landlord."

"Right." Destiny rolled her eyes.

"Not your favorite person, I see."

"Trust me—I'm sure the feeling is mutual." She gave a meaningful sigh.

Before he could ask what she meant, she went on. "Anyway, I had gone through my savings and couldn't afford one more cent. Nessie, God love her, pitched a fit and threatened to leave if he raised my rent and so he backed off. She told Kenny that he owed *me* for all of the improvements I made to the place."

"So did he lower the rent?"

"What, are you kidding?" Destiny wrinkled her nose. "He's kind of a jerk sometimes. He'd freak if he knew about Mike."

Seth said hotly, "Listen, if that guy gives you any

trouble you just let me know, okay?" Seeing her smile, he felt embarrassed. "Sorry. I promise not to beat on my chest."

"It's nice to know that you still care." She reached out and squeezed his hand.

He knew it was just a simple gesture of friendly reassurance, but it affected him on a much deeper level.

She let go too quickly and pointed at the tan faux-suede sectional in the living room area. "Why don't you have a seat? It's ugly, but comfy. Got it at a scratch-and-dent sale when I first moved in."

He went over and obediently sat down. Mike tagged along and scrambled up beside him, wagging his tail.

Suddenly, a plastic statue of Elvis on the end table started moving its head and gyrating its hips, singing "You Ain't Nothin' but a Hound Dog" in a voice that sounded less like Elvis than it did like Alvin from the *Alvin and the Chipmunks*.

"What the ..." Seth stared.

"He's motion-activated," Destiny said with a laugh, as the kitschy mechanical King brought the song home with a high-pitched "Thank you. Thank you very much!"

Gaping, Seth tried to think of something to say and settled on a lame, "Where did you get him?"

"He was a gift from a friend. From Nessie. She gives me all kinds of cool things."

Nessie. Seth found himself relieved that it was a friend-friend, and not a ... *friend.* As in boyfriend.

"She gives you all kinds of things like ... ?"

"You really want to know?"

"I really do."

Destiny closed the dishwasher and crossed the room to open a closet. She pulled out a box and started rummaging through it. "Hmmm . . . let's see if you can still catch, Caldwell." She tossed a rubber chicken at him.

Seth caught it easily and threw it back with a grin. "What else you got?"

"Chinese finger trap, whoopee cushion, laughing mirror, dirty face soap, fuzzy jumping spider, relighting birthday candles . . ." She held up a pair of plastic glasses sporting a fake nose and bushy eyebrows. "You name it, I got it."

"Yeah, I can see that, but . . . why?"

"See, Nessie gives me a gag gift every time I . . ."

She trailed off, toying with the glasses.

Seth prompted, "Every time you what?"

Instead of answering, Destiny slipped on the glasses and tried to laugh. The sound that bubbled up was more of a gurgle than a giggle, though, and she tried to hide it with a cough.

Seth wasn't fooled. He got up, walked over to her, and lifted off the glasses. With his thumb, he gently wiped away a fat tear that was starting to roll down her cheek.

"Hey," he said softly, "what's wrong?"

"Nothing."

"You might be a terrific singer, but you're a lousy actress." Seeing her stricken expression, he quickly said, "Hey, I'm just kidding."

"About my being a terrific singer?"

"No, about—" He realized there was a hint of a smile in her teary eyes. "No one would ever call you anything but a terrific singer."

"Wow, you really haven't ever been in Nashville before, have you?"

"Destiny—"

"No, Seth, listen. I *know* I'm good. I wouldn't be here if I didn't believe that. But I will fully admit that it hasn't been easy. Everybody and his brother seem to be here in Nashville for the same reason. A lot of them—maybe most of them—are good. You have to make yourself stand out from the crowd, and . . . I guess I haven't been able to do that. Yet."

Yet.

He'd been taken aback by her attitude until she gamely tagged on that last word.

Ah, there was the Destiny he knew.

"If anyone can make it here, you can," he assured her.

"That's not what you said when I left."

Maybe I didn't want to see you go.

"I don't think it mattered what I said. You were so pumped . . ."

"On the outside. Inside, I was a mess."

"I had no clue."

She waved a dismissive hand at him. "Trust me, I hid my fear very well."

"But you stuck it out."

"Yeah, well, my father said I'd be home by that first Christmas." She grinned. "It was close enough to a dare for me to dig in my heels and do anything I could to stay."

"Like I said earlier—some things never change. Hey, you still haven't told me about Nessie and the gag gifts."

"Oh. Right. So there I was, not long after I moved in, feeling homesick and having a good cry out on the fire escape. It was a warm night and the windows were open, and I guess my voice was carrying . . ."

"You *guess*?" Back in their adolescent days, Seth frequently teased her about hearing her loud, dramatic sobs resonating through the neighborhood.

"Sometimes I like to have a good, old-fashioned cry, you know?"

"Yeah," he said wryly. "I know."

"Caterwauling, Daddy used to call it. Whenever I got sad, it was like a dam burst behind my eyeballs and these huge loud wails would just erupt. Grace was the same way."

"Maybe it's a genetic thing."

"No—my mother is one of those silent weepers, and it didn't come from my father's side. I've never seen my daddy cry. Ever. I don't even know if he can."

"A lot of men can't," Seth told her. He himself wasn't among them, but he wouldn't be surprised if Colonel John Hart was.

Seth had always been intimidated by Destiny's tough-as-nails father. The man had served countless tours of duty, moving his family all over the world before retiring in Wilmot to please his wife—a compromise, really.

Destiny's mother, Sara, had grown up in Mississippi and longed to return to her roots. John, however, couldn't tolerate the humidity of the deep South. He'd served on a base in Kentucky years ago and grown attached to the Bluegrass state; that was as far south as he'd go when it came time to settle down.

"Anyway . . ." Destiny went on with her story. "I didn't hear Nessie coming up over my carrying on, and when she touched my shoulder she about scared me out of my skin. She asked me what was wrong and I said that I had stubbed my toe."

"Brilliant."

"I know, right? But she knew I'd just moved in and pretty much had the whole situation figured out." Destiny chuckled. "She introduced herself and, of course, I gave her one of my daddy's very firm handshakes, and wouldn't you know she had a hand buzzer curled up in her palm?"

"Oh, that's perfect."

"It sure did make me go from crying to laughing in a hurry. Right then and there I knew we were going to become fast friends. I told her that I wanted to be her when I grew up and she said that was too bad because she was never gonna grow up. And, of course, I said, *exactly*."

"So that's where you got that big box of gag gifts?"

"Yep. Every time Nessie knew I had a bad day or yet another disappointment she would bring me some little gadget to raise my spirits."

"That's a big box," Seth told her quietly.

"I guess there is humor in that observation somewhere," Destiny replied with a small smile.

For a long moment, they were both lost in their own thoughts.

Then she sighed a very un-Destiny-like sigh, and he looked up in dismay to see a dejected expression on her face.

"My parents taught me to aim high and work hard, but lately I'm beginning to think this is beyond my reach."

Sympathy squeezed like a rubber band around Seth's heart. "I'm guessing that no one knows about your struggles other than your friend Nessie."

She nodded glumly. "How could I possibly tell my family? But for the record, I never really lie. I just put a positive spin on everything."

"Destiny . . . you have nothing to be ashamed of."

"Oh really? Seth, look, you're back home teaching.

Cooper is headed for law school, for goodness' sake. Annie's a nurse. And Grace has a marketing degree!" She sliced her hand through the air. "And here I sit over four years later and I'm no closer to my goal than the day I arrived. Now, just how do I tell my parents *that?*"

"This isn't about your parents, Destiny. This is about what you want to do with your life."

She closed her eyes tightly and pressed her lips together like a dam holding back a surge of emotion.

And it stopped him in his tracks.

Not the emotion part, but rather her *mouth*. Her lips, soft and shiny . . .

There was nothing he'd rather do than draw her into his arms and kiss her soundly.

But doggone it, he shouldn't. Wouldn't.

It took every bit of strength he possessed not to haul her into his arms.

"I don't think I can do this anymore," she admitted softly, her eyes still closed.

"Do what?"

"Live here in Nashville chasing this . . . this pipe dream. Everyone else is moving forward and I'm treading water."

Seth longed to tell her to come on home with him, where she wouldn't have to endure one more day of heartache or disappointment.

The scales, he realized, were tipped in his favor. All he had to do was say the word.

Destiny sighed and opened her eyes. "I should have listened to you four years ago and had Plan B waiting in the wings."

Frowning, Seth mulled that over for a minute, but then shook his head firmly. "No."

"What do you mean?"

"Sing something for me."

"What?"

He motioned at her guitar. "Go ahead. Sing."

"Sing what?" She was already walking toward it, slowly.

"Whatever you want."

"Elvis? Patsy Cline?"

"Got anything of your own?"

She picked up the guitar and sat on a stool. "Maybe. I wrote one a couple of weeks ago. It might be a little over-the-top. I was kind of emotional on that particular day."

"The true nature of great country songs . . . and beautiful Southern women. As far as I'm concerned there's nothin' wrong with either one of those things." Seth grinned as Destiny's cheeks colored at the compliment.

She quickly flipped her guitar up from her lap and started strumming.

"It's called 'Restless Heart,'" she announced softly and then began to sing. Seth could tell from the slight tremor in her voice that she was nervous, but she closed her eyes and let the music take over.

The song was about searching and yearning, loving and learning, its lyrics full of sentiment and edged with raw emotion.

"I knew it right from the start . . . that he was the only one who could ever mend"—she drew out the word high pitched and pure and then finished low and soft—"the ragged edges of my restless heart . . ."

After she trailed off and her fingers stilled, Destiny opened her eyes and looked over at Seth expectantly. He opened his mouth to tell her that he was moved by her performance, but words failed him.

He knew what he wanted to say—but somehow, he couldn't bring himself to say it, because it would send her even farther away from him.

"I know . . . too much drama, right?" She looked disappointed, nibbling on her bottom lip as she carefully placed her guitar on the stand. "I need to back it down, don't I?"

Still, he couldn't speak.

"Look, Seth, you don't have to be nice. Say what you need to say. I'm a big girl. I can take it."

"Destiny . . ." He walked over to her and cleared his throat. "I loved the song. *Really* loved it."

She blinked rapidly. "Oh wow, I think I might cry." She sniffed hard and determinedly fanned her hands in front of her cheeks.

"Seriously—you're immensely talented. You should not give up."

She looked at him with luminous eyes and Seth thought to himself that he had never seen a sight so beautiful.

Heaven help him, even though he knew he shouldn't, Seth could not stop from leaning in and kissing her. The moment his lips met hers he was lost in the delicious sensation. Warm, soft, tender, sweet, the kiss went beyond pleasant and touched him on a much deeper level that made him yearn for more . . .

And yet he forced himself to pull back.

"What was that all about, Seth?" Her voice was barely a whisper.

Good Lord, what had he done? Destiny needed encouragement and direction, not confusion.

Seth's heart thumped hard. "I . . . uh . . . guess I got caught up in the emotion of the song."

"Oh." Her face fell and she closed her eyes. "I suppose I should be flattered that my music got to you in such a way."

You got to me.

He opened his mouth to admit it—only to be curtailed by the ringing telephone.

Standing out on the back deck that John had built at her request, Sara leaned into the railing and looked out into the whispering darkness.

She had enjoyed many a cold glass of tea out here on many a warm summer evening, cupped her hands around a coffee mug when the seasons changed.

The cool, gentle breeze usually had a calming effect on Sara. But tonight, as she stood rubbing the goose bumps on her arms, all she felt was inner turmoil, thanks to four issues of *Cosmopolitan*.

Sara inhaled deeply in an effort to let the scent of earth and pine clear her head. The trees were tall, swaying shadows and the leaves rustled softly. She could detect the clean smell of rain hanging heavy in the humid air, and the promise that fall weather wasn't far off.

But she wasn't looking ahead; she was looking back at the countless summer evenings she'd enjoyed on this deck since they'd moved to Wilmot over eight years ago.

Dinner was always a family effort: John would flip burgers as the girls shucked corn and Sara sliced fresh watermelon. After dinner they'd play board games or cards, or sing . . .

"Mom?"

Sara jumped and turned to see Grace standing behind her.

"What on earth are you doing? Didn't you hear me calling you?"

"I'm sorry, sweetie. I guess I was lost in my thoughts."

She saw Grace looking at the glass in her hand. "Tea at this time of night? You know the caffeine's going to keep you up."

"It's not likely to make a difference."

"You mean you haven't been sleeping?"

"Not lately." The bed in the guest room wasn't nearly as comfortable as the king-sized Temper-Pedic in the master bedroom—and that was where she'd been spending her nights lately.

"Where's Daddy?"

"Gone," Sara answered flatly.

"Gone where?"

"He headed up to the camp to fish. Said he might be gone for a few days."

"Would have been nice of him to have said good-bye to me," Grace muttered.

"He left in a bit of a huff." Sara pressed her lips together, holding back tears.

Grace pointed to the Adirondack chairs. "Here, let's sit."

Sara ran her hands lovingly over the wide arms of the white chair as she sank into it. "You know, your father and I found these at a yard sale right after we moved into this house. Boy, were they ever in bad shape, but we sanded them down and made them look like new."

Grace nodded. "I remember that."

I remember everything lately, Sara thought.

Grace lit a fat citronella candle perched on the small table between the chairs. The tangy scent blended with the humid night air, and the flickering flame cast a soft, soothing glow against background music of chirping crickets and croaking bullfrogs.

Grace sat beside her. "Mom . . . what's going on with you and Daddy?"

She opened her mouth to lie, not wanting to burden her daughter with the truth, but then realized it was no use. Grace lived under this roof with them, and she was no fool.

"I guess we're just drifting apart." Sara leaned back and looked up at the inky blue sky glittering with stars. "Now that you girls are grown I feel as if I'm at loose ends . . . restless and ready to go out and . . . I don't know. Do something."

"Like what?"

"*Anything*. As long as it's new and different. Am I making any sense?"

Grace reached over and took her hand. "You're making perfect sense. Mom, you've devoted your whole life to your family, and—"

"And I wouldn't change a thing."

"But maybe now it's time for you to rediscover . . . *you*."

"Maybe you're right."

"And Daddy doesn't get that?"

"No. All the man wants to do is fish and jog and tinker with that old car in the garage. He thinks I'm having a midlife crisis." She shrugged. "Call it what you want, but for the first time I understand Destiny's need to chase her dream."

"So do I, lately. Even after all these years, a part of me was still angry with her for up and moving to Nashville out of the blue, but lately . . ." Grace shrugged. "Maybe I finally get it. Especially now that I'm out of school and haven't got a clue what to do next."

"You have a college degree. In a lot of ways, you're farther along than I was at your age," Sara assured her daughter, who had always been the bubbly blond cheerleader and felt as if no one took her seriously.

"Are you kidding? You were married with two children by the time you were my age, Mom."

Yes, and she'd thought she had everything she could ever possibly want, or need.

"You know, Mom . . ." Grace broke into her thoughts, dragging her back to the present. "I was thinking maybe I could go visit Destiny for a while, and give you and Daddy a chance to have the house to yourselves."

"Oh, Grace, that's not necessary. We don't need you to do that."

"Maybe I need to do it, though. And maybe Destiny needs me, too. When I talked to her today, she sounded kind of . . . lonely."

"You talked to her today?" Sara asked with the pang she experienced every time she thought about Destiny. If only she could go back and do things differently. She should have stood up for her own feelings when her daughter decided to go to Nashville and not blindly followed her husband's wishes. Old habits, however, were hard to break.

Besides, she had known John was having a difficult time dealing with Destiny's sudden need for independence . . .

Just as he was having a hard time with Sara's identical need right now.

"I called because I wanted to give Destiny a heads-up that Seth might be popping in to see her," Grace said, "but her boss kept yelling at her to get off the phone and get on her apron." She paused for a pointed silence, and the last word quickly sank in.

"What? You mean her *costume*, Grace, not—"

"I don't think so."

"But . . . she said she was working at Back in the Saddle, that famous place where all the country music stars got discovered."

"She *is* working there, and not *all* of them got discovered there, Mom—just Tammy Turner."

"*Just* Tammy Turner?"

"Okay, so she's a huge star. But I'm willing to bet that she was singing when she got discovered—not waiting tables."

"Destiny is waiting tables? But . . . she always painted such a rosy picture. How could we have been so in the dark?"

"Because Destiny kept us there. She's got Daddy's independent, stubborn streak. The two of them need to get over each other."

Sara nodded slowly, trying to absorb it all—and remembering why Grace had brought it up in the first place.

"What's Seth doing in Nashville?" she asked her daughter.

"He had to go to Brentwood for a baseball tournament, and he said he might look up Destiny while he was there."

Sara wagged her finger at Grace. "I always knew there might be something going on between those two."

"I don't think there is . . . yet. But maybe there will be."

"I hope you're right," Sara told her. "I'd rather see her with him than . . ."

So far away, waiting tables.

She didn't say it.

Anyway, it wasn't even about that.

Seth Caldwell really had grown into a fine, upstanding young man. Sara had been sorry to see his parents move away, but she still ran into Seth around town from time to time.

Last time she'd seen him, back in May, she'd congratulated him on the high school baseball team's latest win.

"You're doing Wilmot High School proud," she told Seth.

"Well, Coach Reynolds was a great mentor and he left me some solid ballplayers to work with."

"Don't give him all the credit, Seth. I'm sure your coaching has a lot to do with this string of wins."

He'd grinned at her. "Thank you. I hope you and Colonel Hart will come out for some games."

"Oh, you can count on it," Sara had promised—and she'd meant it.

But John was no more interested in attending a high school baseball game than he was in anything else she'd suggested lately: travel, ballroom dancing, even bowling.

Sara's hopes for Seth and Destiny faded as she realized that their lives had taken them in two very different directions. She doubted Destiny was going to give up her dreams—and to her surprise, Sara realized she didn't want her to.

Compromise and understanding were the keys to any relationship. But she knew from personal experience that changing who you are for the sake of your spouse chipped away at your very soul.

She wouldn't wish that on Destiny. Not even for the sake of finding true love.

As for her own relationship . . .

"If you don't allow stubborn pride to get in the way,

John Hart," she said under her breath, "hopefully you'll come to your senses before it's too late."

$\mathscr{H}$earing the phone ring, Destiny snapped her eyes open and her wistful reverie came to a crashing halt.

"I've got to answer that. Sorry," she told Seth, who looked as rattled—and relieved—as she was to have been saved by the bell.

"No problem." He sat on the couch again, petting Mike.

Please don't let it be Kenny looking for the rent, she prayed as she hurried over to grab the phone.

Then again, she couldn't exactly blame him. She had no idea how she was going to come up with it, short of finding a last-minute roommate—and this place was much too small to share with a stranger, so that was out of the question.

"Destiny?"

"Hey, Max." Relieved it wasn't her landlord, she noticed that Seth's hand abruptly stilled on Mike's furry head.

Jealous, was he?

"You're not gonna believe this," Max said in a rush, "but Ralph and Cindy Sue got into it after you left."

"What? No way!"

"Yeah. Some dude who was apparently Cindy Sue's boyfriend came into the bar while Mandy was on break. She took off with him and never came back to do her final set."

"Wow . . ." Her mind only partly on what Max was saying, Destiny watched Seth. "So what did Ralph do?"

"Oh man, he was livid! He called Cindy Sue up and told her not to bother coming back. Ever."

Suddenly Max had her full attention. "Ever?" she echoed incredulously.

"*Ever*. But that's not the best part. He told me that *you* were going to take over for Cindy Sue. For good."

"Shut up!" Destiny shouted, and saw Seth wince. "Sorry. I didn't mean to bust your eardrums," she said to him, and then back into the phone, "Do you think he's serious, Max?"

"Oh yeah, definitely. You're already on the schedule for tomorrow night. He'll be calling you, but I wanted to give you a heads-up. Congratulations, Destiny. This could be the break you been waiting for. You deserve it. You're gonna rock the house and Ralph is gonna wonder what the heck he was thinkin' all this time."

"I hope you're right. Thanks so much for calling, Max. I'll see you tomorrow night." She flipped the phone shut and then looked at Seth. "You're not going to believe what just happened."

"Your boss finally came to his senses?"

"Did you overhear?"

"I wasn't trying to, but, yeah, most of it. Especially the *shut up* part."

"Sorry about that," Destiny said again, and put a hand to her pounding heart. "I can't believe it. I know it's not Honky-Tonk Row or Second Street or the Grand Ole Opry, but still! I'm suddenly a nervous wreck."

"Don't sell yourself short. You just scored yourself a gig in Nashville. Next thing you know, you'll be discovered by some record executive who comes in for a Back in the Saddle burger."

"You make it sound easy."

Billy Jackson popped into her head, and a wave of nausea swept through her. But she couldn't tell Seth about the charismatic con man who'd taken her last cent with a promise to create and deliver demos to the industry powers-that-be, then disappeared off the face of the earth.

She'd promised herself she'd never tell a soul about that, and anyway, she didn't want to ruin this moment with thoughts of that jerk.

Or, for that matter, with thoughts of that soul-shaking kiss a few minutes ago. She had no idea what it had meant to Seth—or what it meant to her, either. And now wasn't the time for clearheaded thinking.

"I don't think for a minute it will be easy," Seth was saying. "But what was it that Nessie told you?"

"Just because you put your boots in the oven don't make 'em biscuits?"

He laughed. "Not that—but it does sound like her. She said, 'The sun don't shine on the same dog's butt every day,' or something like that. You have your shot. Now take it."

Destiny nodded, but something didn't feel exactly right. While she knew Seth was sincere, there was an edge of sadness about his demeanor. She could hear it in the tone of his voice; see it in his eyes. "What aren't you saying?"

He glanced away and hesitated just long enough for her to believe she was right.

But all he said was, "It's getting late. I need to get going and you need to get some shut-eye."

"I'm sure you do, too."

"Right. Just remember that I'm always just a phone call away and I want to hear from you, Destiny. To share good news and to bend my ear with frustrations. I didn't know how hard this has been for you, and you deserve more support than you've been given."

"Thanks, Seth." Destiny wished she could read his expression, because for some reason his offer sounded like both a beginning and closure wrapped up together. "Are you coming to Back in the Saddle to hear me sing tomorrow night?"

"I wouldn't miss it. Well, as long as you want me in the audience?"

"Of course I do. Why would you even ask that?"

"I didn't want to add to any nerves you might be feeling."

"No, I really want you there. The moral support would be awesome. I've done lots of open mike nights over the past four years and landed a small gig here and there, but to be a regular would be a giant leap forward. I could develop new songs, work on my stage presence, and try to get over my stage fright . . ."

"Stage fright?" he echoed in surprise. "*You*?"

"Mercy me . . . *yes*. My heart starts pumping like a jackhammer when I have to get up onstage. I get lightheaded and weak-kneed even in front of small audiences. I can't imagine being in front of thousands."

"Well, you'd better start imagining it, because it's gonna happen."

"You think?"

"I *know*. Believe in yourself, Destiny. Get rid of any negative thoughts. Listen, I've seen baseball players who have the talent but not the drive. If this is really what you want, don't pussyfoot around."

"You know me, Seth. I'm not a pussyfootin' around kinda girl."

"Then get fired up! You can do this!"

Destiny rolled her eyes at him. "Sure thing, Coach Caldwell."

"Well, come on, get ... *pumped*! Gimme a woo-hoo, Destiny."

"Woo-hoo."

"That was weak."

Destiny laughed and then shot a fist skyward. "Woooooo-hooooo!"

"That's what I'm talkin' about!"

"Ohmigosh, I'm really glad that you're here to share this with me."

She was a little embarrassed when her voice came out husky with emotion, and wondered if she'd scared him off, because he quickly said, "And I'm glad I was here. But now you seriously need to get some rest."

"You're right."

They walked to the door, and she opened it.

"This has been one long, eventful day."

"Sure has." And she hated to see it come to an end.

Looking at Seth, she wondered whether he was thinking the same thing. Uh-oh.

What if ... ?

No. No way. Destiny knew not to hope for another toe-curling kiss ... let alone anything more.

"Thanks again for kissing—I mean, coming!"

He grinned. "You sure about that?"

"Positive." Yet in her hurry to put some distance between them, she stumbled. He steadied her, closing his hands around her waist.

Oh boy.

For a couple of seconds, as they stared at each other, it seemed as though the pause button had been pushed on a remote and time felt suspended.

Then he leaned in—just as thunderous footsteps raced up the stairs.

"Just what in tarnation's goin' on up here?" Nessie looked from Destiny to Seth, and her painted-on eyebrows shot toward her platinum hairline. "Oh . . . was I interruptin' somethin'?"

"Nothing like what you're thinking," Destiny assured her.

Seth eyed the broom. "What are you doing with that thing?"

"Protecting Destiny." At his raised eyebrow, she retorted, "It was all I could find on short notice. I heard all kinds of commotion, including a very loud scream, and thought I was comin' to Destiny's rescue, but it doesn't look as if she wants to be rescued. Not from you, anyway. Am I right, sugar?"

"No, you're not right!" Destiny rolled her eyes. "Nessie, that's not why I—"

"It's getting hotter in here than two possums in a mailbox." Nessie jammed her thumb over her shoulder. "I'll just see my way back downstairs and y'all just go back to whatever y'all weren't doin'."

"Go on, tell her," Seth whispered in Destiny's ear.

"Tell me what?" Nessie almost toppled sideways in her mile-high shoes and had to use the broom as a cane. "Destiny, I'm not gonna budge from this here spot until you tell me what's goin' on."

"Cindy Sue skipped out on her final set tonight and Max said that Ralph fired her. He wants me to take her place!"

"Well, butter my butt and call me a biscuit!" Nessie thrust the broom into Seth's hands and threw her arms around Destiny. "I'm so happy for you, baby doll!" She turned and hugged Seth as well.

"What was that for?" he asked with a chuckle.

"'Cause you're as cute as a sack full of puppies and it was as good an excuse as any." She turned back to Destiny. "Listen, I'm gonna be there tomorrow even if I have to shut the shop down early."

"You don't have to do that."

"Are you kiddin'? I wouldn't miss this for the world. Let me know what time and I'll be there with bells on!"

"I will."

Destiny's wobbly smile didn't escape Nessie, who patted her shoulder. "I know you've got some nerves goin' on, but you'll do just fine."

"I hope so."

Seth gave Destiny a little nudge with the broom handle. "Excuse me?"

Destiny rolled her eyes. "Okay, Coach . . . I *know* so."

"That's more like it."

"I knew I liked you." Nessie gave Seth a wink, then turned back to Destiny. "Girlfriend, I do believe the tide is turning. Okay, I'll leave you two alone."

"That's all right. I was just leaving. I'll walk you downstairs," Seth offered.

"Are you sure?"

"Positive." He gave Destiny a quick squeeze. "See you tomorrow night."

"Me, too." Nessie started down the stairs with him. "Oh, what am I gonna wear?"

"Something flashy for a change?" Destiny called after her and was rewarded with laughter from both Nessie and Seth.

As she closed the door after them, she suddenly remembered: She and Seth were supposed to have a date tomorrow night. She hadn't even given it a thought when Max told her she was scheduled to perform.

Oh well. Seth had to understand that her music came first.

And if he didn't . . .

Well, she had her shot, and she was going to take it— just like he himself had told her.

Mike followed her into the bedroom and hopped onto the bed, watching her as if he sensed her inner turmoil.

"You know what's weird, Mike?"

He seemed to tilt his furry head.

"This started out ordinary, just like any other day. But you mark my words: From this day forward, everything is going to change. I can feel it in my bones."

She just wished she knew whether it was because of her career—or Seth Caldwell.

FIVE

Back in the Saddle was always packed on Saturdays, and tonight was no different.

As Destiny wove her way through the tables toward the stage, all of the things that could go wrong flashed into her head. What if she tripped up the steps? Knocked over the microphone? Broke a guitar string? Forgot the lyrics? Hit a sour note? What if they hated her?

What if Seth was here?

What if he wasn't?

She deliberately kept herself from scanning the room for him as she walked, focusing on the small stage instead. Her light supper felt like lead in her stomach and her mouth was completely dry.

At least she knew she looked good. After a two-hour wardrobe-changing marathon, she'd settled on jeans and a sexy black button-up shirt. She'd added a little sparkle: a double-stranded turquoise rock necklace with a crystal-studded spur rowel pendant and a matching bracelet.

Terrific. You look good, but how are you going to sing without saliva?

She tried to swallow, but her tongue felt stuck to the roof of her mouth.

Shooting a panicky glance toward the bar, she caught Max's eye and made a drinking motion with her free hand. When he nodded and held up a bottle of water, she mouthed, "Yes, please!"

Okay, that was better. Now all she had to worry about was . . . everything else.

At last she reached the stage, which suddenly seemed like a skyscraper. She wished there was a handrail or something to grab on to and hoist herself up.

Inner strength . . . where the heck are you? Out for a coffee break?

Her pulse pounded in absolute panic.

This is silly.

You're finally right where you want to be. All you have to do is get on up there and sing your heart out.

She gave herself a mental shake and was almost able to lift her leg when a familiar voice stopped her in her tracks.

"Just what in the world do you think you're doin'?"

Awash in dismal dread, Destiny turned around and came face-to-face with Cindy Sue Smith. Well, not exactly face-to-*face*. For the first time in ages, Destiny was glad for her superior height. In her heels she really towered over Cindy Sue.

Unfortunately that didn't seem to faze her. "I saaaa-id *what* in the *world* do you think you're doin'?"

Destiny somehow managed to unglue her tongue. "Ralph said you've been fired, Cindy Sue."

"Yeah, like he's gonna stick to that. Excuse me."

Destiny arched an eyebrow. Heart pounding wildly, she managed to respond with a firm, "I don't think so."

Cindy Sue jutted her chin in the air and gave her blond hair a toss. "Then I'll just have to move your big ole Amazon-ass outta my way," she announced so loudly that the microphone picked up her voice. Of course, almost everyone in the restaurant stopped eating and suddenly all eyes were focused on them.

Destiny calmly tilted her guitar case against the steps, then turned back to face her snooty little foe. She could easily lift Cindy Sue up and flip her out of the way like a Frisbee. Too bad physical intimidation wasn't her style; she preferred brain power. Unfortunately, her brain was already on overload and she had no idea what to do or say next.

Luckily, Max intervened. "Here's your water, Destiny."

"Oh . . . uh, thanks." Destiny reached over and took the cold bottle from Max's outstretched hand, aware that all eyes in the room were still on her.

Mind racing, she unscrewed the cap and took a much-needed gulp.

"Cindy Sue, you need to leave. Destiny is singing," Max said quietly, but firmly.

"Get back to polishing the bar, Max," Cindy Sue hissed. "This is none of your concern."

"Seriously, you need to leave."

"Seriously, you need to shut your piehole. Don't you have beer to pour or bathrooms to clean or something?"

"I'm giving you one last chance . . ."

"Bite me."

"You asked for it."

Destiny's eyes widened as she watched Max—the big teddy bear of a guy who was terrified to sing in front of an audience—hop right up onto the stage.

He took the mike and signaled for silence. "Ladies and gentlemen, may I have your attention, please?"

Except for the clinking of glasses and silverware, the restaurant got quiet. With all eyes focused on him, Max swallowed hard, but managed a smile.

"I think what we need here is a little sing-off. Whaddaya say?" he asked, and was answered with cheers and whistles.

Destiny's jaw dropped.

"Let's listen to Cindy Sue Smith sing first, and then Destiny Hart. Then y'all decide who you want with your applause. Whoever gets the biggest cheer will be our performer at Back in the Saddle tonight."

Oh boy. Destiny glanced around for Ralph and found him over by the hostess stand, looking as if he was going to march up to the stage and give Max what for. But when the audience roared in wild approval of the little wager, Ralph crossed his arms over his chest and grinned as though this had been his own brilliant idea.

"You ready, Cindy Sue?" Max gestured toward the stool.

Detecting a slight twitch to his lips, Destiny could tell that this wasn't easy for him, and she loved him for it. Besides, with his deep baritone, he had terrific stage presence, and she dearly hoped that someday he got to use it.

"I . . . uh . . ." Cindy Sue narrowed her eyes and glared up at Max.

"Or would you rather Destiny went first?"

"No, I—I—this is just plain stupid. I'm outta here!" She turned on her heel and marched out the door with her hips swinging.

Max saluted her back, and the crowd cheered.

"Well, now that we have that unpleasantness out of the way, allow me to introduce a talented young lady with a voice that will knock your socks off. Put down your burgers and beers and give it up for Nashville's own Destiny Hart! Show them who really owns this stage, Destiny!"

Max jumped down. "Go get 'em, girl!"

"That took some guts," Destiny whispered back, giving him a quick hug. "You're a good friend and I can't thank you enough."

Max squeezed her hard and she took a deep breath, then stepped up into the spotlight.

Destiny was welcomed with cheers and whistles. At the realization that after all that build-up, she definitely couldn't disappoint, Destiny felt light-headed. Her heart pounded wildly and her knees felt so weak that she had to immediately sit down on the stool. The sea of faces blurred and ran together and her panic mounted.

She was about to blow her big chance.

The crowd settled down, watching her, and Destiny sensed a ripple of disappointment that might very well kill the earlier buzz. She blinked and tried to think of something clever to say.

Don't say anything! Just sing!

Good idea! But her fingers were frozen on the guitar strings and her voice seemed to have taken a sudden leave of absence.

A hush had fallen over the crowd. Any moment now they would be booing and chanting for Cindy Sue. Oh, this wasn't good . . .

"Hey, Destiny Hart!"

That familiar voice snapped Destiny out of her stage fright. She shielded her hand above her eyebrows and over the crowd to be sure.

"I dare you to sing Gretchen Wilson's 'Here for the Party'!"

Seth.

She couldn't see him out there, but she recognized his voice—and the challenge. He knew as well as she did that Gretchen's kickin' song would get the crowd rocking. He also knew she couldn't back down from a dare.

Although her heart was still pounding like crazy, Destiny adjusted the microphone and shouted, "Hey there, Nashville, Tennessee! I know *I'm* here for the party, too! How about you guys?"

Whoops and "hell yeahs" rang out through the audience and suddenly the magic was back.

"I can't *hear...* you!" Playing to the crowd, she cupped her hand to her ear and waited. When they roared in approval, she shouted, "Well, then, let's get this party started!"

Destiny dove into the song, gaining strength and confidence when she had the whole room singing along.

"I'm here for the party ... yeah!" Destiny raised her fist into the air at the conclusion of the kick-butt song. Deciding to keep right on riding the wave, she asked, "Are there any redneck women out there?"

Of course her question was answered with cheers and "hell yeahs."

In the front row, she spotted Nessie, who put her thumb and pinkie between her lips and gave a shrill whistle of approval. "Come on, girl! I know I'm here to have some fun!"

Her last bit of fear thrust away by a surge of adrenaline, Destiny shouted, "Well, then, get your redneck selves up here on the dance floor and sing along with some Southern pride!"

Destiny slid right into "Redneck Woman" and within moments, had the dance floor packed.

To keep the energy going she went right into Miranda Lambert's "Gunpowder and Lead."

"Thank you!" Destiny told the cheering crowd and then paused to take a long swig of water.

She'd watched Cindy Sue perform too many times not to feel the difference in the crowd tonight. Maybe this was only Back in the Saddle Bar and Grille, and maybe she was far from making it in this business, but this was what she had been working toward and waiting for.

"My mother introduced me to the country classics when I was a little girl moving from one air force base to the next. I'm a military brat—'born, raised, and transferred'— and no matter where I lived, even overseas, I never lost my love of bluegrass, gospel, and country music. I was teased for not listening to boy bands or Top 40, but I can sing along with every Tammy Turner song you can name. Another one of my idols, Barbara Mandrell, sings, 'I Was Country When Country Wasn't Cool,' and I'd like to perform her signature song for y'all right now." She grinned and added, "I know y'all have been right there with me on this one. Am I right?"

When Destiny was met with more wild cheers, she learned that connecting with her audience on a personal level was crucial. The amazing thing was that she was being completely honest and simply herself . . .

And they liked her. Incredible.

The rest of the performance flew by, and before she knew it, she was thanking the band and the audience to a thunderous round of applause.

As she stepped down from the stage, her knees still felt a bit wobbly and her heart pounded like mad but she felt good. Great.

She planted a big smile on her face and looked around for Seth, but before she could find him, a distinguished-looking silver-haired gentleman walked up to her.

"Hello, Destiny Hart," he said in a whiskey-smooth voice laced with a touch of the South. "Allow me to introduce myself."

Immediately wary, she took a step back, experiencing déjà vu. This was exactly how she'd met Billy Jackson, who'd come up to her after a pinch-hit performance here last year.

"I'm Nick Novell of Sundial Records."

Nick Novell! The man was a country music industry icon. But recognizing the name as legitimate didn't exactly relax her. On the contrary, she found her hand shaking as she reached out to shake his.

"It's nice to meet you, Mr. Novell."

"Likewise." Nick angled his head toward the doorway. "Could we walk out into the hallway where it's not quite so noisy?"

"Sure." As she followed him through the crowd, Nessie grabbed her arm. Today her jeans were eye-popping pink with bright yellow piping. Big white sunglasses held back her puffed-up platinum-blond wig, which fell past her narrow shoulders in fat curls instead of little ringlets.

"You were dynamite, kiddo! Come here, I want you to meet—"

"Hang on, I'll be right back, Nessie." She pointed at Nick, and saw her friend's eyes widen. Nessie gave her a big grin and a thumbs-up.

In the hallway leading to the break room, Nick Novell told her, "I don't come in here very often, but luckily I had a craving tonight for a Back in the Saddle bacon cheeseburger. Once I have it on my mind, I have to have one."

"Oh, I'm the same way about chicken and biscuits at the Loveless Café," she heard herself say, and wished she hadn't.

"You know," he said with a grin, "there are lots of other biscuits in the world."

"True, but these are really special."

"I know what you mean."

"Well, butter my butt and call me a biscuit," Destiny replied without stopping to think.

Holy cow, had she really just said that to Nick Novell?

To her blessed relief, he tossed his silver head back and laughed.

"You are something else, young lady."

"Thank you ... Oh wait. You meant that in a good way, right?"

"Sure did. I've been going to lots of showcases lately, searching for someone with a cool, sexy sound laced with some sass."

"Did you find it?"

"There's plenty of talent in Nashville."

"Oh." Destiny tried to sound upbeat. "That's so true."

"But like those biscuits, you have some extra-special ingredient that I can't quite put my finger on . . ."

Her heart began to race. Maybe this really was her big break.

Nick pursed his lips, eyeing her thoughtfully. "You've got the cool sexy sound and more than a little sass, but there's a vulnerability about you that softens the edge. I saw it when you stepped up onto the stage."

"I was terrified for a minute there," she admitted.

"Maybe, but determination won out. You'll need that in this business. It's not for the faint of heart. You also have a gift for songwriting. 'Restless Heart' was a beautiful song with a fun, honest edge."

"Really?"

"I don't give out compliments lightly. Ask anyone who knows me." Nick reached into his pocket, pulled out a slim leather case, flipped it open, and handed her a card. "This is a music publishing house. Contact them and drop my name."

"Oh, I will," she said breathlessly. "Thank you!"

"And here's my card. I've been doing this for more years than I care to count and I can instantly spot talent and stage presence. You've got both, but you need some polish. If you have a manager in mind, give them a call."

Destiny nodded vigorously. "I've done my homework. I have someone in mind."

"May I ask whom?"

"Miranda Shepherd."

Middle-aged Miranda was well-known around Nashville, and occasionally came into the restaurant with her clients. She was rumored to be hard-nosed and polished in the boardroom, but Destiny was impressed with her down-to-earth attitude toward the waitstaff and her clients: celebrities and up-and-comers alike.

Nick gave an approving nod. "Excellent choice! If this works out the way I think it will, you'll need Miranda's guidance." He winked. "I'm sure glad I had a burger on my mind tonight. Once in a while it just works out that way. See you soon."

"Thank you. I'm looking forward to it." Destiny shook her head mutely as he walked away, then stared down at the cards in her trembling hand. "Wow."

"That's what I was going to say."

She looked up to see Seth standing there.

"Actually, maybe I'll still say it. Wow. You brought down the house, Destiny." He grabbed her in a hug, then released her with an apology. "I came straight here from the game. I mighta just gotten some field dust on that shirt of yours. I'd wipe it off, but . . . well, maybe not here in public."

Seeing the gleam in his eye, she forgot all about her performance, and Nick Novell, and the business card she was holding.

Then Seth asked, "What's that in your hand?"

She opened her mouth to tell him, then closed it again, telling herself she might jinx it by talking about something that wasn't a done deal.

Or was there some other reason she didn't want to tell Seth that she might be on the brink of something huge?

Maybe you're afraid he'll give you a reason to turn your back on your career—even now that you're on the brink of taking off.

Twenty-four hours ago she'd have said that was impossible.

But twenty-four hours ago she'd never been kissed by Seth Caldwell.

"I suppose you're too drained after that performance to let me take you out to celebrate?" he asked.

"I definitely am." She looked him in the eye. "But we can go back to my place instead, if you want."

"Oh, I want." He broke into a slow grin, and she wondered what she'd just done.

SIX

As Destiny fit the key into the lock, Seth had to laugh at the ferocious sound of Mike's bark.

"You know, Destiny, he might look like a little alien, but he sounds like a huge dog that could take someone's head off."

"I know. It's like having a built-in alarm system. Mike, hush!" She turned the key, opened the door, and the so-called dog came running, barking and jangling his tags.

Laughing, Destiny gathered him into her arms and he licked her face. "Yes, Mike, yes. It did go well. Thanks for asking. And look who's back to see you. It's your friend Seth."

"Hey there, Mike. I'd pat you, but I've kind of got my hands full here." He was holding both Destiny's guitar and the duffel bag he'd grabbed from his car—not because he had any hopes of spending the night with her, but because he needed to get cleaned up. Not that he was in any hurry to get home . . .

"Remember, I didn't know you were coming over tonight," Destiny told him, flipping on a light, "or I would've cleaned for you."

"It wasn't bad last night. How much messier can it be?"

She raised an eyebrow at him. "It was kind of a whirlwind day."

"Whirlwind? As in cyclone?" Stepping over the threshold, Seth took in the clothing strewn over every surface and wondered if there was anything left in her closet.

"I had to figure out what to wear."

He flicked his gaze over to her. "Good choice."

His heart kicked into high gear. He knew he was staring, but she took his breath away. It wasn't the clothes or makeup or hairstyle that captivated him; it was Destiny herself. Her beauty radiated from the inside, intertwining with her personality to create the sweet and spunky package that had enchanted the audience back at the bar and grill.

He'd jumped on her obviously spontaneous invitation for him to come back here with her, worried she might take it back—but she hadn't.

She'd even asked whether he, too, had something to celebrate. "Did you win?"

"No, but it was a great game."

"Then it was worthwhile," said the girl who, just last night, had told him winning was the only thing that mattered.

Seth smiled and reached over to tug on a lock of her hair. He meant it as a playful gesture, but the softness curled around his finger like spun silk. When he pulled his hand free, fine strands caught against his calluses.

He cleared his throat. "You really should wear your hair down more often, Destiny. It suits your personality."

"You mean wild and crazy?" she teased, but there was a husky quality to her voice.

"More like untamed and beautiful, like your music . . . heartfelt but with an edge of honesty that hits you right in the gut," he said, and immediately felt foolish. "There goes my man-card again."

"Your what?"

"Never mind. Where should I put this?" He indicated the guitar, handling it like the precious cargo it was.

"Oh, you can set it over there on the stand," Destiny told him. "I've got to go walk Mike."

"By yourself? At night?"

She gave him a look. "What do you think I do, hire a bodyguard every time my dog has to go?"

"Here—I'll trade you." He held out the guitar. "You take this. I'll take Mike."

"But—"

"I know, I know. He's not supposed to be here. We'll be very quiet and careful, won't we, Mike?"

"Mike? Quiet?" Destiny shook her head, but she took the guitar and handed him the dog and a leash.

"Should I make some coffee while you're out there?" she asked.

"Nah, it's too hot tonight for that. I'll just take some sweet tea, if you have it."

"Lots of ice, no lemon. Right?"

He smiled in surprise. "Good memory."

"For some things."

Seth carried Mike down the steps and out to the small yard behind the building.

"There you go, guy. Get busy." He set Mike on the tiny patch of grass and watched him sniff around.

He could hear the lively sounds of lower Broadway in the distance—so very different than sleepy little Wilmot, where the only sound at night was chirping crickets.

But then, there were crickets here, too, and a familiar, sweet scent of summer in the sultry city air. Honeysuckle, he realized, and looked around for the source before spotting the telltale vine that determinedly twisted its way around the chain-link fence.

He thought about Destiny and how hard the past four years must have been on her. Behind the in-your-face strength and sassy humor was an emotionally vulnerable woman needing a strong shoulder and a sympathetic heart.

I want to be the one who gives that to her.

I want her to come back home with me—and that's never going to happen now.

Seth looked up at a nearly full moon and stars glittering like rock candy against blue velvet. At least Destiny could come outside and look up into the same night sky he'd be seeing at home. From now on, he'd think of her here . . .

Suddenly, a new sound reached his ears: the soft strumming of a guitar.

He looked up at the fire escape and saw her silhouette against the brick building. She didn't see him; her head was tilted down and her hair tumbled forward to shadow her face. Barefoot, she'd changed into shorts and a T-shirt.

She began to sing, and Seth smiled, remembering the

Patsy Cline classic as one of Destiny's many old-school favorites.

"*Crazy . . .*"

Seth let the song wash over him like steamy-cool summer rain. Destiny's husky pitch gave the timeless song a modern edge, yet evoked the haunting beauty of the original.

Mike trotted over and sat on his haunches beside Seth, tilting his head as if he, too, were captivated by the song.

Then he joined in, tossing back his spiky head and howling.

"Ahhh-eoowwaaaa!" His doggie lips curved in a perfect O.

Overhead, Destiny laughed and kept right on singing, right through to the end, accompanied by a final canine wail as she sang, "For lovin' . . . ya-oooooah!"

Seth applauded, laughing, and she called down, "Any requests?"

"For you or for your sidekick down here?"

"We're a duo, just like Brooks and Dunn."

"Hmm, let me think . . ."

"Nah, show's over." She gave the guitar one last strum. "Bring my little sidekick on up here, would you, before he gets me into trouble?"

"Sure thing." Seth scooped up Mike and returned to the apartment, where he found her packing her guitar away.

"Thanks for the private performance," he told her as he set Mike on his feet.

She smiled. "Sometimes, on warm summer nights, I like to sit out on the fire escape with my guitar. It makes me remember how much I love this city."

Again, he was reminded that this was her home now—not Wilmot. He forced himself to look enthusiastic. "So what do you love most about it?"

"Oh, you know . . . that you rub elbows with all walks of life here. You can walk into the Stage or Tootsies or Legends and see all ages from crusty old cowboys in worn Wranglers to college kids in Lucky jeans. Same thing at concerts. Country music is about real life, real people."

"You're going to be a part of the music that makes this city famous."

"Yeah, well, if that's the case, then this town will never be the same," she joked.

"I was serious."

"So was I. Listen, why don't you have a seat and I'll get us our sweet tea?"

"I don't want to go near your furniture"—*or you*—"until I get a shower, if you don't mind."

"Sure, go ahead. There are clean towels in the linen closet. Help yourself."

"Thanks." Seth picked up his duffel bag. "I won't take long."

earing the shower go on in the bathroom, Destiny shook her head. After all that had happened tonight, this might be the most surreal event of all: Seth Caldwell at her place, naked.

Well, in the next room, behind closed doors, but still . . .

"Talk about crazy," she told Mike, who gave her a blank stare. "Oh, never mind."

She gave him a bone-shaped biscuit, then sliced cheddar cheese into squares and located some wheat crackers. As she poured two glasses of sweet tea, she let herself wonder what it would be like if this were a typical Saturday night and she and Seth were settling in for a movie or a baseball game.

But then she closed her eyes and swallowed hard, firmly reminding herself that Seth was only here by chance, just for tonight. He belonged back in Wilmot, and she belonged here—especially now.

Thinking or hoping for anything else was only setting herself up for heartbreak, and she had all the disappointment in her life that she could handle right now, *thank you very much*.

She was going to enjoy Seth's company this evening, then say good-bye and go back to her life as he went back to his.

Two separate and very different lives.

Destiny carried the tray to the coffee table and sat down to wait. In the bathroom, the shower stopped running.

She picked up a magazine and flipped through it, but her brain refused to focus on anything other than the fact that Seth was undoubtedly toweling off his naked body on the other side of the door.

A few minutes later it opened. "There. I feel much better now."

Seth reached up to run his fingers through his wet hair, and Destiny couldn't help but notice a delicious ripple of muscle beneath the Wilmot Panthers T-shirt stretched across his wide shoulders. And while there shouldn't have been anything attractive about his basic black sweatpants, Seth managed to wear them well.

"Hmmm . . ." He brought his forearm up to his nose

and sniffed. "Peaches-and-cream bodywash," he said with a grin. "I smell like a girl."

"Well, you sure don't look like one," came out of Destiny's mouth. Dangerous territory, but she couldn't stop herself. Something sizzled between them, making her feel feminine and alive and daring—just as she had earlier, onstage.

"Thanks. Although I have to say that those little exploding beads I read about on the bottle made me tingle all over."

That pretty much stole coherent thought from her head, and she could only look him over from head to toe.

"What?" Seth asked with an amused frown. "Do I have a Q-tip sticking out of my ear or something?"

Oops. Embarrassed, she blurted the first thing that popped into her head. "No, but your barn door is open."

"These sweatpants don't even have a barn door."

Oops again. "Gotcha!" She forced a laugh.

"What are you, twelve?"

"And holding. Just ask my father."

Talk about an effective mood dampener.

"Destiny—" Seth came over to the couch, shaking his head. "Don't do that to yourself."

He sat beside her, and Mike settled at their feet.

"All I meant was that Daddy's been waiting impatiently for me to come to my senses and finally become an adult. Maybe it's about time I did."

"You're an adult. Look at you. Better yet, let me look at you." It was his turn to let his gaze ride over her. "Yep—you're all woman, all right."

Unnerved, Destiny thrust a glass of sweet tea into his hand and turned the conversation back to her father, the buzz kill.

"I guess I should be grateful that Daddy raised Grace and me with the belief that you create your own luck and seal your own fate."

"And yet he named you Destiny."

She nodded. "In that you create your own. And Grace was named as a reminder that if we stray from our path in life, through divine grace we will find our way back."

Seth reached over to put his glass back on the coffee table. Droplets of condensation fell onto a drowsy-looking Mike, but it didn't faze him in the least.

Destiny smiled fondly at the little dog. "Too many nights sleeping in the rain."

"But he'll never have to be cold, wet, or hungry ever again, thanks to you."

"You got that right. Truth be known, though, I needed him as much as he needed me."

The warm concern shining in Seth's deep brown eyes was so comforting that for a long moment Destiny simply sat there and soaked it up like a dry sponge. Life, she thought, would be so much easier with a soft place to land at the end of the day.

But that—*this*—wasn't going to happen. Not for her. Not with him.

Resigned to the fact, she inhaled deeply.

"You know, you really do smell like a peach," she heard herself say. "Not that there's anything wrong with that."

"You sure?" He opened his arms. "In that case, why don't you come on over here."

"Oh, I—" She slid away from him and crashed into the arm of the couch, rattling the end table.

The statue of Elvis immediately began swiveling his plastic hips and singing a high-pitched, "You Ain't Nothin' but a Hound Dog."

Destiny rolled her eyes. "Oh, for the love of—"

Seth gave her a smug smile. "There's a good way to make sure it doesn't happen again, you know."

"Really? What's that?"

With a challenging glint in his eye, he wordlessly patted the cushion beside him.

"Oh, I don't know . . . I kind of like this song," she teased. "Don't you?"

"Not this version. And the King is dead. But if you want to grab your guitar and give it a whirl . . ."

"No, thanks. I'm exhausted from all that singing."

"Then come on over here"—he patted the cushion again—"and let me give you a good old-fashioned back rub."

"I don't think that's a good idea."

"Why not?"

She just shook her head, looking at him, unnerved by the challenge in his eyes.

"You know, I prefer friendly persuasion, but . . ."

Destiny shook her head. "Don't you even . . ."

"Dare?" Seth grinned. "Hey, I know how you can't refuse a dare, so that wouldn't be fair of me, now, would it?"

"No, it certainly would not."

He tilted his head. "Actually, I was thinking of leaving it up to fate."

"Don't you remember how I feel about fate, Seth?"

"So you're still a nonbeliever?"

She nodded.

He slid toward her.

"What are you doing?"

"Taking *your* advice. You said you have to make things happen, not sit back and wait for them to happen, so . . ."

"You remember everything I said that evening?"

"Pretty much," he responded with a soft smile. "In fact, seeing you flooded my brain with memories. I've missed you, Destiny."

He reached out and pulled her into an embrace.

A warm little tingle slid down her spine and she closed her eyes to savor the moment. Hugging him close felt more than just wonderful . . . it was simply delicious. His wide shoulders stretched the soft cotton of his T-shirt and his muscles rippled beneath her fingers. She longed to slide her fingers into the hair at the nape of his neck, and when the sandpaper tickle of his five-o'clock shadow slid against her smooth cheek, it was all she could do not to nuzzle closer.

She pulled back to look at him and saw that his eyes were fixated on her mouth. Okay, so they were definitely on the same wavelength.

Destiny was no stranger to romance; she'd dated her share of men since she'd arrived in Nashville. She knew exactly where this was headed.

But this was *Seth*. The stakes had always been high where he was concerned. That hadn't changed.

"It's getting late," she said, and faked a yawn.

"I know."

"I really am wiped out."

"I know that, too."

She started to stand up; Seth put a hand on her shoulder.

She swallowed hard.

"Now, how about that back rub?"

*P*acing through his fishing cabin, John clutched his cell phone and thought about calling Sara for the millionth time since he'd left home yesterday—heck, probably the millionth time tonight.

He'd been trying not to think about her, but he couldn't seem to help it. She should be here with him.

Although he had bought the property for fishing and hunting, Sara loved summers in this rustic setting, and would often accompany him on the weekends to read and needlepoint.

Not anymore. She'd lost interest in the cabin—or maybe just in him. Not only did the cabin look a mess without her tidy hand, but normally this time of year she would have flowerpots full of blooming annuals to bring a shot of color to the place.

Now it was all browns and grays, musty and quiet.

He shook his head, telling himself that it was too late to call. Still, he opened his contact folder and started scrolling with his thumb, finding some small measure of comfort at seeing her name.

Sara—home, the entry read.

He didn't really mean to follow through with a call, but his thumb seemed to have a life of its own. He pressed the dial button.

She answered right away, and the sound of her voice made John's heart pound like it used to when they were kids dating. Now, as a grown man sitting in a remote cabin in his boxers with the phone to his ear, he couldn't begin to find his voice.

"Hello? John?"

Damn caller ID! He couldn't just hang up, but he didn't know what to say.

"Hey, Sara. How's it going?" He winced.

"Fine," she responded shortly.

"Good." John looked up at the shadowy ceiling and ran his fingers through his short cropped hair.

Met with stony silence, he cleared his throat. "Well, I was just checking."

He longed to tell he her that he missed her, *loved her*, but his pride was in the way, and the words stuck in his throat.

"I talked to Grace about something. You should know . . ."

"What? Don't tell me she changed her mind and got back together with that fool boyfriend of hers. The kid's going nowhere."

There was a long pause. Then Sara said, "That's not what it was about."

"Oh. Well, good," he said gruffly.

"We talked about Destiny."

His heart sank. "What about her?"

Again, Sara hesitated. "It seems she might be a little worse off than she led us to believe."

"No surprise there," John said immediately, and hated himself for it.

"You know what? Never mind. I don't know why I even bothered to—"

"No, tell me what's going on, Sara. I deserve to know. I'm her father."

Sara said nothing to that. He could just imagine what she was thinking, and he wanted to tell her she had it all wrong. He was a good father. That was why he had to take a stand.

"Sara, tell me."

"It's nothing, really. Not that big a deal. She's just . . . she's a waitress."

No surprise there. Relieved, John asked, "Well, what did you think she was? A rock star?"

"Not a rock star, John. Destiny isn't into rock—she's into country. And I thought she was making a living at it, but—"

"Who makes a living singing songs?"

"Plenty of people do, and if you believed in her, then you'd—"

"I believe in *her*. I just don't believe in throwing away your life on a stubborn whim."

"Oh, really?" Sara said in such a loaded tone that John had to clutch the phone to keep from tossing it across the room.

"What does that mean?"

"Nothing," Sara said.

He shook his head.

"You just don't get it, do you?"

"What don't I get?"

"I think we should help her out."

"I've tried. She doesn't want my advice."

"Not with advice. With money, maybe, so that she can—"

"Handing her money isn't going to make her wake up and smell the coffee."

"That's not what I—"

"Look, I love my daughter," John managed to spit out. *I love you, dammit.*

"Then support her dream."

A muscle jumped in his jaw and he gripped the phone tighter. "Don't you see, Sara? That's all it is. A dream! She needs to build a solid future. Dreams don't pay bills," he ground out. "Destiny needs to get her head out of the clouds and come down to reality!"

"Oh, really? If everyone felt that way, we wouldn't

have music or art. Theater. Movies. We wouldn't have the pro sports that you love to watch, for that matter. We need dreamers, risk-takers."

"You said yourself you're upset that she's waitressing. I don't get why I'm the bad guy just because I—"

"No, I'm disappointed. It's not that I don't approve. I just wanted something better for her."

"That's the point! So do I. She's my daughter, for Pete's sake!"

"*Our* daughter! And do you think this isn't a sacrifice for *her*? Leaving her friends and family? Living alone? Waiting tables? She's doing what she has to do to make her dream come true."

"She's wasting her life away, Sara!"

"You don't know that!" she said fiercely. "What she *will* be wasting if she doesn't give this a shot is her talent." He heard her inhale a deep breath while she waited for his response. "What I'm wasting is *my* time trying to reason with you. Talk sense into that thick, stubborn head of yours and get you to see that Destiny needs us."

"This isn't about money—not about my money—*our* money," he quickly amended. "It's about—"

"Good-bye, John." She cut him off in such a firm tone that a cold shot of fear slid down his spine.

And then the line went dead.

John muttered a harsh oath and stood there for God knew how long, gripping the phone, staring into the silent, shadowed darkness.

A *back rub? Did I really just offer her a back rub?*

Seth held his breath, expecting Destiny to bolt off the couch and order him out of her apartment.

To his shock, she turned around and presented him with her back.

His hands were shaking as he eased her hair out of the way to expose her shoulders. Beneath the thin cotton of her shirt, he could feel the firm muscles that reminded him that she was strong in body, mind, and spirit. And yet the delicate arch of her neck gave her a sweet vulnerability. Seth longed to lean in and kiss her there, but concentrated on massaging away her tension and easing past her fear.

"Just try to relax," he said in her ear.

"I am."

Her curls brushed across his hands, and he became acutely aware of her soft skin and her light floral scent.

It felt so good, so natural to be here with her like this that Seth wondered how he was going to return to Wilmot and resume his life without her.

No—don't think about that. Not right now. Just be in the moment.

He leaned in and kissed her neck. "That feels nice," she murmured, and he knew that they'd reached the point of no return.

He could play it safe and leave right now—or he could throw caution to the wind and kiss her again.

Her own words ran through his brain, and his mind was made up.

You have to make things happen . . .

Gently, Seth cupped her chin to turn her face toward him, and kissed her.

Ten days later, Destiny found herself in the board-room at Sundial Records, thighs pressed together beneath the gleaming mahogany table to keep her knees from knocking.

"You're about to get some serious writer's cramp," Nick Novell commented as he slid a sleek silver pen over to Destiny. "But I think it'll be worth it, don't you?"

"No doubt."

Was this really happening?

Funny—that was the same thought that kept flitting through her mind the night she and Seth had spent together. Even now, the memory sent butterflies flitting through her.

It had really happened.

This, too, was really happening.

Before reaching for the pen, she dried her damp right palm on the skirt of her new business suit.

She eyed the crystal water pitcher with longing, but was afraid that her hands were shaking too hard to pour.

Then, as if reading her mind, Miranda Shepherd, seated beside her, reached over and filled her glass.

"Thanks," she told her manager, who discreetly patted Destiny's leg beneath the table.

That she actually *had* a manager—let alone one of the best—was going to take some getting used to. And now she was about to have a record label as well.

Sundial Records . . . Nick . . . Miranda . . .

Seth.

Wow. Dreams really do come true.

Destiny took a big sip from the tall glass. The cold water slid down her dry throat and splashed into her empty stomach.

"Ready?" Nick asked Destiny, who nodded. He looked over at Miranda.

"Everything is in order," Miranda answered crisply.

"Then let's get this show on the road." Nick handed out the contracts and Destiny picked up the pen. "Just sign at the red arrows. I'll explain each section as we go, but don't hesitate to ask questions."

The process seemed so surreal that as she signed her name over and over, Destiny felt as though she might wake up curled up on her sofa with Mike, eating Cheetos and watching reruns of *Friends*.

She signed the final page with a flourish and gently laid down the pen.

"This is exciting!" Nick Novell announced in his deep, booming voice, and reached over to shake Destiny's hand. "I've been in this business for a long time, and my gut tells me that your star is going to rise quickly, Destiny."

"Has your gut ever been wrong?" she couldn't help asking.

"Hmmm . . ." Nick arched one eyebrow and rubbed his chin as if in serious thought, then grinned. "Never."

Destiny let out a little whoop, then put her hand over her mouth. "Sorry. Sometimes I tend to get caught up in the moment."

Nick Novell tilted his head back and laughed. "I knew you had spunk. Now, we have to get a great road band behind you, set you up with an A and R rep, and you'll be on your way to the top of the country-music charts."

"I can't wait."

"Well, don't get too anxious," he said with a smile. "For a new unknown artist, it can take a year or more from signing to getting a first single on the air."

"A whole *year*?"

"Sometimes less—if you get some kind of break. Look, don't worry, Destiny, we have big plans for you. We're going to get you into the studio as soon as possi-

ble, and once we have a couple of songs in the can, we'll
get our other departments involved—promotion, creative, marketing . . ."

"What do they do, exactly?"

"They all weigh in with their two cents, basically. The
creative team works on your brand image—head shots,
video shoots, album packaging. They get to know you
and figure out what your style is—or should be."

Should be?

As determined as she was to rise to the top, Destiny
wasn't crazy about that terminology—or the idea of
changing herself to fit someone else's image.

"The promotion guys are responsible for getting your
songs on the radio. They're the ones who are in tune
with what's working and not working on radio across
the country, so basically, they have a lot of say in what
you record."

She nodded. Her head was spinning.

"The marketing team is responsible for marketing
the album launch, and the sales team sells it into retail."

"That's an awful lot of people."

Nick laughed. "Don't worry. I'll be observing and
guiding the whole way, and Miranda has been doing this
forever."

He went on with more detail, and Miranda took
notes, and Destiny tried to concentrate, hoping she was
nodding at all the right places. But she was buzzing with
such excitement that it was difficult to stay focused. Finally, when she thought her brain would explode from
too much information, Nick's assistant poked her head
in and informed him that he was late for a luncheon.

The meeting ended with a flurry of handshakes and
hugs.

"I'll call you soon," Miranda told her. "And congratulations. I'm very excited about this! Drive, ambition, talent, sex appeal . . . you've got all the right stuff!"

"Thank you, Miranda. My parents taught me to always give a hundred percent."

"That's good to hear, because if you're going to make it in this industry, it's going to take nothing less." Miranda put her hands on Destiny's shoulders. "There's lots of talent and competition out there, Destiny. You have that special, elusive . . . something, no doubt. But continued hard work will separate you from the pack." She gave her a gentle squeeze. "As busy as your life is now . . . well, let's just hope you're ready, 'cause you ain't seen nothing yet!"

"I'm ready," Destiny answered with conviction and gave Miranda a hug, but a troubling thought entered her brain.

If she gave a hundred percent to her career . . . then what would be left over for Seth?

SEVEN

October had always been Destiny's favorite time of year—whenever she lived in an area that saw the change of seasons, anyway.

Nashville certainly fell into that category. The summer's humidity gave way to crisp, clean air, and the city was more scenic than ever, set against a backdrop of fiery foliage and cobalt sky.

As she stepped outside after a Friday-afternoon rehearsal at Back in the Saddle, though, Destiny's thoughts weren't on the landscape or the weather.

Nor were they on her career, despite the encouraging response the label was giving her on "Restless Heart," which was slated to become her first single.

It had all happened so fast, in a chicken-or-the-egg kind of way: Nick Novell signing her with Sundial Records and Miranda agreeing to take her on as a client. She'd been an invaluable source of advice and encouragement.

"Think of me as the captain steering your career ship with a full crew of attorneys, agents, accountants, and publicists," she'd told Destiny at the beginning—back when she couldn't imagine that she'd ever need all those people in her life.

Maybe the reason it was all such a blur was that her thoughts at the time had been preoccupied with Seth— kind of like they were right now.

It had been three months since they spent that first glorious night in each other's arms. There had been many more romantic evenings since—but not nearly enough of them.

Destiny's days were spent songwriting or in the recording studio, and her nights performing with her new band. That left little time for anything else. She did manage to talk to Seth most every night, but he couldn't come to visit very often—at first due to the success of his summer baseball team, then because school was back in session.

She'd been hoping they could see each other tonight, but Seth had sent her a text message while she was onstage rehearsing.

CAN'T MAKE IT AFTER ALL. LEAGUE
SCHEDULED A MAKEUP GAME FOR LAST
NIGHT'S RAINOUT.

She understood, of course, that circumstances were beyond his control, but still . . .

Why, once the summer league had ended, did he have

to take on another coaching position for the town recreation board's league? Fall wasn't even baseball season, as far as she was concerned.

Okay, maybe that wasn't fair. Baseball was in Seth's blood the way music was in hers. He understood that she spent her weekends singing, and just about every other waking hour on her songwriting and recording. Could she really blame him for indulging his own passion?

No. You absolutely cannot, and you know it. Not if you want this to work.

Their relationship was working so far, and the last thing she wanted was to shake things up.

So she'd texted back:

NO PROBLEM. CAN U COME TOMORROW?

The reply was exactly what she expected:

CAN'T. WE HAVE PRACTICE. REMEMBER?

Yeah. She remembered.

And she knew he wouldn't miss practice, because it wasn't just about coaching. Seth's most talented player, Chase Miller, was going through a rough time at home. His father—who, along with his stepmother, had been raising him—had been killed in a car wreck a year ago.

Now Chase's mother, who had left when he was a toddler and lived in a remote part of Alaska with her fisherman boyfriend, wanted custody. The boy didn't want to be uprooted just when everything he'd worked for was about to pay off. His stepmother wanted to keep him, but his mother appeared to be gearing up for a custody battle.

Seth was becoming more and more emotionally engaged in Chase's dilemma. He was convinced the boy could win an athletic scholarship if he could just stay put for the remainder of his high school career, but there would be no chance of that in the Alaskan wilderness.

Seth worked with Chase every chance he got. Destiny didn't resent it. She just missed him.

She supposed she could try to squeeze in a trip back to Wilmot sometime next week. That was just about the last thing she wanted to do, though. She'd been home for a couple of visits since she'd started seeing Seth, and although she'd spent most of her time with him, she couldn't avoid her parents.

Well, she didn't *want* to avoid her mother. Grace, either.

But Daddy . . .

He seemed more distant than ever, if that was even possible. Not just from Destiny, Grace assured her—but from the rest of the family as well. Especially Mom.

When he wasn't out fishing, he was puttering around the house in stony silence.

"I don't know how you can stand it," Destiny had told Grace the last time she'd visited, in late September.

"I can't. Believe me, as soon as I find a job, I'm going to get an apartment."

"I'm sure something'll turn up soon," Destiny assured her sister with a confidence she didn't feel. Seth had told her that there weren't many job opportunities in Wilmot.

"But if your sister has an ounce of your determination, she'll land one," he'd added with a grin.

"Oh, she's determined." If only to get away from their parents—a real shame, because Grace had always wanted to stay in their hometown, just like Seth.

The two of them would have been perfect for each other, Destiny couldn't help thinking sometimes. Much more suited than she and Seth were.

Now that school was back in session, she could see his enthusiasm for teaching and knew it was his life's calling. She knew he was still house hunting, too, though he didn't seem to want to discuss it much with her.

Every time she thought about Seth putting down roots, she tried—and failed—to imagine herself settling down with him in Wilmot.

Maybe, if they'd been reunited a few months sooner . . . or even a few days sooner. Twenty-four hours would have done it.

She'd been right about that one day changing the course of her life, in more ways than one.

Big things were finally happening for her career-wise, and she wanted success more than ever before, if that was even possible.

Nothing was going to hold her back now. Not even her feelings for Seth.

"Hey, Destiny! Wait up!"

Turning to see Jesse Jansen hurrying to catch up, she thought, *Uh-oh*.

Jesse was—or rather, had the potential to be—trouble with a capital T.

With his shoulder-length hair, dark stubble shadowing his cheeks, and Celtic tattoos hugging big, bare biceps, he looked every bit the rock and roller he'd once been. He'd drifted around after his band broke up back in the nineties, eventually ending up a studio musician here in Nashville—and Destiny's lead guitarist.

"Hey, Jesse."

"You sounded good today."

"Thanks. So did you."

"You walking home?"

"Yep."

"Want a ride?" He gestured at the Harley parked by the curb.

"Thanks . . . but no thanks." It wasn't the first time Destiny had turned down a ride—or other things—Jesse had offered her.

He definitely had charisma, but so far she'd managed to sidestep his advances. It wasn't easy to keep her distance when they worked together every day, but a walk on the wild side would definitely ruin things with Seth.

"You sure about that?"

"I'm positive. See you tomorrow."

She walked on without looking back. A few minutes later, he roared past on his bike with one of the lunchshift waitresses on the seat behind him, arms wrapped around his waist.

Destiny smiled and shook her head, feeling sorry for the girl and hoping that one day Jesse would fall head over heels for someone and get a taste of his own medicine.

As Seth stepped into the parking lot outside the high school, he found that this morning's sunshine had given way to an overcast sky. Terrific. If it rained tonight, he'd have canceled on Destiny for no reason.

Well, if it rained early enough, maybe the game would be called in time for him to make the drive to Nashville after all.

Then again, his upstairs neighbors had thrown a wild weeknight party last night that kept him up into the wee hours, and today had been grueling. Was he really up for another six-hour round-trip drive?

He'd done it as often as possible, always forced to spend far less time with Destiny than he did in the car.

"Hey, there, Coach. TGIF, right?"

He turned to see Tracy Gilmore, the girls' gym teacher. The fresh-faced, ponytailed brunette was a fellow Wilmot alum, having graduated a year behind Seth. She'd been an all-star tennis player and a couple of lunch-hour sets this fall had shown Seth that her backhand was as fierce as ever.

"How's it going, Tracy?"

She looked up at the sky. "Not well. It looks like it's going to storm, doesn't it?"

"I was just thinking the same thing. We've got a game tonight."

"And we've got a match." Tracy coached the girls' tennis team. "Tell you what, if we both get rained out, why don't we get together and go over the winter team practice schedules?"

Seth blinked. While their jobs required them to coordinate the seasonal usage of the school's athletic facilities, they'd never met on their own time to do it.

"Um, that would be . . . I, uh, I'm not sure that I can . . . I mean, I have the game, so . . ."

"Not if it gets rained out, right?"

"Right."

Yet meeting Tracy after hours on a Friday night seemed like a bad idea, even if it was strictly professional. She was well-toned, pretty . . . and single. In other words, *dangerous*.

"I'll tell you what, Seth . . ." She reached into her canvas tote bag and pulled out a pen and a scrap of paper. "I'll give you my cell number. If you get rained out, call me."

What was there to say to that? "Okay."

She scribbled her number and handed it to him. "There. Ball's in your court."

He had to grin at that.

Watching her walk away, he decided it was a good thing Tracy hadn't started teaching here before this fall. If she'd been around last spring, chances were he'd have gotten involved with her.

And that would be a bad thing because . . . ?

Because of Destiny.

It would have been so much easier to fall for someone who lived here in Wilmot.

Tracy rented a condo in the next town over. Knowing he was house-hunting, she'd suggested that he come take a look at the available units in her building. He hadn't ruled it out—yet.

"But I really have my heart set on a house," he'd told Tracy the last time she'd asked.

"A condo is like a house, only you don't have to do the maintenance."

"No, I know, but I want something with a front porch and a backyard . . ." *And plenty of room to raise a family.* But he hadn't said that.

"You're an old-fashioned guy," she'd said with a smile.

"Guess so."

She nodded, and he could tell what she was thinking: that she was an old-fashioned girl.

She didn't have to say it; he knew that. Tracy was part of a large extended local family that went back generations; like her siblings, she probably intended to get married and settle down here.

She had everything in common with Seth . . .

Everything that Destiny doesn't, he couldn't help thinking as he walked slowly toward his car.

And yet opposites attract. Everyone knew that.

They were both determined to make this work; there was no reason why it shouldn't.

No reason at all.

That was what Seth had been telling himself, anyway, every chance he got. Some days, he honestly believed it.

Today wasn't one of them.

As he drove home listening to the car radio, he knew the day was going to come—very soon—when Destiny's first single came blasting through the speakers.

Then there would be no turning back.

Heck, there was no turning back even now.

He hoped that all her dreams came true—really, he did. But he felt as if she were slipping away from him before he even had a chance to explore his feelings for her.

Talking to her on the phone for hours on end had helped at first, but lately she had been so busy in the recording studio during the day and performing at night that their conversations were short and bittersweet, leaving him longing for so much more. He had wanted to head to Nashville on several occasions, but they could never quite make their schedules mesh.

At this point he wanted to hold her in his arms so badly that it was a constant ache that simply wouldn't subside.

Would success change her? Would she forget all about him along the way?

She was so young, so eager, so darned innocent in a lot of ways. She could easily be gobbled alive by the wrong people.

Seth clenched his jaw. He'd never, *ever* allow that to happen. Not as long as he was around.

What if you're not, though?

Again, he thought of Tracy. With her, it would be so easy. They could see each other anytime they felt like it; they'd both have summers off; they could even drive back and forth to work together . . .

She wasn't Destiny.

But Destiny wasn't here.

Who are you kidding? She's never going to be here again. She might want Seth, but she didn't want his lifestyle . . . and he didn't want hers.

He'd made that decision years ago, when he failed to get drafted into the minor leagues the first time out. Rather than feeling disappointed, he found that he was relieved. He loved baseball, but not the prospect of life on the road.

Accepting that it wasn't meant to be, he knew that God had other plans for him; that he was meant to mold and influence young minds and spirits in a world sorely lacking in leadership.

Just look at how far Chase Miller had come now that Seth had taken him under his wing. When Seth first met him in the wake of his father's death, the boy had been lost and angry at the world. Still, Seth had recognized in Chase not just talent, but raw determination to rise above his circumstances. All he needed was a chance— and Seth meant to see that he got it. The boy's mother, on the other hand, seemed—perhaps selfishly, or just misguidedly—hell-bent on taking it away.

Chase was depending on Seth to be there for him; Seth wasn't going to let him down.

How right he'd been: Teaching and coaching were his

true calling. And until Destiny had literally tumbled back into his life, he'd been looking forward to the beginning of another school year.

Now he seemed to spend every day torn between living his own life and wondering about hers.

Even his fantasies about building a life together felt wrong. If she ever returned to Wilmot, it should only be with the realization that she'd chosen the wrong path when she'd gone to Nashville—but that wasn't the case, and he knew it.

Even if things didn't work out in Nashville, he didn't want her coming home in defeat and years later wondering what might have been.

"And now for the WKCX Kicks Country weather forecast. Don't let these clouds mislead you, folks. They're going to blow right on out of here, so keep an eye out for a nice sunset and plenty of stars tonight. Speaking of stars, here's an oldie from Tammy Turner . . ."

Glancing up at the sky through the windshield, Seth saw that a patch of blue had already broken through the gray.

That, he decided, was a good omen. Tonight's game wouldn't be rained out after all—and he wouldn't be tempted to call Tracy Gilmore.

Reaching her building, Destiny grabbed her mail from the box and flipped through it quickly. Bills, bills, and more bills. At least she'd managed to pay her rent these last few months with money from the tip jar, along with some of the hefty credit card balance she'd run up, thanks to Billy Jackson.

Even now, she was stung by the thought of what he'd done to her.

What you let *him do.*

But it was a lesson well learned. She'd never be that gullible again. She'd tread very carefully where Nick and Miranda were concerned, even though they were well-respected names in the industry.

But things were different with them. Neither had promised to move mountains for her, the way Billy Jackson had. They both believed in her, but they knew—as she did—that in this town, dreams rarely came true overnight.

Again, she thought of Seth, remembering what it was like to wake up that first morning in his arms—and have to say good-bye as their days carried them in opposite directions.

She wasn't used to it then.

Maybe I never will be, she thought as she stepped into the vestibule.

Then she saw a figure sitting on the stairs, and her heart lurched.

"Hi, Destiny."

Her momentary fright gave way to utter surprise. The person lying in wait couldn't have been less threatening: petite, blond, and dearly familiar.

"Grace? What are you doing here?"

"I just couldn't take it anymore." Her sister stood up and they hugged each other.

Grace could be a drama queen, but Destiny saw real anguish in her blue eyes.

"Come on upstairs," she said, and saw that her sister had an overnight bag with her.

So she was planning to stay over—maybe more than just a night, Destiny thought, as she bent over to pick up the bag and found that it weighed a ton.

As she led the way upstairs, she asked, "How long have you been here waiting for me?"

"Only about an hour. I figured I could browse around in that shop downstairs, but the sign on the door said out to lunch."

"Yeah, Nessie's at her kids' parent-teacher conferences this afternoon," Destiny remembered. "Otherwise, she could have let you into my apartment. She has the key."

As they approached the door, Mike burst into frenzied barks inside the apartment.

Grace let out a whoop of delight. "You have a dog?"

"Sure do, and believe me, his bark is worse than his bite." Destiny unlocked the door, set down Grace's bag, and scooped Mike into her arms.

"Oh, isn't he the cutest little thing?" Grace reached over to scratch beneath his scraggly chin, and Mike nearly launched himself out of Destiny's arms to get to her. Destiny handed him over and closed the door behind them.

"What kind of dog is he?" Grace asked, laughing as Mike joyfully licked her face.

"Heinz Fifty-Seven."

"What?"

"A mutt," Destiny explained. As if in defense of his lineage, Mike demonstrated his deep, commanding bark.

"You're so lucky. We always wanted a dog, remember?" Grace reminded Destiny.

"I know, but Daddy would never allow it, and Mom would never stand up to him."

"So what else is new?" Grace muttered, setting Mike on his feet again and crossing the room to sink heavily onto the couch.

Fear gripped Destiny's heart. She followed and sat beside her sister. "What's going on with Mom and Dad?"

"They're still barely speaking, and it's been getting worse and worse the past few months," Grace told her glumly. "It's been like this silent war between them, and I finally just had to get out of there. I hate to ask, but . . ."

Uh-oh. Destiny suspected what was coming.

She was right.

"Can I move in with you for a while?" Grace asked. "Maybe with me out of the house they'll have the privacy to work things out, or figure out how to move on if that's what has to happen."

"You . . . you don't think they might . . ."

"Split up?"

Destiny nodded. "Yeah."

"I never thought I'd say this"—Grace gave a sad lift of her shoulders—"but maybe."

Destiny closed her eyes, battling the overwhelming urge to cry. Sensing her distress, Mike licked her leg.

"I should have never left home," she said, shaking her head.

"What does that have to do with anything?"

"They've fought about my choices and you know it, Grace. It's always put a wedge between them. And I've been home more lately than I have the entire time I've been away, so if things are worse, then obviously—"

"Stop that right this minute. You can't take the blame for this! They're both being as stubborn as mules—that's the problem. Not you."

"But they love each other. Mom always said that true love conquered all."

"I just hope that she was right and that their love is

strong enough, because right now, that's about all they have."

Grace was talking about their parents, but she could have been talking about Seth and Destiny, as well.

If the Harts couldn't make it after twenty-five years of marriage and two kids, what chance did she and Seth have?

"I guess all we can do at this point is have faith and pray," Destiny told her sister, and she wasn't talking about just her parents, either.

"I know." Grace shifted her weight on the couch. "There's one more thing . . ."

"Uh-oh. What is it?"

"I've been thinking . . . I know a lot about business and marketing . . . and I have a good eye for fashion, too. Don't you think?"

"Definitely, but—"

"Destiny, I'd make a great personal assistant."

"I bet you would."

"So am I hired?"

"Hired?" She feigned confusion, but her thoughts were spinning. She felt for her sister—really, she did—but—

"As your personal assistant!"

"Grace—"

"I've been working on your online presence ever since we talked about it the last time you were home, and—"

"I know you have, and thank you, but—"

"Oh, Destiny, I've got so many more ideas! For one thing, you really need to start Twittering."

"About what?"

"About anything. Your fans want to know what you're up to on a daily basis."

"What fans?"

"The ones you're going to get when I pimp your social-networking pages and get more people to friend you." Grace was up and pacing now. "That will help create a built-in fan base."

"Sounds like you have it all figured out."

"I do. Where are we at with choosing the first single from your new record?"

We? Destiny couldn't help but grin. Her sister might be jumping the gun, but it was kind of nice to feel a whole new level of support from someone other than Nick, Miranda, Max, Nessie—and, of course, Seth.

"The first single's going to be 'Restless Heart,' and we're hoping to get some airplay. The A and R reps at the record label are already working with promotion and marketing, so . . ."

"What about branding you?"

"I'm sure they've got everything covered, Grace. They have a whole creative team on it."

"But I know how you operate, Destiny. I've known you your whole life. I could be the glue that holds you together here in Nashville and with you on the road. I can take care of details and take charge whenever you need me . . ." She stopped pacing and looked at Destiny. "Trust me."

"I do. But, Grace, I barely make enough money to support myself." She took a deep breath. "Look, I know everyone thinks I'm rich because I signed with Sundial, but my advance needs to be used for business expenses, and the money I make at Back in the Saddle barely pays the bills. I can't hire an assistant."

"I have it all figured out. All I need is free room and board. I have a little nest egg saved up from moving back home this past year. I thought maybe I could find some kind of part-time work in retail, or a restaurant . . ."

Destiny nibbled on her bottom lip. "Well, my boss at the bar and grill *is* looking for another waitress."

She didn't mention that business was stronger than ever on nights when she took the stage. Ralph was grateful.

"Perfect." Grace clapped her hands. "Then we're all set. Unless I'm forcing you into this?"

"Are you kidding? You're *totally* forcing me into it." Destiny broke into a grin. "But I wouldn't have it any other way. I'd love to have you here with me."

"Yeah!" Grace pumped her fist in the air. "But when you make it you have to pay me the big bucks."

Destiny laughed.

Grace raised a salon-arched blond eyebrow. "I'm dead serious. Never underestimate the power of a personal assistant."

"Are you going to drive me crazy?"

"No doubt. But I'll do an amazing job, and I'll handle everything."

Destiny could just imagine the many things Grace would take charge of, her toenail polish to her wardrobe. She'd want to dress Destiny right down to her underwear and want to throw away everything in her closet like an episode of *What Not to Wear*.

Still . . .

Destiny gave her sister a hard hug. "I'm glad you're here. I've missed you so much."

"Same here. And I'm sorry it took me this long to get over being mad at you for leaving. It was just—I felt abandoned. During all those times we had to move . . . we still always had each other."

"Yeah, to argue with," Destiny tried to joke, but her voice cracked.

"I mean it, Destiny. You deserved more support than any of us gave you, and I know Mom feels as terrible about it as I do."

"Just Mom?"

Grace shook her head. "Who knows about Daddy? He's never been one to talk about his feelings. But you know he loves you. He loves all of us."

"Including Mom?"

"Definitely. I just don't know if love is enough, where those two are concerned. I never realized how different they were."

"Maybe they didn't, either."

Grace sighed. "I just hope they can figure things out now that I'm gone."

"Do you have to go back home and get your stuff?" Destiny asked, thinking she might be able to catch a ride to Wilmot to pay Seth a quick visit.

"Not for a while. I loaded my car down with as much as it would hold."

"So you were sure I'd agree to this?"

Grace grinned. "I'm pretty persuasive. And that's going to work on your behalf. You just made another giant leap toward stardom, Destiny Hart."

And away from Seth, Destiny couldn't help thinking.

EIGHT

"Please don't tell me that you've got good news and bad news," Destiny told Miranda as she slid into the chair opposite her manager's desk.

"Why would I say that?" With her reading glasses perched low on her nose, Miranda leveled a curious gaze at Destiny, who shrugged.

"People say it sometimes."

"Well, I only have one piece of news for you today."

"Is it bad?" Destiny had been to countless meetings here in the last five months, and she'd walked into every single one of them feeling as though the bottom was about to drop out.

So far, it hadn't.

But in the too-good-to-be-true scheme of her life these days, it was probably only a matter of time.

"Now why," Miranda said, "would I ask you to drive all the way over here on a holiday, no less, just to hear bad news?"

Today was Veterans Day, and every time Destiny thought about it, her father popped into her head.

Now that Grace was living here in Nashville with her, she had no way of knowing how things were going back home. Mom always sounded the same on the phone—cheerful and wistful—and Dad never seemed to be around to say hello.

Destiny wanted to ask about the state of their marriage, but somehow, she could never bring herself to do it. Maybe she was afraid of what the answer would be, and she wasn't ready to hear bad news.

But good news? She was always ready for that.

"So what's going on?" she asked her manager, grateful, as always, to have someone like Miranda in her corner. She understood Destiny's core small-town beliefs and values, and would never steer her away from that comfort zone.

"Ever hear of *Cowgirl Up*?"

"You mean that reality show on Country Music Television?"

"That's exactly what I mean. Do you watch it?"

Destiny shook her head, wondering where this was going. She knew enough about CMT's version of *The Bachelor*—which involved country girls trying to win the heart of a city slicker—to hope that Miranda wasn't going to ask her to be a contestant.

Grace—who had been working tirelessly to get her sister's name out there in every which way—would probably say the exposure would be priceless, and she'd probably be right.

But Destiny's heart wasn't up for grabs. She and Seth had managed to see each other three times over the last month—twice when he'd come to hear her sing here in Nashville, and once when they'd met halfway for a quick lunch date.

Since schools were closed for the holiday, he'd driven into Nashville late last night, and was waiting for her at this very moment in a coffee shop down the street.

"The next season airs in January. The producers have been looking for a new theme song for the show," Miranda told her, "and it looks like they've found it."

Destiny's breath caught in her throat. "What is it?"

Her manager broke into a broad grin. "It's 'Restless Heart,' Destiny."

"I . . . that's . . ." She shook her head in wonder. "Am I dreamin'?"

"No, Destiny, you most certainly are not. It's really happening. All of your work in the studio has paid off. This is huge. The song will be available for download on the CMT Web site. And now that the album is in the can, we'll ship your single to radio stations to coincide with the start of the new season of *Cowgirl Up*. I really think you're going to have a hit on your hands. Now, go on . . . get out of here and go celebrate!"

"I'm planning to." She thought of Seth waiting for her. "Why don't you come along, Miranda? My . . . boyfriend is in town, and you could meet him . . ."

Boyfriend. The term didn't do justice to the depth of her relationship with Seth, but she'd taken to calling him that lately, for lack of anything better.

"You can always call him your lover," Grace had slyly suggested, which made Destiny blush.

As much as she loved having her sister around, she

hadn't welcomed Grace's regular analysis of her bur-
geoning relationship with Seth. According to Grace,
they were perfect for each other, and were destined to
live happily ever after "and make me a maid of honor
and an aunt."

Just how she expected Destiny to do that—while becoming a country-music superstar, with Grace as personal assistant extraordinaire—hadn't been clear.

"You'll figure it out," she'd said with a shrug. "You
guys love each other. Love conquers all, right?"

Grace made it sound so simple.

Besides, the only L word that popped up regularly in
conversations between Destiny and Seth was "leave"...

As in, "I wish you didn't have to ..."

Meanwhile, Miranda was saying, "I'd love to join you,
but I've got piles of work to get to. You're not the only
one who believes in giving one hundred percent." She
winked at Destiny. "But tell that boyfriend of yours that
I'm looking forward to meeting him some other time—
and that he's going to be seeing even less of you. But if he
loves you, he'll understand that this is once in a lifetime."

"He does," Destiny assured her on her way out the
door.

But, she wondered, as her heels clicked on the hardwood floor of the corridor, *do you mean he does love
you, or that he does understand?*

She wasn't sure about either of those things.

She could tell he'd been disappointed when Miranda's summons interrupted their leisurely morning, but
as she'd tried to explain, when your manager calls, you
come running.

And boy, had it ever been worthwhile today.

Overtaken by excitement once again, she wished she

could beam herself to Seth's side to share the news. The best she could do was pick up her pace, practically running by the time she hit the lobby.

"Either you just had a very bad meeting," said the receptionist who sat behind a small circular desk there, "or a very good one."

"Definitely good," Destiny said with a grin, and paused to quickly sign herself out of the building.

"Are congratulations in order?"

"Definitely."

"Then congratulations!"

"Thank you!" Beaming, Destiny pushed through the door and out into the brilliant autumn morning, where a light fall breeze toyed with her hair.

A stone's throw from Sundial Recording Studios, Miranda's office was in the heart of Music Row, a semiresidential neighborhood. Mature trees and vintage brick buildings lined the lovely streets, where private homes were nestled amidst the publishing houses, recording studios, and quaint old houses that contained offices for lawyers, agents, and managers. Here and there, colorful banners announced a hit record or award for the studios' artists.

Someday, my name will be hanging out in front of Sundial Records.

It wasn't the first time the thought had occurred to Destiny, but it was the first time it actually seemed likely.

Waiting on the corner for the light to change, she adjusted the portfolio strap that was digging into her shoulder. She did her best to wear a dignified expression as she stood in the crowd of Music Row executives, but it was all she could do not to bounce impatiently.

When the light turned green, she forced herself to

walk, not run, down Sixteenth Avenue. Only when she turned the corner did she pick up speed, covering the short block like a track star and bursting into the café where Seth was waiting at a table for two.

"You'll never believe it!" she shrieked, hurtling toward him.

"What? What happened?" He was on his feet in a flash. "Are you okay?"

"I'm great!" She told him the news in a rush, and he threw his arms around her.

"It's finally becoming a reality, Seth! 'Restless Heart' is going to be on TV and the radio! Is that the craziest thing you've ever heard, or what?"

"Destiny, it's amazing. *You're* amazing!"

"After all these years, it's finally coming together! My very own song!"

"When do I get to say I told you so?"

She grinned. "Feel free to say it right now."

"Great. I told you so." He pulled out the chair opposite the one where he'd been sitting. "Here, sit down. What can I get you? I'm afraid they don't serve champagne here, but they make a mean latte."

"You know what? I'd rather have champagne. Let's go over to Back in the Saddle. Grace is working the lunch shift and I can't wait to tell her." Seeing a spark of disappointment in his eyes, she hesitated. "Is that okay with you?"

"Of course! Let's go."

"Are you sure?"

"Positive," he assured her so sincerely that she wondered if she'd been wrong a moment ago.

She was so eager to get to Back in the Saddle that the usual fifteen-minute walk took only ten.

Seeing a familiar motorcycle parked at the curb, Destiny rolled her eyes and told Seth, "Guess who you get to meet?"

"Who?"

"Remember Carrie Underwood's song 'Cowboy Casanova'?"

"I remember the video. I get to meet Carrie Underwood?"

"No, you get to meet a real live Cowboy Casanova. As in my lead guitarist, Jesse Jansen."

Seth narrowed his eyes. "Does he ever flirt with you?"

"Jesse flirts with everyone. Trust me, I'm not the least bit tempted. I just hope Grace can keep her distance. He's exactly her type—or what she *thinks* is her type."

They entered the restaurant and found Ralph working on the specials board in the vestibule. "Well, look who's here. What brings you in at this time of day?"

"Lunch," Destiny answered, and gave Seth a discreet nudge with her elbow. She didn't want Ralph to know about her business dealings until she had all of the details. "Do you remember my boyfriend, Seth Caldwell?"

"Sure do. I've seen him in the front row when a certain someone performs on Saturday nights." Ralph shook Seth's hand and added grandly, "Listen, you two order whatever you want. It's on me."

It was amazing—and amusing, for that matter—how differently Ralph treated her now that she brought customers in the doors in droves.

It was early, and the place was still pretty empty. Destiny spotted Grace over by the bar, chatting with Max, who was stocking it. Destiny knew that her cute and curvy sister had a crush on the bartender, and suspected Max shared the attraction, but was too shy to do anything about it.

Grace wasn't so sure. She didn't get "shy," having

gravitated toward the opposite type for years: tall, dark, and with an attitude.

Destiny had thought about saying something to get the ball rolling on Max's end, but then decided not to butt in. Grace tended to jump into relationships; it would probably do her good to ease slowly into this relationship—if there was going to be one.

Catching sight of Destiny and Seth, Grace broke off whatever she'd been saying to Max and called, "Hey, what are you guys doing here?"

"Having lunch. Where's your section?"

"You're standing in it. I got Ralph to let me work the bar tables today."

"Gee, I wonder why," Destiny couldn't resist saying as she and Seth slid onto stools at one of the tall tables.

"Kind of like I'm wondering why you two are here when you could've had the apartment to yourselves this morning," Grace said slyly as she put two place settings and glasses of water in front of them.

"We're celebrating," Seth told her, and looked over at the bar. "Hey, Max, we need some champagne . . . What've you got?"

"Champagne?" Grace grabbed Destiny's left arm. "Oh my gosh, let me see it!"

"See what?"

Grace, who had raised Destiny's hand up close to look at it, frowned, and Destiny realized what she'd been thinking.

Don't say it, Grace, she begged silently. *Please don't say it.*

But her sister, who had never been known for her tact—much less her mind-reading skills—blurted, "You're not engaged?"

"Engaged?" Destiny echoed as though she'd never

heard such a ridiculous thing in her life. She didn't dare glance at Seth. "Why would you think *that*?"

"You know . . . champagne."

"People celebrate all kinds of things with champagne," she retorted. "Not just getting engaged."

"I know, but the way you two have been—"

"For Pete's sake, Grace, we've only been going out a few months," Destiny cut in. She could feel her cheeks flaming.

"Oh, please . . . you two have known each other forever," Grace said dismissively. "So tell me—what's the big celebration about?"

Talk about anticlimactic . . .

It was Seth who announced the news. "Grace, 'Restless Heart' was chosen as the new theme song for *Cowgirl Up*!"

"Shut up!" Grace squealed and hugged Destiny, pulling her off the stool. "Are you serious? Do you know what this *means*?"

"It means we need champagne!" Seth stood and walked over to the bar.

"Wow . . ." Grace breathed, looking emotional. "Wow! Destiny, this is going to give 'Restless Heart' a big push! Aren't you excited?

"Are you kidding? Do you know how hard I've worked for this moment? And now everything is coming together so fast . . ."

"Mark my words." Grace swiped at both corners of her eyes with her knuckles. "'Restless Heart' is going to shoot to the top of the charts. You just wait!"

"I'm tired of waiting. Bring it on!"

"There's the Hart attitude! Cowgirl up!" she added with a wink.

"Cowgirl up!" Destiny swiped at her own eyes as well. "I was meant to do this, Grace . . . to sing, to write songs . . ."

"To bring joy to people," Grace put in. "Music does that, you know."

Destiny gave her a wobbly smile. "Ya think?"

"Are you going to tell Max?" Grace asked, glancing over at the bar.

Destiny nibbled on the inside of her cheek for a moment. "I'm dying to, but I'm worried . . ."

"He'd never say a word to anyone if you didn't want him to."

"No, I know—it's not that." More than anyone else, Max knew how long she'd been waiting for a break like this. "I guess I'm just afraid that if I tell anyone else, I'll jinx myself and Nick Novell will wake up one morning and realize signing me was a mistake or something, and the whole thing will go up in smoke."

"That's so not going to happen, so get that nonsense out of your head. Listen, I know you must be feeling overwhelmed right now, but like you said, you were born to do this."

Destiny closed her eyes and inhaled deeply. "I know, but . . . sometimes, I just wonder if I've been so focused on the future that I forgot to enjoy the present. Composing songs for the sheer joy of it when an idea would come to me . . . Creativity isn't something that you can do on command or force and now that I'm published there's pressure to create commercial hits. I don't want that to interfere with the fluidity or beauty of the lyrics or what I have to say. Do you know what I mean?"

"Sure, you don't want to compromise yourself."

"Yes. And you know, as much as I complained about

eating canned soup, those days were special too. I'm going to miss Nessie coming out here to listen to me sing while she would unwind after a long day. I'll miss singing into broom handles with Max." She pushed up and looked over at him, and Seth.

"It's like the Trace Adkins song 'You're Gonna Miss This,'" Grace told her.

"Exactly." Destiny smiled. "So you do get it? You don't think I'm crazy?"

"I wouldn't go that far . . ." Grace teased but then nodded. "I do get it."

"Is it crazy to say I'm afraid I might miss this place, and writing songs on my fire escape, and . . ."

And Seth.

That was the real reason she was worried, she realized. It wasn't about jinxing herself, or doubting her ability.

It was hard enough for them to find time for each other as it was. If her career took off the way Miranda had predicted, she was going to be busier than ever with interviews and photo shoots, making videos, performing, touring as the opening act for a big name . . .

What about Seth?

"Don't worry," Grace was saying. "Once you take off, I guarantee you'll never look back."

I know. That's what I'm afraid of.

She opened her eyes and glanced over to see Seth surveying the row of champagne bottles Max had set out on the bar.

He looked up as if he felt her gaze, and smiled a bittersweet smile.

He's happy for me—but he's worried, too, Destiny realized with a pang.

And there's nothing I can do about it, unless I want to give up my dream . . . or ask him to give up his.

"I think we'll go for the Veuve Clicquot," Seth told Max, and tapped the orange label.

He looked up at the bartender and saw that Max's attention was zoned in on Destiny and Grace. Rather, on Grace, who was being chatted up by a tattooed musician type in black jeans and boots.

"Let me guess . . . Jesse Jansen?"

"You got it. You said you want the Veuve?"

"Yeah, but no rush on that." Seth was in no hurry to meet Jesse, and he didn't particularly want him to join in the toast.

Max nodded as if he got it, and began returning the other bottles to the fridge behind the bar, keeping one eye on Grace.

When the hotshot lead guitarist leaned in and said something in her ear, Seth heard Max mutter something under his breath and plunk a bottle down with more force than necessary.

It clinked against the others and Grace looked their way. Max quickly averted his gaze and concentrated on wiping down the bar.

Seth shook his head. "Come on, dude."

"What?" Max asked defensively.

"That's the same look I once gave you."

"Huh?"

"When I was here with my baseball team, you were whispering in Destiny's ear and I wanted to kick you into next week." Seth tipped his head in Grace's direction. "I know how you feel. Go after her or you'll always regret it."

Max tossed his towel over his shoulder and flicked another glance at Grace.

Jesse was playfully lifting a lock of blond hair from her shoulder, and Max's jaw tightened. "Right. Jesse Jackass over there is a lead guitarist. I'm a bartender. How do you think that will work out for me?"

Seth angled his head. "Did you seriously just ask *me* that question?"

"Dude, whaddaya mean?" Max's eyes widened at Seth's deadpan look, and he immediately backpedaled. "Hey . . . no! Your situation is nothing like mine."

"Really?"

"Absolutely!" Max insisted. "It was a lame thing for me to say, anyway."

"Exactly, and it was a lame thing for you to think. Besides, I've heard you have some *skills*," Seth added, but Max shrugged.

Following his gaze back along its familiar path, Seth was just in time to see Destiny shove Jesse's wandering fingers from her own hair. She did it firmly, but with a laugh.

For a moment, watching the exchange, Seth was seized by pure doubt and insecurity.

"Hey, heed your own advice there, Coach," Max advised.

"What?"

"You know something? You're right. I grew up poor, but my father always reminded me that we all put our pants on one leg at a time."

"You're damned straight." Seth tilted his head in

Jesse's direction. "Some pants are just tighter than others."

That drew a chuckle from Max, and Seth joined in.

Hearing their laughter, Destiny looked over and met his gaze. Her smile was tired around the corners, but all for him. It did funny things to his insides and lifted his spirits.

"Listen, you've just gotta trust that everything will turn out the way it's supposed to in the end," Seth said, as much to Max as to himself.

"What?" Still watching Jesse, who'd gone back to flirting with Grace, Max accidentally knocked a champagne flute off the edge of the bar. "Ah . . . hellsfire!"

"Hey, are you okay?"

"Nothing I haven't done a thousand times before," Max muttered as blood welled up on the pad of his thumb. "I'll live."

As Max wrapped a white bar towel around the wound, Seth saw that Jesse had wandered away and Destiny and Grace were headed in this direction.

"Hey, I thought we were going to have some champagne," Grace announced.

"We are," Seth told her. "But . . ." He motioned with his head toward Max.

Grace's eyes widened when she saw bright red seeping through the white towel. "Did you cut yourself?"

"Yeah, I'm fine," he assured her, but she hurried behind the bar anyway.

"You think you need some stitches?" Destiny asked in concern.

"Nah."

"Are you sure, Max? Let me see!"

"Grace!" Destiny warned. "You're not good with stuff like this."

"Destiny, don't be silly. I just want to make sure he's okay." One glance at the cut, and she turned white as a sheet.

"My stupid thumb is fine," Max told her.

"You sure?" Grace managed in a barely there whisper. The sight of blood had always made her woozy. She couldn't even look at a skinned knee.

"Yeah, I'm just a klutz. That's—"

"Max!" Destiny warned, "She's gonna go down!"

"What?" Max turned just in time to see Grace starting to sway, and grabbed her in his arms.

"Ohmigod, baby, are you okay?" he asked, and cupped her cheek in his uninjured hand. "You need some water? A sip of brandy?"

"Maybe some water." Grace's lashes fluttered; then her eyes snapped open and she smiled. "Wait, did you just call me 'baby'?"

"It just slipped out," Max admitted and his face flushed a dusky shade of pink. "Sorry."

"No . . . I thought it was sweet," Grace assured him with a lazy smile. It was obvious she no longer needed to be held in his arms, but that didn't seem to matter to either of them.

"Really?" Max's eyes widened slightly. "I didn't think you'd be . . . interested . . ." He trailed off and glanced away.

"Well, that's what you get for thinking," Grace teased, drawing Max's attention right back.

Seth shook his head at Destiny and looked pointedly at the waiting bottle of champagne, but Max and Grace were too wrapped up in each other to notice.

"You okay to stand?"

"I believe so." Grace nodded with obvious reluctance.

"Gracie?" Destiny interrupted and arched one eyebrow. "Can we open the champagne now, or are you still suffering from the vapors?"

"Destiny, I was having a *moment*. You know how squeamish I am," she snapped, then turned back to Max and said, in a delicate voice, "Okay, I can stand."

"You sure?"

"I think so."

Destiny cleared her throat in an effort not to chuckle, and her sister shot her a don't-you-dare look.

Maybe, Destiny realized, she was finally ready to give up her weakness for bad boys. Max was a really good guy, and so was Seth . . .

She turned to see him watching Grace with a hint of amusement before he caught her eye and shook his head, grinning.

For most of his life, every time John Hart came home, he felt the weight of the world lift from his shoulders.

These days, though, it was just the opposite, he noted grimly, as he pulled into the empty driveway and looked up at the house.

It was modest by modern standards, but neat as a pin with a lush front lawn that he meticulously mowed and manicured. The hedges were trimmed, the trees pruned, and a dandelion had better not dare raise its yellow head. Sara's flowerbeds overflowed with colorful fall flowers.

After years of moving, he loved having his own home—and now, ironically, all Sara talked about was traveling. They had spent a lifetime being uprooted and he'd be damned if he'd start traipsing all over creation.

He liked his quiet little existence, and for the life of him he couldn't understand what had suddenly put a burr up Sara's butt, just as he couldn't comprehend why his bright and gifted daughter would choose to wait tables in Nashville.

What were they thinking?

They weren't thinking. That was the problem. They were simply letting their whims guide them, all of them, even Grace, without a care for the future—or, for that matter, for the past.

John walked up to the door, checked the mailbox, and removed several envelopes. Sara must have left the house before noon, as that was when the mailman made his rounds.

He stepped into the front hall and called, "Anyone home?" He knew the house was empty, but it made him feel better, for some reason, to pretend that he didn't.

"Hello?" he called, as if someone might be waiting here for him, just like the old days.

Whenever he came back from a tour of duty, his wife and daughters would hang a Welcome Home banner and greet him with kisses and excited chatter.

Now there was only an empty house.

But you're only coming back from a fishing trip, he reminded himself. *And the girls are gone, living their own lives in Nashville, and Sara . . .*

She was here, but not really; it was just the two of them left rattling around in their dream house, sad strangers with nothing left to say to each other.

Wondering where she was, he went into the kitchen to see if she'd left a note in the usual place: on the countertop in front of the toaster.

No note.

But then, she wouldn't have known he was coming home this afternoon. He never told her when he was coming and going, because he didn't know himself. He took off for the cabin as the spirit moved him, and he came home when he could no longer stand being away.

The house was too quiet.

Even though he had complained about Grace moving back home last spring, John desperately missed Grace's laughter, her constant chatter, and even the music blasting from the bathroom while she showered.

He dearly missed Destiny too. It had been four long years of barely seeing his daring daughter who was always so full of life and laughter.

When Destiny had hightailed it off to Nashville, he had been livid and let her know in no uncertain terms that he would have absolutely no part of her foolishness.

Maybe it scared him, seeing so much of himself in her. Having grown up feeling abandoned and unloved, he had spent his youth pulling stunts and taking chances.

Later, he learned to live life conservatively, serving his country and providing for his family. He had made darned sure his girls could go to college so they could have a secure future.

When Destiny ignored his wishes and left home, she took a piece of him with her—although he'd never let her know it.

God help him, he missed her. He missed them all. He only wanted the best for his children and his wife. How could that possibly be wrong?

John pulled his cell phone out of his pocket to see if he'd somehow missed a call from Sara.

He hadn't.

With a scowl, he flipped the phone shut and tossed it

onto the countertop. It skittered across the shiny surface and he lunged forward to catch it just as it went sliding over the edge. He carefully placed the phone next to the shiny silver toaster.

Ever since he'd gotten past his youthful indiscretions, he'd taken pride in exercising self-control, but today he was about to lose it. He closed his eyes and swallowed—a lonely man in an empty house, with nothing left but his own pride.

That was the one thing he'd had before all this, and the one thing he'd never let go.

Not like he had everything else.

Seth glanced at his watch as he and Destiny settled on her couch back at the apartment, with Mike curling up at the opposite end.

Time was running out. He had a long drive ahead of him, and a stack of papers to grade tonight, and he'd promised to help Chase with his college essay, and . . .

And I don't want to leave her yet.

Or even today.

Or . . . ever.

So what else was new?

"How do you feel about everything?" he asked her. "Is it sinking in yet?"

"I can't even tell. All that celebrating made me tired." She leaned her head back against his arm with a yawn.

"Why don't you take a nap? I should get going anyway."

He started to get up, but she put a hand on his arm. "No, don't. You can stay for a while longer, can't you? Having you here is kind of keeping me from freaking out about this whole thing," she admitted in a soft voice that went straight to his heart.

"Sure. I can stay awhile." He kissed the top of her head, then nudged Mike out of the way to give them both room to lie down. The sofa was so roomy they'd have fit without being too snug, but he pulled her closer against him anyway, breathing the herbal scent of her hair.

"You know," she murmured, "when Miranda called this morning, all I could think was that something had gone wrong."

"Why would you think that?"

"Because everything's been going right. *Too* right. My career, and having Grace here, and being with you . . ."

"There's no law that says you can't have it all, Destiny."

"Are you sure about that?"

No. I'm not.

"Sure, I'm sure. You're going to be a star, Destiny—like you always wanted. Just don't ever forget what matters most."

"What?"

"The simple things that were there all along—the things that would be there even if your career went away tomorrow. Your family, your friends . . ."

"You."

"Yeah. Me."

"Seth, I could promise you that no matter what I'll stay humble and grounded and God help me, I'll try. Believe me when I say that it's important to me that I do. But since you brought it up . . ." She lifted her head to look at him, and her serious expression caught him off guard. "I want you to promise that if I do make it big and start acting like a diva you'll keep me grounded."

"You got it," Seth promised.

"Good. You know, everybody thinks my goal is to become rich and famous. Don't get me wrong . . . that would be just fine and dandy, but it's not my real reason for being here."

"What is your real reason, then?" He brought her hand to his mouth and kissed the back of it tenderly.

"From the time I was a little girl, music would play in my brain. At first it was songs that I knew and loved and then I started to have my own melodies spring to life." She tapped her temple and laughed. "It was like having an internal iPod always on shuffle. Eventually I started writing down the words and music in a journal."

"And let me guess . . . nobody knew."

"Of course not. I was afraid of being laughed at."

"So what are you afraid of now?"

The question seemed to take her by surprise, but she didn't hesitate to answer. "Failure," she said flatly.

"That's not going to happen. Not now."

"It might. Anything could go wrong. Even now."

"Then don't give up. Give it all you've got and sing your doggone heart out, and you'll make it."

"Ha—if only it were that easy."

"No one said it would be easy," he reminded her gently and then tucked a curl behind her ear. "Look, if you're ready to come home then I'll help you pack your bags."

"Come home?" she echoed in horror, shaking her head vehemently. "*Now*? No way!"

"There's my girl." Seth forced a smile despite the odd sense of panic that welled up in his throat.

She yawned. "Sorry I keep doing that. I guess champagne in the afternoon makes me useless for the rest of the day." She laid her head against his chest again.

He stroked her hair and listened to the soft sound of her breathing, wondering just what life had in store for them.

At least she assumed he was going to be around in the future. But in what capacity? Friend? Boyfriend? More?

Did she ever think about getting married?

Remembering her reaction back at the bar when Grace had assumed they were engaged, he felt his earlier optimism evaporating.

She hadn't exactly seemed thrilled by the prospect. More like . . . horrified.

What did that mean?

Are you kidding? Nothing good, that's for sure.

But she'd just asked him to keep her grounded when she made it big, so . . .

Maybe he should just come right out and ask her where she thought they were headed; whether there was a chance she might actually want to settle down someday, somewhere . . . with him.

"Destiny?"

No reply.

"Destiny?" he repeated, wondering if she somehow sensed what he was going to ask her and was trying desperately to avoid the question . . .

Not *the* question, of course.

He wasn't going to propose. He just wanted to know whether she'd ever considered that someday, he actually might . . . and that she might want to say yes.

About to say her name again, he heard her breathing, slow and steady, and realized she'd fallen asleep.

It was just as well, Seth decided. The last thing he wanted to do right now—or ever—was force her to make a choice.

Because he knew what it would be.

NINE

"Here, taste ..." Destiny lifted a forkful of stuffing to Seth's lips as he came up behind her at the kitchen counter. "What do you think?"

"Mmmmmm." He wrapped his arms around her and turned her around.

She laughed, shaking her head. "I have to finish making this—"

"I'd say it's delicious as it is. And so are you." He nuzzled her neck.

"And I have to get the pie into the oven ... and you said yourself that your oven's slow."

"Yeah ... that'll give us some extra time."

"We're supposed to be over at my parents' house in an hour."

"They won't care if we're a little late."

"Are you kidding? You know my father."

"Maybe he'll be in a more relaxed mood. It's Thanksgiving."

"Trust me—I don't think dried-out turkey will relax him. Here, do you want to crack some more pecans for the pie while I roll out the crust?"

"Sure," Seth told her. "As long as I have you next to me, I'd do anything."

"Are you flirting with me?"

"No, I'm not just flirting." He pulled her close. "I'm dead serious."

He lowered his head and kissed her long and sweet until her head was spinning.

"The pie," she said weakly when he pulled back at last.

"Let 'em eat cake."

Destiny laughed and swatted his arm. "Now I'm dead serious. Get cracking." She pointed to the bowl of pecans on the table.

Grumbling good-naturedly, he sat down and picked up the nutcracker as she covered the tray of stuffing with tinfoil, then reached for the rolling pin.

Seth's galley kitchen was surprisingly well equipped for a bachelor pad—much better equipped than her own back in Nashville. These days, with Grace sharing the small space and her own life more hectic than ever, the place was so cluttered that she couldn't find tinfoil or a rolling pin even if she knew she owned it. Which she didn't.

"We really should clean up before we hit the road," she'd told Grace late last night, as they threw their belongings into suitcases to make the long drive back to Wilmot for Thanksgiving.

"We'll do it when we get back. Grab your guitar and let's go."

They didn't get into town until the wee hours, and Grace dropped Destiny—with Mike in tow—here at Seth's place. He was waiting up, of course. It had been so long since they'd seen each other that the first place they headed was the bedroom—and the last thing they wanted to do was sleep.

"It's so unbelievably good to have you here," Seth commented, and she looked up to see him watching her.

"Yeah, well, it's so unbelievably good to be here— and to be doing something like this." She waved the flour-dusted rolling pin.

"Been a while since you baked a pie, huh?"

"Or anything like it. *Sometimes* I miss the simplicity of just being me. Don't get me wrong, I'm not complaining, but it keeps hitting me that my life has changed pretty drastically in the blink of an eye."

"You haven't even told me how the music video shoot went."

"Well, we're not finished. As a matter of fact, we're going to be shooting some footage tomorrow night."

Miranda had arranged with WKCX for her to perform a special hometown concert tomorrow night— right back where it all began. She and the record company's PR team thought it would be a great opportunity to generate some press in advance of the single's debut on *Cowgirl Up* after the holidays.

"I'm sure it'll be great to have some familiar faces in the crowd," Seth told her.

"One in particular." She pointed at him. "Others . . . I'm not so sure about."

"Did your father say he'll come?"

"He didn't say he wouldn't. He hasn't said anything at all, in fact. I haven't talked to him. But my mother told me she's working on him, and of course, she'll be there . . ."

"Annie and Cooper, too."

"How do you know?"

"They both happen to be in town for Thanksgiving, and I may have mentioned it to them . . ."

"Okay, now I'm nervous." She started to pace.

"Why? They love you. Everyone around here does."

"That's why." She shook her head. "It's easier to perform in front of strangers. There's a lot less to lose. Oh well. I guess if I want to make it in this business, I'd better get used to performing in front of people I know and love. And anyway . . . I always do better when I know you're there with me." She leaned close and captured his mouth with hers, then placed her forehead against his. "I miss you so much. Every second of every day we're not together."

"I feel the same way."

"How are we going to keep doing this, Seth?"

"Trust."

"You mean in fate because you—" she began, but he put a fingertip to her mouth.

"Trust in us. It's the only way long-distance relationships can survive."

"Well, then, that's not a problem, is it?"

"Not at all." Seth slid his fingertip across her bottom lip and then kissed her gently.

He had such a simple, direct way of looking at things. She dearly hoped it would be their lifeline, and not their undoing.

With a sigh Destiny rested her head on his shoulder,

savoring the solid muscle beneath her cheek and the steady beat of his heart under the palm of her hand. She knew she had to tuck these memories away and take them with her when she left . . .

And that they couldn't sit around holding each other all day, because they had a Thanksgiving dinner to get to.

At the thought of her father, she suddenly realized something and gasped.

"What?" Seth asked.

Destiny raised her head and looked at him. "I'm sitting here moaning about how much I miss you when we're apart, and it made me think about how tough it must have been on my father whenever he had a tour of duty. I'm heading back to Nashville to *sing* for goodness' sake. I'm not going off to war. You're always just a phone call, text message, or e-mail away."

"And I can get in the car and drive to see you as often as possible, and we'll be together for a whole week at Christmas . . ."

"Right." Destiny had arranged to take the time off. "I need to stop whining and just deal, don't I?"

Seth laughed. "There's the Destiny Hart I know and love."

Destiny laughed and hugged him hard. "I might be leaving you again in a few days, but my heart's not going anywhere." She smiled to herself, thinking that was a pretty darned good song title.

That was an incredible dinner, Mrs. Hart," Seth announced, after taking the last bite of turkey.

"You outdid yourself, Mom."

"You really did," Grace chimed in with Destiny. "Don't you think so, Dad?"

"It was good."

Sara tried not to show how stung she was by the grudging praise. "Thanks," she said, more to Seth and her daughters, "but it really was a group effort."

John had been noticeably quiet throughout the meal, sitting in his usual place at the end of the table.

Sara knew what was wrong with him. He finally realized that Destiny's impossible dreams were coming true. Not only had he been wrong to take such a stubborn stance against her going to Nashville to begin with, but now he was going to lose her all over again . . . just when she'd started coming back into their lives, thanks to Seth.

"So, Seth," Sara said, "you haven't told us how the house hunting is going."

"It's . . . going. Actually, maybe it's gone, for the time being. I've pretty much seen everything that's on the local market, and it slows down around the holidays. Maybe after that, some new inventory will come on."

"Let's hope so. And how are your parents doing in Florida?"

"They're loving it. This is their first Thanksgiving away from Wilmot, and when I talked to them earlier, they said they weren't the least bit homesick. They were having turkey on the beach."

"That sounds like fun!" Sara turned to John. "Wouldn't it be nice to do something different some year? Not that I don't love having all of you kids around, but I'm not naive enough to think you'll be here every year . . ."

John pushed back his chair abruptly.

"Where are you going, Dad?" Grace asked.

"Out to the garage for a little while to work on the car. Call me in for dessert."

They all watched him go.

If Seth caught the sudden undercurrents he was polite enough not to let it show. Pushing back his own chair, he said, "How about I get the dishes while you three catch up?"

"Absolutely not. You're a guest."

"Trust me, it would be my pleasure. I'm not used to sitting around for hours at a time."

"I'm not either," Destiny said, "but right now, I'm too full to move."

"Just relax, ladies. I'm on it."

"You really don't have to do that, Seth," Sara told him.

"Seriously, I want to. I know my way around a kitchen."

"He cooks, too," Destiny informed them proudly. "And not just breakfast and barbecue stuff, either."

Not like Daddy.

Destiny didn't say it, but Sara sure as heck thought it. She remembered many a backyard party when she slaved all day long making several salads, complicated casseroles, and delectable desserts, and all John did was flip a few burgers and burn a few hot dogs. Yet he would get all the credit.

At the time, it had been amusing.

For some reason, it wasn't anymore.

"Oh, come on, Destiny," Seth was protesting. "You make it sound like I should have my own show on the Food Network. Just because a guy can bake a potato and broil a steak doesn't mean—"

"What about the lasagna you made for Chase for his

birthday last week? You said the two of you finished off an entire tray of it in one sitting."

"Would that be Chase Miller?" Sara asked, familiar with the tragic accident that had taken the life of his father last year. "How is that poor boy doing?"

"He's had interest from quite a few college scouts," Seth told her. "If he can just stay here in Wilmot for his senior year, he'll be set. But his mother wants to drag him away."

"I imagine she just misses her son and wants him close to her," Sara said mildly.

"Then where was she for the past fifteen years?" Destiny shook her head, her eyes flashing in anger. "She has no right to step in now and take away Chase's opportunity to make a dream come true."

"Hey, calm down, Destiny," Grace said. "Don't take it so personally. You barely know these people."

"No, but I know about dreams, and how hard it is to make them come true, and how much it hurts when . . ."

The words dropped off into silence, and Sara contemplated them, wondering if Destiny was drawing some kind of parallel between Chase's unsupportive mother and the way she and John had handled their daughter's unexpected exodus to Nashville.

But now wasn't the time for making amends. Not with Seth here, and John . . . not.

"I really hope Chase realizes his dreams," she told Seth simply. "You could have brought him for Thanksgiving dinner, you know. There's always room for one more."

"Thank you, but he flew out to be with his mother. Judge's orders."

"All the way to Alaska and back in just a few days?"

Seth nodded and started gathering wineglasses. "I

just hope she lets him come back home when the holiday is over."

"Something tells me she's not thinking of Wilmot as his home, Seth," Destiny said with a shake of her head.

There was another long moment of thoughtful silence before Seth resumed collecting the glasses.

"Don't spend all kinds of time on the dishes, now," Sara told him. "Just throw them all into the dishwasher."

"Careful when you tell him to throw something, Mom." Grace grinned. "He's got a pretty strong pitching arm, remember?"

"Nah, those days are over. Now I'm just an old guy sitting on the bench."

"That's not true," Destiny said. "You're out there on the field with the kids at every practice."

"How do *you* know?"

It should have been an innocent question, Sara thought, and yet there was an accusatory hint in his tone. *He resents her for not being here,* she realized. *Maybe he doesn't even realize it.*

But Destiny sure did. Sara didn't miss the flicker of concern in her daughter's eyes.

"I'll throw the rest of it into the dishwasher, Mrs. Hart, but I'll be sure to hand wash the crystal," Seth said, carefully clustering the wineglasses by their stems and disappearing into the kitchen.

"Wow . . . Destiny, he's a keeper," Sara informed her daughter, who looked distinctly uncomfortable at the comment.

"We're just dating, Mom. Not . . ."

"They're not getting engaged anytime soon," Grace supplied. "Maybe not ever."

"Grace!"

"What? That's what you told me."

"I never said *never*."

"So you *are* getting engaged at some point?"

"Shh!"

Seth had reappeared. He picked up a couple of plates, then looked around at them. "Y'all are bein' awfully quiet."

"We're just enjoying one another's company, thanks to you," Sara told him. "I miss my girls, and this is my one day to spend with them."

"Mom, we'll be around till Saturday."

"I know, but tomorrow you'll be running around getting ready for the performance ..."

"So come with us," Grace told her. "Not to the rehearsal and sound check, but to Chez Mia."

Chez Mia was Wilmot's fanciest salon, and the girls were planning to spend much of the afternoon there.

"What would I do at Chez Mia?"

"Get a facial, a manicure, a pedicure ..." Destiny started counting off on her fingers.

"Maybe even a new hairstyle," Grace put in, and Sara's hand defensively went up to her sprayed-stiff head. "What do you think, Seth? Isn't it time Mom went for a new look?"

"I think this is girl talk," he said tactfully, and walked back toward the kitchen with a stack of plates.

Looking after him, Sara mouthed, "Nice butt."

"Mom!" Destiny said, looking as shocked as she did dismayed.

Grace, however, was grinning. "That was so *not* a prim-and-proper Sara Hart comment."

"Maybe I'm not as prim and proper as you girls think," Sara said with a shrug.

Grace turned to Destiny. "Maybe Daddy's right about her having a midlife crisis."

"I am not having a midlife crisis! I'm having a midlife . . . revival."

"Good for you, Mom." Destiny nodded in approval. "You've spent all these years worrying about everybody else. Maybe it's time you just worried about yourself for a change."

"And maybe you girls are right about Chez Mia." Feeling restless, Sara pushed back her chair abruptly and marched over to the mirror above the buffet.

Looking at her reflection, she felt as though she were seeing it for the first time. "Mercy me, my hair looks like a helmet sitting on my head." She looked at her daughters. "Why didn't y'all tell me?"

Destiny and Grace exchanged a glance.

"I, um, just thought it was your signature look," Grace ventured with a tentative smile. "You know, like Grace Kelly or Jackie Onassis."

"Neither of those women went around with a hair helmet on their head."

Suddenly she felt like a big old dinosaur. She had been getting her hair done the exact same way for the past twenty years without thinking twice about it.

John liked it this way. He might have a fit if she changed it . . .

Wait a minute. Why was she worrying about what *he* wanted?

For years she had lived in her husband's shadow. She'd become everything he wanted—the quintessential military wife and mother. And although she loved John and the girls, he was retired now and her children were grown.

It was high time Sara reclaimed her free spirit.

Again, she looked in the mirror.

This was *her* hair. Her life. For once, something could be about what *she* wanted.

"Girls," she said, "I've used my last can of Final Net. Chez Mia, here we come!"

*T*he next morning, enticed by the aroma of coffee and bacon, Destiny fumbled her way into Seth's kitchen with Mike trotting at her heels. She rubbed the sleep from her eyes as she reached the doorway, but the sight standing before her stopped her in her barefoot tracks and curled her toes. "Wow."

A shirtless Seth turned around and gave her a smile that was much too cheerful for the crack of dawn. Oh, wait, the digital clock on the microwave said it was nine. Oops. She hadn't meant to sleep in. She had a huge day ahead of her. . . .

And now, all she wanted to do was go back to bed, with Seth in tow.

For a moment, she wished she were wearing something more appealing than her XXL NASHVILLE IS FOR LIVERS T-shirt, a Nessie castoff.

But then, she wasn't a Victoria's Secret kind of girl, and Seth knew it.

"Wow . . . *what*?" he echoed.

Wow, you look amazing even with rumpled hair and dark stubble shadowing your jaw.

But there was no time for romance now, Destiny reminded herself sternly; she had to get moving.

"Wow," she improvised, "is that coffee and bacon I smell?"

"You betcha."

That familiar pang of wishing this wasn't just temporary—waking up together—fluttered in Destiny's stomach, and without thinking she put her hand on her midsection.

"Hungry?" He nodded toward her hand and turned back to the stove, deftly turning over the sizzling strips of bacon.

"Starving," she admitted as Mike trotted into the kitchen. Destiny bent to pet him.

"How do you want your eggs?"

"Eggs?"

Seth took one from the carton on the counter and held it up for her inspection. "These here are eggs, little city girl. They come from chickens."

"Ha-ha. Very funny. It's just that . . ."

Again, she looked at the clock.

I don't have time for breakfast. I barely have time to jump into the shower before I have to be at rehearsal.

"I wasn't expecting you to cook for me," she said, not wanting to hurt his feelings.

"Well, you deserve a little pampering. Especially on a special day like this. So . . . the eggs. How do you want them?"

Her mouth was watering. Maybe she could spare a little extra time.

"Over easy," she said, "and Mike likes his scrambled."

"You want me to scramble eggs for your dog?"

Her chin came up. "It's good for his coat."

Seth removed the bacon from the skillet and placed the strips on paper towels to drain. "Yeah, I can see how that fur is the envy of all the local dogs."

"Don't you be pokin' fun of crazy hair," Destiny warned with a wag of her finger. "I might just take offense."

"What are you talking about?" He turned around and looked at her in question.

Destiny rolled her eyes and pointed at her wild bed-head.

"I like your hair. Like I keep telling you, you should wear it down more often."

"Yeah?"

"Yeah."

Their eyes locked. She knew, from his expression, that he was thinking not about her bed-head, but about her . . . *in* bed.

Sure enough, he started toward her, nearly knocking an egg to the floor, but catching it just as it rolled over the edge of the counter.

"Nice save."

He set the egg on the counter and turned toward her again.

She took a wary step back. "Um, shouldn't you be cracking that into the skillet?"

"I will. In a minute."

"But I'm starving, remember?"

"So am I." He reached for her, and the look in his warm brown eyes melted Destiny's resolve like saltwater taffy on a hot summer day.

"Seriously, Seth . . ."

"Here. This'll hold you over." He grabbed a slice of bacon and held it to her mouth.

"Yum," she said as she took a crispy bite.

Mike, at their feet, barked, and then sat up to beg.

"What, you want some too?" Seth asked.

"He can have a little nibble, but then I should take him outside. His bladder must be ready to burst."

Seth shook his head. "I took him out earlier while you were still sleeping. Don't worry—I have it all under control."

"I can see that." Destiny broke off a piece of bacon and tossed it to Mike.

Seth wrapped his arms around her and kissed her.

Laughing, she shook her head. "Not now."

"Yes, now." He backed her against the counter and buried his face in her neck, sending shivers through her.

But she really didn't have time.

Blindly reaching behind her, she found the carton of eggs. Her fingers closed around one. Without stopping to reconsider, she pulled it out—and cracked it over his head.

Seth sprang back with a yelp.

"What was that?"

"That there was an egg. Eggs come from chickens, and—"

"Oh, you are gonna pay for that!" he shouted, and lunged for her.

"You gotta catch me first." She tugged her arm free and took off running for the living room.

Mike scampered after them barking with doggie delight.

"I can run a lot faster than you!" Seth's bare feet slapped against the hardwood floors as he came after her in fast pursuit.

"Yeah, but I've got some moves, see?"

She took a flying leap over the couch, bounced off the wall, and kept on running. She laughed when she heard him grunt in frustration when he had to circle around, giving her time to tear down the hallway.

That was where she realized her game plan was lacking, since she basically had nowhere to go but the bedroom—which was exactly what she'd been trying to avoid when she'd cracked the egg over his head in the first place.

She decided she'd circle toward the window, scramble across the bed, and head back to freedom. But her plan was thwarted when she tripped over her own duffel bag left on the floor, went airborne, and landed on the bed with a big bounce. She rolled over with the intent to scoot away, but he dove on top of her with a whoop of triumph.

"Gotcha now!"

She squirmed, laughing.

"Hmmm . . . just what am I going to do with you?"

"Let me go?"

"Not a chance."

He gathered her into his arms, and she knew she was helpless to resist.

The rest of the world—the rehearsal and sound check, her mother and sister, the salon trip—would just have to wait.

On the opposite side of town, the Harts faced each other stubbornly across the breakfast table.

"Sara, I just can't support something I believe is wrong." John threaded his fingers through his short hair. "You know that simply isn't me."

"Just how can pursuing a dream be wrong?"

"It's not wrong if you go about it in the right way, but—"

"The right way or *your* way?" Sara cut in.

"Those two things don't have to be mutually exclusive, you know."

She knew he was trying to joke, but she failed to see the humor. "She's your daughter, John. Everyone else in town is going to be there, and—"

"And you really think that means everyone else in town loves her more than I do, Sara?"

"Well, you sure have a funny way of showing it."

"It's not in me to stand back and watch my children make mistakes."

"Mistakes are part of life, John. Stop controlling and start supporting before it's too late. Please . . . just come to see her perform tonight."

He shook his head.

A hot wave of disappointment washed over Sara. She pushed back her chair.

"Where are you going?" he asked with an edge of panic in his voice that clawed at Sara's heart.

She clenched her fists and fought the urge to sit down again. "Outside for some fresh air. I have some serious thinking to do."

He didn't ask about what, and Sara didn't offer. "Maybe you should do the same," she advised, and stepped out onto the deck.

It wasn't fair. It was a holiday weekend, and the first time her entire family had been together in ages. Grace had found happiness in Nashville with her sister, Destiny's career was going well and she was seeing Seth Caldwell . . .

If only John Hart would come to his senses, all would be right with Sara's world.

"It shouldn't be this way," she whispered, and tried to swallow the hot moisture gathering in her aching throat.

While she knew that John's stubbornness was born of love, he had to learn that it couldn't always be his way or the highway.

Sara gripped the railing harder and raised her face to the blue sky with a silent prayer that her husband would learn that it's possible to bend without breaking.

After all, I've been doing it for years, Sara thought grimly.

"All right, Mrs. Hart, what can I do for you?" asked Mia, who sported bright chunks of pink in her platinum-blond spikes and a piercing in the corner of her eyebrow.

Definitely not what you did for—or rather, to—yourself, Sara thought.

Aloud, she said, "I do believe I'd like my hair frosted."

"Frosted?"

"She means highlighted, Mia," Destiny explained.

"Full or partial?"

Mia might as well have been speaking Greek. Sara looked at her daughters for help.

"I think she might like to go short," Destiny said.

"But Daddy might not like it," Grace told her.

That did it!

"Make me short and . . . sassy!" Sara instructed Mia. "With lots of blond frost—I mean, *highlights*."

"So you want a full?" Mia started threading her fingers through Sara's hair, only to get stuck in the stiffness.

"A full? That means all over, right?"

"Right."

"Okay, then, all over. Do me up good and proper." Sara folded her hands on her lap and nodded with conviction that she wasn't quite feeling.

"No problem!" Mia picked up a big book. "Look through here for some styles and color while I get started on Destiny. I'll be back in a few minutes."

Left alone in the chair with Grace standing by, Sara frowned at her reflection in the mirror. "There was a time when I was carefree and pretty," she said, more to herself than to her daughter.

"You are pretty, Mom. Just look at your skin—it's perfect. And you have a great figure with all that healthy living. You just hide it under layers of clothes. And you need more color in your wardrobe—and jewelry. We can stop at the mall and hook you up."

"No, Grace. This is Destiny's day, not mine." She put her hands on the arms of the chair and started to push up. "In fact, I shouldn't really even be here."

Grace put a restraining hand on her shoulder. "When was the last time we got to spend a day together, the three of us?"

"You're right."

"Here, look at the book and find yourself a style."

Heart pounding like a hummingbird's, Sara started turning pages, not really seeing the photos until Grace stopped her.

"There!"

"What? Where?"

"Turn back a page."

Sara obliged, and Grace tapped the picture of a woman with soft layers framing her face. It was short, but not too radical. Feminine, but with a hint of sass.

"Throw in some highlights in honey blond, Mom, and you'll be a knockout."

"A knockout? Get out of here." Sara nibbled on her bottom lip.

"I mean it."

"Really?"

"Really."

Sara had birthed two babies and sent her husband off to war. This was a haircut and color, for pity's sake.

Mia reappeared. "Your turn, Mrs. Hart. Did you decide on a cut?"

"Sure did." She pointed to the picture on the page. "And don't be stingy with that blond, now, sugar. Give me some attitude."

TEN

Coming in from a long Friday-afternoon run, John Hart wiped the perspiration from his brow with the edge of his T-shirt. It was a warm, sunny day for November. He pulled open the refrigerator door and the cool air seeped into his sweat-soaked shirt as he snagged a bottle of water. He chugged half of it before the door even had a chance to close.

John realized he'd pushed himself too hard, but he'd been so full of frustration after this morning's confrontation with Sara that he just kept going, mile after mile.

Now his legs felt like wet noodles, his knees ached, and his lungs burned. So what? He welcomed the exhaustion. Maybe tonight he'd be able to fall asleep instead of tossing and turning yet again. Since Sara had been sleeping in the guest room he hadn't been able to get a good night's rest.

He missed Sara in his bed.

He missed her, period. Missed her bright smile, her easy laughter, and her gentle touch that had been fading fast over the past few years.

"Sara?"

No reply. Her car was in the driveway, but she must have gone out with Grace.

The house felt empty, so silent that when the ice maker suddenly dumped cubes into the container, John jumped as if he'd been startled by a rumble of thunder.

Annoyed by his unaccustomed skittishness, he polished off the water and tossed the bottle into the trash with more force than needed. Pushing away from the counter, he decided he needed a long hot shower to ease his aching muscles—and the tension in his brain.

But just as he reached the bathroom, he heard the front door open and Sara and Grace chattering happily.

For a moment, he considered getting right into the shower anyway. But then he heard Grace calling him.

"Daddy? Come out here and see!"

"See what?"

Grace didn't answer. Frowning, he left the bathroom.

The living room was empty, but several shopping bags were heaped on the sofa.

Hearing the door open again, John turned to see Grace and a friend, both wearing big sunglasses, returning with another round of bags.

"Grace, what is all that?" he asked as her friend deposited her load and hurriedly went back out, presumably for more. "Are you moving back in?"

"No, just coming from the mall, and believe it or not, most of this stuff belongs to Mom!"

John raised an eyebrow. "Mom? Where is she?"

"She'll be right back. This should be the last trip."

"Back? Where . . . ?" Confused, John stared at his daughter—and then the light dawned. "Wait . . . that woman who breezed in and out of here just now was your *mother*?"

Grace grinned. "Who did you think she was?"

"I don't know . . . a friend of yours or something." Dazed, John shook his head and turned just in time to see his wife standing in the doorway.

At least, it sounded like his wife. "That was it," she told Grace, and dumped the bags she was holding on the floor before collapsing in a chair. "I feel like I just ran a marathon!"

John—who until a few minutes ago had felt like he'd just run a marathon, and pretty much *had*—now felt as though he'd been zapped to an alternate universe.

"Where . . . who . . . what did you *do*?" he asked the woman who sounded like Sara.

She took off the sunglasses and looked up at him for the first time, putting her hands up and touching the feathered ends of honey-blond hair that softly framed her face. He saw tears in her eyes—which suddenly looked enormous, rimmed in rich brown liner that brought out the hazel.

"You . . . you look so . . ." He just shook his head, at a loss for words.

"You don't like it?" Sara asked in a tiny voice.

"Mom, come on, how could he not?" Grace spoke up when John didn't. "Your helmet hair is gone forever. You look fresh and pretty and years younger."

Still, John couldn't speak.

"She looks amazing, doesn't she, Daddy? Between the haircut and the makeup and the new clothes . . . I can't remember when I last saw her in a pair of jeans that didn't have elastic at the waist. And she bought five styles!" Grace held her palm up and wiggled her thumb and fingers.

"I seriously thought she was a friend of yours," he said at last, to Grace.

For some reason, he couldn't bring himself to address Sara directly.

"It's amazing what a new hairstyle can do, and Mia showed Mom how to apply makeup in shades that suit the new hair color."

John just nodded, taking it in.

She looked like the old Sara—the one he'd known decades ago; the girl whose hair and clothes were feminine and flowing, much like her personality. That Sara wore mascara and lipstick, and bangles on her wrists— and had fresh flowers in her hair on their wedding day.

She'd been even more beautiful and radiant during her pregnancy with Destiny.

But then—at his insistence—her appearance began to change. Gone were the long skirts and bright colors, and she rarely wore makeup. He knew why.

He didn't want her to stand out. He wanted her to blend in. She had dutifully transformed herself into the wife of an officer—pretty, but in a much more understated way that didn't draw attention.

"I don't know about you, Mom, but I'm going to take a nap," Grace announced. "You wore me out, but I truly had fun today, and you look fantastic."

Sara smiled. "Thanks, Gracie."

"Don't let me sleep for more than an hour."

Grace grabbed a couple of bags—leaving the vast majority behind—and left the room.

John cleared his throat and said at last, "You do."

Sara looked at him in surprise. "What?"

"You do look fantastic."

"Really?"

He nodded fervently. "The blond becomes you, Sara, and I love the way it frames your face."

"Thank you," she said softly, and added, "That doesn't sound like you."

"I have my moments," he said with a grin—then eyed the shiny pink Victoria's Secret bag at her feet with interest. "Is that yours?"

"Sure is."

"What's in it?"

"Don't ask," she teased. "Let's just say there might be a Playtex 18-Hour Bra burning tonight."

"I'm not sure what that is, but I bet it doesn't have any lace—and I'm betting whatever's in that bag just might."

Sara laughed.

"You're blushing."

"Am I?"

He nodded and sat on the couch, patting the cushion beside him. She stood, crossed the room, and sat down—close enough for John to drape his arm around her, just like old times.

"That feels good," she said. "I'm plumb wore out. The girls ran me ragged."

That reminded him. "Where's Destiny?"

"Getting dressed, and then Seth is going to drive her over to get warmed up for tonight."

Tonight. The concert.

John immediately deflated.

"I hope you've changed your mind about coming."

"I haven't."

She promptly slid out from beneath his arm and stood.

"Don't let this come between us."

"Destiny's career isn't the only thing that's come between us, John." She looked at him with accusing eyes that made guilt settle like a lead ball in his gut. "But since we're on the subject—she's an adult and this is the path she's chosen. You need to let her be who she wants to be and not who *you* want her to be."

"The odds are stacked against her, even now. Be realistic."

She put her hands on her hips and looked him straight in the eye. "I don't want to be realistic! I want to dream with her. Support her. Shower her with praise and encouragement. Like I should have been doing all along!" She hesitated, then said with quiet conviction, "Like *you* should have been doing all along."

"Don't tell me what to do."

"Oh, heaven forbid!" She raised her chin with defiance. "Well, guess what? The days are over when *you* can tell *me* what to do. For once this isn't all about you."

He, too, was on his feet, facing her, cold, hard fear pounding at his temples. "What are you saying, Sara?"

She blinked at him, and he wondered for a moment if she even knew. Then she said quietly, "I'm tired of being everything you want me to be and not being myself. It's your world and I'm just living in it."

"What the hell does that mean?" he growled, even though down deep he knew.

"Figure it out." She left the room, and a moment later slammed the door to the guest room.

John started to follow her down the hallway leading to the four bedrooms and two baths. Lining the walls were framed pictures beginning with their wedding and progressing over the years.

Something made him stop and look at them. At Sara. At photos of their engagement, and their wedding, and their young family . . .

Sara had been so pretty, so sweet. He could never quite get over why a girl like her had fallen for a guy like him in the first place. Every time he had left her for months on end, he worried that she would get tired of him being gone; that someone better would come along and sweep her off her feet. Someone more deserving than him.

Looking at the old photos, remembering what it had been like, John shook his head. There was a stark difference between the early pictures and the later ones—particularly at the girls' graduations. Sara was still smiling, but John could see that some of the life had been sucked out of her.

Shaken, he turned away.

"Still . . . I don't deserve this treatment," he grumbled under his breath, and stomped down the hallway to the master bathroom. He wanted to slam the door, but controlled his anger.

He ran the water, stripped off his clothes, stepped into the stall, and stayed there for a long time.

Though the hot water eased his aches and pains, he tasted salt on his tongue.

Crying had always gotten a backhand from his father, and he had learned early in life to control his emotions.

His throat closed up now, and he refused to let tears flow.

"*D*estiny, you still in there?" Seth knocked on the closed bedroom door.

"Sure am."

"Can I come in?"

"Not yet. I'm getting dressed."

"Hey, don't be shy. It's just me. I've seen it all."

"I'm not being shy," Destiny answered. "I'm trying to focus, and I know what'll happen if I let you in here. This time, I can't let you make me late."

Seth had to grin, remembering this morning. He drifted back over to the couch and looked at Mike, who was lying on the rug.

"She's gonna be late for her own concert, and this time, it won't even be my fault."

Mike wagged his tail. Shaking his head, Seth hummed "Waitin' on a Woman."

The bedroom door creaked open. "Seth, have you seen my red heels?"

"I put 'em in the closet so I wouldn't keep tripping over 'em. I thought you were going to wear boots."

"No, I was just yessing Grace. I'm wearing my favorite shoes!"

The door closed again.

"It's her night," Seth told Mike. "If she wants to wear the red shoes, then she should wear the red shoes, right?"

Mike raised one eyelid, looked at him, and lowered it again.

"I know, I could use a nap myself."

He went back to humming until at last the bedroom door opened and footsteps tapped down the hall.

"What do you think?" Destiny asked.

Seth's heart caught in his throat.

She looked absolutely stunning.

Her hair, misted with sparkles, was piled high on her head with soft curls escaping to frame her face and kiss her neck. She wore snug-fitting jeans, a simple yet sophisticated midnight blue V-neck shirt trimmed in silver piping, a heart pendant at her throat, and chunky cuffs on both wrists.

"Earth to Seth," she said.

"Oh . . . uh . . ." He cleared his throat and then had to ask, "Um, what was the question again?"

"How do I look?"

"Incredible. The wait was worth it."

"You don't think the shoes are wrong?"

He flicked his gaze to her feet. "I'm no fashion expert, but in my opinion they give the jeans a real dressed-up touch."

"Nicely said, for a guy!" She glanced down at her watch. "I need to grab my guitar and hightail it down to the stage. Sure you don't mind driving me?"

"What, are you kidding? It's an honor."

He grabbed his keys as Destiny left the room, returning a moment later with her guitar case in tow.

"Wow, Seth . . ." Her smile trembled a little. "This is going to be quite a night, isn't it?"

Seth gave her shoulders a squeeze. "It sure is. And I'll be right there in the front row."

"Thanks. It means the world to me to have you there."

Outside, the sun was dipping lower in the sky and the orange glow glinted off her hair. Seth admired the straight set of her back and her determined step as she headed toward his car.

But he had seen her vulnerable side, and it had touched him deeply. How he wished he could gather her in his arms and show her the love and tenderness he was feeling right now.

Instead, he put her guitar in the back cargo, opened the passenger door, and looked at her. "Ready?"

"I was born ready," she assured him. "Let's go."

"Well, now, don't you just look amazing!" Amy Dale, Destiny's A and R rep, breezed into the makeshift room with an airy smile.

"Thanks," Destiny said, standing before the lone full-length mirror, examining her reflection. Her eyes seemed enormous, and not just because of Mia's expert makeup application.

She'd snuck a peek outside a few minutes ago, and the town square was jammed. She'd spotted her mother right there in the front row, in special seats reserved for her family—but the seat beside her had been empty.

"Hey, there, Ms. Hart, you need to look like you believe in your very sexy self!" Amy demanded with an arch of one thin eyebrow.

Destiny tossed a cascade of curls over her shoulder, sending a flurry of sprayed-on sparkles—also courtesy of Mia—fluttering to the floor. "Oh, you know I'm bringing sexy back," she said in a sultry tone and sucked in her cheeks.

"That's more like it! Now give me a little hip action while you're at it. Shake it like a salt shaker!"

Destiny gave her hips a good wiggle and tried not to laugh.

"Perfect. Now do just that while you're out onstage, and we'll be in business. So listen—"

"Okay, let's give Destiny a few minutes of quiet time before she goes onstage!" Miranda Shepherd announced, breezing into the room wearing her no-nonsense don't-argue-with-me expression.

She was trailed by Cassie Cook, who was directing the music video.

"I just want to remind her of a few things for the video footage, Miranda, and then I'll be out of your hair," Cassie said, and turned back to Destiny. "Make sure you try to hit your marks on the stage. The cameras are set up to get the best angles from there. 'Restless Heart' is the song we're going to focus on, but we'll film the whole performance."

Destiny nodded and tried not to panic.

"Remember what I said about expression, too. We need energy with a sexy edge. Vamp it up, okay?"

"Gotcha."

"Fantastic. Just forget about the cameras and have fun with it, okay?"

"No problem," Destiny replied with more conviction than she was feeling.

Forget about the cameras, remember to hit the marks . . .

It all seemed so complicated and contradictory.

And Amy had her share of advice as well.

Finally, Miranda cleared her throat and gave them both a polite but pointed look. "Um, guys?"

"Okay, okay," Cassie said.

"Break a leg, girlfriend!" Amy called over her shoulder and wiggled her fingers in the air.

The two of them sashayed out the door . . . just as Grace slipped in.

"Destiny, people are going nuts out there. It's awesome. I just saw Cooper and Annie, and—"

"Grace?"

Her sister blinked and spotted Miranda, who gave her a pointed look. "Oh, sorry I didn't see you there. Hi, Miranda," she said briefly, and turned back to Destiny.

"Is Daddy here, Grace?"

Her sister hesitated. "I didn't see him, but like I said, the place is packed, and—"

"He's not here."

Grace met her gaze and said quietly, "No, he's not."

Destiny squared her shoulders and shook off her disappointment. Colonel Hart pretty much had the market cornered on stubbornness, and though she knew it was a childish notion, she realized something. One of the reasons she'd hoped so hard for success was to prove her worth to her father. She had him to thank for that—if nothing else.

"It's okay," she told Grace. "I didn't think he'd come."

"He still could show up."

"He could," Destiny said, feeling herself getting choked up, "but he won't."

"It's all about the stubborn Hart pride," Grace grumbled. "And I'm just as guilty. I can't tell you how sorry I am that it took me this long to jump on board."

"You were going to school!"

She lifted one shoulder. "I know, but still . . ."

"You're here now," Destiny said, "and that's all that matters."

"You know, I really believe that Daddy will come to his senses. Mom might just have to knock it into him, but she's got a different attitude and I think she's gonna do just that. Squash that Hart pride. Boom!"

She banged her fist on the wall, and the trailer shook.

Miranda, standing by, narrowed her eyes and exhaled an audible breath.

"I hope you're right, Grace. I really miss him," Destiny admitted with a little catch in her voice.

"Me too." Grace patted Destiny's hand. "But now that everything is coming together for you, don't dwell on the hard stuff. You've got a show to put on."

"What if I blow it?"

Grace turned on her stool to face her. "You won't!"

"You don't know that . . ."

"Just think, a whole team of experts has been grooming you for this! The creative team knows what they're doing. All you needed was some spit and polish, and . . . well, a bit of glamour."

"And *you*, Grace. I needed you. Thanks for all the positive energy."

"No problem," Grace said breezily, covering Destiny's hand with hers and giving it a squeeze.

"Grace, I'm sorry"—Miranda stepped forward and made shooing motions with her hands—"but your sister needs some breathing room."

"All right, all right." Grace hugged Destiny. "I'm so proud of you."

"I haven't done anything yet."

"Sure you have. And it's just the beginning."

"She's a dynamo," Miranda commented as Grace left. "Must run in the family."

Destiny smiled and nodded, thinking of her mother—and then of her father, and her smile faded.

"What's the matter?" Miranda asked, watching her.

"Stage fright?" she guessed, sparing Destiny an explanation about her father.

"I'm used to being onstage, but not in front of a hometown crowd."

"That's okay. Make those nerves work to your advantage. Harness them into energy."

"I'll try. I just—" Destiny broke off as Miranda's cell phone rang.

She pulled it out and examined the caller ID window. "I have to take this," she told Destiny. "I'll be right back."

Miranda left the room, and Destiny sighed. As always, she couldn't quite shake the sadness that came with thoughts of her father.

"You look like a star, Destiny Hart." At the sound of Seth's voice, Destiny spun around and her breath caught in her throat. He looked incredibly handsome in a light blue polo shirt and khaki pants.

He held out a simple bouquet of wildflowers tied with a pink silk ribbon. "They're hard to come by this time of year," he said softly, "but nothing else would do. Wildflowers remind me of you. Untamed and beautiful."

"Thank you, Seth." She swallowed hard. "They're perfect."

Seth nodded his head toward the door. "There's lots of excitement in the air out there. "Your band's been warming up. They're kick-ass. And the place is packed."

Destiny put a hand to her stomach. "Everyone keeps telling me that."

"You're gonna go out there and kick some butt tonight."

"Well said, Coach." She tried to laugh, but it came out husky.

Seth took a step closer and lifted a lock of her hair. "I want to hug you, but I don't want to mess anything up." Instead he leaned in and brushed his lips ever so lightly against hers. It was a barely there kiss, but it rocked her to the core.

"I'm so proud of you," he whispered softly, "and I want you to know that I l—"

"Destiny, I have—" Back, with her cell phone in hand, Miranda stopped short in the doorway.

Shaken, Destiny longed to beam her away so that she could hear whatever it was that Seth wanted her to know.

Was he going to say that he loves me?

"I'm Miranda Shepherd, Destiny's manager. And you must be her boyfriend."

"Seth Caldwell," he said, and shook her hand as Destiny stood by mutely.

"It's good to meet you, and I'm sorry to do this, but it's time for Destiny to take the stage."

"It's okay." Seth turned and took both of Destiny's hands in his, giving them a hard squeeze. "Get on out there and knock 'em dead. I'll see you after the show."

She couldn't quite keep the catch out of her voice. "I'm so glad you're here."

"Me too."

Destiny watched him walk away and then turned to Miranda. "Okay, I'm as ready as I'll ever be. Let's get this party started."

Miranda grinned. "You got it!"

Destiny's heart pounded hard and fast as she followed Miranda outside. The lights in the square had been turned down low and her band played in the background.

Destiny inhaled deeply. The anticipation in the room felt like a living, breathing thing. Trembling with excitement, she smiled at the familiar faces of friends and family scattered in the crowd as she made her way to the stage, where WKCX's Rex Miller was waiting for her. He caught her eye, winked, and addressed the audience.

"Some of you might remember our Kentucky Idol contest four summers ago right here on the town square. A special little lady brought down the house with her a cappella performance of 'America the Beautiful.' She headed to Nashville shortly thereafter and the rest is history. Allow me to introduce singer-songwriter extraordinaire . . . *Destiny Hart!*"

ELEVEN

$\mathcal{A}$s she stepped up onto the stage, the thunder of applause sent Destiny's pulse racing. She thought she had her nerves under control, but when she faced the spotlights' glare, she forgot everything. *Everything*—including which song was first on her set list and where to stand.

Stage fright had once again reared its ugly head.

"The set list is taped to the floor and the X is where you stand," the rational side of her brain said, but the words didn't make sense. The cameras seemed to loom beyond the stage like big monsters eager to capture her fright for all to see.

Flight or fight . . .

Flight or fight . . .

Flight seemed her best option by far. Her eyes flicked to the exit sign but luckily her legs refused to budge.

You're gonna go out there and kick some butt tonight . . .

Seth's words ran through her head. She looked out into the audience, thinking that if she could just see him, she'd feel better. But the lights were blinding.

And then, by some miracle, she heard Seth's voice hollering her name. She couldn't see him, but he was there, right up front.

Determination took over. Destiny looked at the microphone and a surge of white-hot adrenaline shot through her from her red high heels to her hair. She wouldn't have been surprised if her sprayed-on sparkles suddenly started shooting up in the air like fireworks.

With a pounding heart, Destiny grabbed the microphone and shouted, "How y'all doin' tonight?"

She waited for the loud response to die down and then waved her hand toward her band.

"Give a warm welcome to my amazing band, Hart Rockers!" She waited for the big round of applause to dwindle. "Okay, let's get things started with a cut from my album called 'Kiss Me in the Moonlight.' It's a song I wrote about love and loss." She put a hand to her chest and sighed but then arched one eyebrow. "Or in other words, getting dumped. Raise your hand if you've been there."

She could hear Grace's distinctive two-fingered whistle reverberating from the front row, and grinned. She'd written the song for her sister.

"Thought so." Her fear melting away, Destiny shaded her eyes as she looked out over the audience. "Well, then, listen up because although the title sounds sappy, it's about *not* drowning in your sorrows. It's about picking up the pieces and moving on with your life. Y'all know what I'm talkin' about! Don't be that girl and for pity's sake do not send him one more text message! Put on that red dress and move on, girlfriend!" Destiny grinned at the female cheers. "Oh, I knew you'd be with me on that one!"

Finding her mark, she smiled at the camera and gave the band the hand signal to begin.

Low and throaty, sweet and sorrowful, Destiny crooned into the microphone, keeping her eyes closed as she tapped into the emotion of the beginning, letting the pain of love lost pour from her soul.

Then, after a two-beat rest, the band suddenly kicked it up and the sad song took a sudden turn. Destiny grabbed the mike, tossed her head, did an Elvis move, and belted out the refrain. The crowd seemed to love the rockin' lyrics. Maybe, Destiny thought, this song could be her next release, after "Restless Heart" had made a big splash.

Oh, feeling confident now, are we?

Destiny sang two more upbeat songs from the CD and then sat down on the stool. "Whew, that was fun, but I'm going to slow it down here and cover one of my all-time favorite classics, from Patsy Cline.

"'Crazy . . .'" Destiny began, and sank her teeth into the soulful ballad. She forgot about the camera and the audience—except for Seth.

She sang the song straight from her heart, to him alone. After she drew out the last line of the lyrics, she had to take a deep, shaky breath.

The crowd had fallen silent, she realized, and she slowly raised her head. From the lighted stage, it was next to impossible to see people's faces. Her heart pounded wildly. What was wrong? Why weren't they clapping? Had she sung off-key?

All at once, the audience collectively rose to their feet, clapping and whistling in approval.

Destiny's eyes widened with surprise and then immediately filled with tears. "Thank you! Thank you so much!" She swiped at a tear but then knew she had to keep her emotion under control so she could keep on singing.

After clearing her throat she said, "Y'all having as much fun as I am?"

"'Free Bird'!" someone yelled.

Destiny's eyes widened. There was no mistaking that voice.

"Sorry, 'Free Bird' boy," she said with a grin. "Not tonight. But don't y'all go sittin' down out there. I think we need to shake our tail feathers. Ya know what I'm sayin'?" She cupped her hand over her ear and was rewarded with a loud response. "That's what I'm talkin' about!" Destiny cheered and her confidence level shot through the roof. She sure hoped she was vamping it up enough for Amy's approval.

"I wrote this next song after a night of line dancing at the Wildhorse Saloon when I first moved to Nashville. Well, okay, I watched line dancing and ate lots of their famous fried pickles. See, I'm not very . . . um, what's that word? Oh yeah . . . good. I tend to turn the wrong way and crash into people, and the other dancers aren't very happy with me. I found out very quickly that serious line dancers don't giggle or stop and stomp their foot in frustration in the middle of a song. They also don't say the heck with it and go freestyle." She wagged her finger. "Big no-no."

The audience laughed, hard and long, as she performed an exaggerated freestyle dance.

"Anyway, this was one of those written-on-a-napkin songs and I called it 'Kick It Up!' I would be oh so thrilled to have y'all dance with me! See, I didn't want lots of stompin' and scootin' and spinnin' around! Just a simple dance that even I can do. So stay on your feet because this song is high energy, meant to get y'all up on the dance floor, chair dancing while sitting in traffic or boogieing around the kitchen while cooking up dinner. Basically, it's meant to getcha in a good mood no matter what you're doin'! Here we go!"

With a signal to the band, Destiny jumped into the toe-tapping tune. Out in the crowd, hips swayed and hands clapped. Everyone seemed to be getting into the spirit of the song. Music had that special magic to transform a bad mood into a good one, and the only thing better was dancing along.

When the song was over, she grabbed a quick drink of water, recognizing her chance to take a short breather while showcasing the talent of Hart Rockers.

The band continued to play softly in the background as she said, "Allow me to introduce my band—mercy, I've always wanted to say that!" she admitted, and the crowd applauded.

"Okay, on bass guitar is Nashville native Pete Reeves," Destiny shouted and waved her hand in an arc toward Pete, who did an energetic riff that drew a big round of applause.

She swung her hand in the opposite direction. "From Brentwood, Tennessee, let's make some noise for Matt Carter on keyboard!"

She waited for his solo to end and then shouted, "Hailing from Lexington, Kentucky, and backing me up on vocals is the lovely Zoe Carter!" Destiny pointed her hand in Zoe's direction and the bodacious backup singer belted out some scat singing in her amazing range, and then gave Destiny a high five.

"From Atlanta, Georgia, we have Murphy Quinn on drums!" Destiny shouted. Murphy performed a smoking-fast drum solo that had the crowd applauding like crazy.

"And last but certainly not least, hailing from Cincinnati, Ohio, is hotshot Jesse Jansen on lead guitar!" Jesse performed a wicked guitar lick with lots of flash and then flicked his pick into the crowd. As expected, the women went wild.

Destiny turned and applauded her band before pivoting back to the audience. "Give it up for the Hart Rockers!"

When the applause died down Destiny looked out to the audience and smiled. "Y'all have been great. It means so much to me to see familiar faces in the audience! God bless!"

The lights dimmed and she bounced down off the stage to her dressing room to freshen up her hair and makeup.

"Hear that? They're going nuts out there, Destiny," Miranda told her with a big grin, bursting in behind her. "People are holding up their cell phones as lights and starting to clap and stomp their feet for an encore. Just listen! Hear that?"

"I hear it. How do people do this day in and out? It's physically and emotionally exhaust—" Destiny broke off and wrinkled her nose as she was shot with a cloud of hairspray.

"Ready?" Miranda asked.

"Ready."

Her heart was once again beating wildly, and she felt like she was going to collapse in sheer exhaustion. But the moment she stepped back up onto the stage to the opening strains of "Restless Heart," the wild applause and warm acceptance made her fatigue dissolve like sugar in hot tea.

Destiny forgot about the cameras and her fear and exhaustion, simply pouring her heart into the song, which had been written beneath the stars on a warm summer night.

She might have glitter in her hair and fringe on her shirt, but in the end, she realized, it was still all about the music.

*W*atching Destiny up there singing, Seth had tears in his eyes.

If he'd held a last shred of doubt about where she was headed—or what she meant to him—it was gone.

Why in the world had it taken him this long to figure out that he was in love with her? The realization couldn't have come at a worse time, and he didn't know what—if anything—to do about it.

He'd tried to tell her backstage, but the timing wasn't right.

The timing between them *never* seemed right. They lived in separate cities and had vastly different dreams; that they might possibly build some kind of life together was against all odds.

"Thank y'all so much!" Destiny called out over the thunderous applause and then waved her hand in an appreciative arc toward her band.

She was about to walk off the stage, but Rex Miller

stopped her. "Destiny, that was quite a performance—and you wrote that song yourself, didn't you?"

"Sure did. Songwriting is my passion. I love the stories that country music tells. Music can take you back to a place and time in an instant."

"Well, if that's the case, Destiny, you might just be writing about this moment someday, because we happen to have a special surprise in store for you."

Seth frowned. What was he talking about?

Judging by the expression on Destiny's face, she didn't have a clue, either.

Seth looked at Sara beside him. She shrugged, and then like everyone else, they turned their attention toward the stage and waited.

Maybe the mayor was going to give Destiny the key to the city or something.

Miranda Shepherd came out onstage, smiling broadly, and accepted the mike from Rex. "Destiny, I got a phone call from Tammy Turner just before the show tonight. Y'all know who she is, right?"

The crowd roared with approval for one of the biggest names in country music today.

"It seems Tammy saw you perform down in Nashville not too long ago, and she was so impressed she wants *you* to open for her Christmas show at her new concert theater in Pigeon Forge, Tennessee! What do you say?" Miranda asked over thunderous applause.

"Are you . . . are you serious?" Destiny pressed a fluttery hand against her throat. "I . . . I . . ."

Mesmerized, Seth watched her as Sara clutched his arm, shrieking, "Can you believe it?"

"No, I can't. Looks like she can't, either." He knew Destiny had just made yet another giant leap toward stardom—and away from him—but in this moment, he felt only a sweeping sense of joy.

Onstage, Rex took the mike back from Miranda. "Wow, this is amazing news. Congratulations, Destiny! How are you feeling right now?"

"Well, I'm a huge fan of Tammy's, so you can't begin to imagine how thrilled I am!"

"And now Tammy Turner is a fan of yours," Rex commented. "What do you think about that?"

"It just blows me away. I . . . I'm so honored just knowing that she's heard me sing, let alone . . . *this.*"

Watching her, Seth was moved by how humble Destiny was—and said a silent prayer that she'd stay that way.

"Guess this means she won't be coming home for Christmas after all," Sara said low in his ear, and he nodded glumly.

He could feel her looking at him, but he didn't dare catch her eye.

"You know, Seth, everything happens for a reason," Sara said, "even though you can't always figure it out until much later—sometimes years later."

Destiny took one last bow, and the stage went dark.

"Think we can get backstage?" Sara asked.

"Hell, yes. Pardon my French," Seth added. "I just . . . I can't wait to see her."

"I feel the same way. You push your way through, and I'll be right behind you."

He started shouldering through the crowd, filled with familiar faces and kids who called, "Hi, Coach!"

He wondered how many people here knew that he and Destiny were . . . well, whatever they were.

One person who definitely didn't was Tracy Gilmore.

He saw her coming at him, looking flushed and pretty, and gave a little wave, but meant to keep his distance. She still kept hinting around about getting together after hours, but she hadn't come right out and asked. If she had, Seth would have had a good reason to bring up the fact that he was seeing someone. It didn't seem right to announce it out of the blue ... even though he'd been involved with enough women in his day to know Tracy was most definitely interested in him.

Behind him, Sara stopped to talk to someone who wanted to gush about Destiny, leaving Seth with two choices: abandon Destiny's mother, or stop, too—right in Tracy's path.

He stopped. No big deal. It wasn't as if Tracy was going to make a pass at him right here in public.

"Seth, wasn't she terrific?" she asked.

"What?"

"Destiny Hart. She was really something. That girl is going to go places. I'm so glad I let my nieces talk me into coming."

"Your nieces?"

"Aunt Tracy, at their service." She pointed at a nearby gaggle of giggling, gossiping middle school girls. "I'm babysitting while my brother and sister-in-law are out—which I was planning to talk to you about, actually, but I couldn't find you after school on Wednesday."

No, he'd bolted as soon as the kids were released that afternoon, wanting to get home and get things ready for Destiny's visit—not realizing she wasn't going to get there until two a.m.

"You wanted to tell me about your brother and sister-in-law's date night?" he asked Tracy incredulously. "Isn't that a little ... strange?"

She laughed. "Not really. And actually, it's not date night—or funny in the least. Tim and Joyce are splitting up and I thought you might be interested."

He blinked. "In your sister-in-law?" Maybe he'd been mistaken about Tracy's attraction to him.

"No!"

"Oh—in your *brother*?" Clearly, she'd had the wrong idea, too.

"Seth, you idiot—I'm talking about the house!" She laughed and poked him in the chest.

"Oh! The house!"

"They're getting ready to put it on the market, and they're both anxious to get out and move on. It's a great house, and if they could sell it without getting Realtors involved, it would be much easier, and they could pass the savings along to the buyer. You, if you're interested. Are you?"

"I'd have to see the house, but . . ."

"Trust me, it's right up your alley. Brick, close to the school, affordable . . . and it has a front porch."

He smiled. "Sounds good. I'll take a look."

"Great. I'll put you in touch with Tim. Do you still have my number?"

"I do."

"Call me over the weekend and we'll set something up."

"I will. I'll call you," he promised, and she smiled and moved on.

He turned away to see Sara, watching and listening and wearing a thoughtful—and disappointed—expression.

"I, ah . . . I work with her," he said hastily. "She's going to—"

"You don't have to explain anything to me, Seth."

"No, it's not what it—her brother is getting divorced and selling his house, and she thought it might be right for me."

Sara's troubled expression vanished—but only momentarily. "Seth, if you're thinking about settling down with Destiny, I'm not sure now is the time to—"

"No, I know it isn't," he told her, not wanting to hear her say the words. "I'm really happy for her."

Sara nodded. "We all are. Come on, let's go find her and tell her."

Seth resumed pushing through the crowd, wanting desperately to believe, even now, that he and Destiny were meant to be together.

If they were, fate would find a way.

And if they weren't . . . well, he figured fate would take care of that, too.

*B*ackstage was bedlam.

There were hordes of people and all of them seemed to be talking at once, calling Destiny's name, congratulating her, literally patting her on the back.

All she wanted—needed, desperately—was to find Seth. But he was nowhere in sight, and even if he tried to get back here, she wasn't sure he'd be able to.

Grace materialized and grabbed her shoulders. "Tammy Turner!"

"No, it's me, Destiny Hart," she cracked, and her sister grinned and shook her head.

"I can't believe we're going to Pigeon Forge!"

"*We?*"

"Sorry to break it to you, but this isn't just about you. Or even me. It's much bigger than that."

"Gee, thanks for the added pressure."

"You'd better get used to it!"

Destiny smiled, but she felt a cold ball of fear slide down her spine. Until this moment, she hadn't really considered that becoming successful meant that there would be lots of people depending on her. Holy cow. Grace was right. This really wasn't just about her ...

"Hey, you're not scared, are you?" Grace asked, seeing the look on her face.

"What do you think?"

Grace narrowed her eyes and poked a finger into her chest. "I think you're a Hart. You're made of stronger stuff than that."

Destiny squared her shoulders and angled her head at her sister, who always seemed so full of fluff, and realized that they shared some pretty doggone strong genes. "Damned straight!"

"Now you're talkin'." Grace grinned and gave her a fist bump.

"Listen," she asked her sister, again surveying the crowd, "have you seen Seth?"

"He was right in the front row, with Mom. I imagine he's somewhere in this mob scene—oh, hey, look, there's Annie!"

Destiny turned and her old friend grabbed her and hugged her tight. "Destiny, you're on your way! I'm so excited for you!"

"I've got a long way to go to make it in this business," Destiny said, "but tonight truly was special for me. Thanks so much for coming!"

"What about me?" Cooper popped up beside her. "I was the person who dared you to sing in the first place, right on this very spot. Remember?"

"Of course I remember," Destiny said, "and you're never going to let me forget it, are you?"

"No. You should have heard him busting Seth's chops earlier," Annie told her. "Ever since he found out you two are together, he's been obsessed with getting his share of the credit for that, too."

"Just how are you responsible for that?" Destiny asked Cooper.

"I always knew you and Seth were meant for each other, even when you guys didn't, that's how."

"Oh, come on. You were way too busy flirting around to pay any attention to what I was up to—and for that matter, so was Seth," Destiny told him.

"Yeah," Annie chimed in, "you were both hot stuff."

"*Were*?" Cooper echoed indignantly, and she gave him a playful punch in the arm.

Destiny had to smile, watching sweet little Annie try not to make moon eyes at Cooper.

Cute as a button with strawberry-blond hair, a winning smile, and a bubbly personality to match, Annie was adorable and quite a catch for any guy, Cooper included. But being petite and full figured, she always worried about her weight and fair skin in a world where blond and tan still seemed to be the yardstick for beauty.

She might not be the arm candy Cooper ran around with even now, but she was pretty as a picture and had a warm, giving heart. Hopefully, he'd sit up and take notice before someone else beat him to the punch, Destiny thought.

Aloud, she said, "Speaking of Seth . . ."

"We weren't speaking of Seth. We were speaking of me."

"You're wearing thin, Coop," Destiny told him. "Have you seen him?"

Annie shook her head, while Cooper grumbled, "Why does Seth always get to steal my spotlight?"

"Maybe because you're always being a pain in the butt."

"But a lovable pain in the butt, Annie. Admit it."

"Oh, please. Give me a break." She turned her attention back to Destiny. "Listen, we'd better let you go. A lot of people are waiting to talk to you. Guess you won't be coming home for Christmas so we can get together, huh?"

"Guess not." She felt a wistful pang. "Maybe you guys will be able to come down to Pigeon Forge, though, and see the show."

"I don't know . . . that's an awfully long way to go." Annie was teasing, Destiny realized, suddenly missing her old friend more than she had in years.

I have to do a better job at staying in touch, she told herself—then realized that if anything, it was going to be harder now than ever before.

"I wouldn't miss seeing you open for Tammy Turner," Annie said, and hugged her.

"Yeah, and don't worry," Cooper said. "You can ride down to Pigeon Forge with me. I'll keep you entertained in the car."

"Talking about yourself?" Annie arched an eyebrow.

"It's my favorite subject."

"Annie, just turn the radio up real loud and drown him out," Destiny suggested, and they were all laughing as they parted ways.

"Destiny, there's someone I want you to meet," Amy said, and pulled her along.

She kept scanning the crowd for Seth as she shook hands, smiled for pictures, and said all the right things about how excited she was about this wonderful opportunity.

That was true—but what if Seth didn't see it that way?

What if he'd left in a huff after the big announcement?

At last, Destiny heard him calling her name.

"Excuse me," she murmured to the aspiring country singer who was chewing her ear off, and turned to see Seth pushing his way toward her. Their eyes locked, and the crowd seemed to melt away.

"Destiny." He reached her, grabbed her, held her close.

"I'm so sorry, Seth."

"Sorry! What are you sorry for?"

"I didn't know about Pigeon Forge. I swear I didn't, or I'd have told you."

"Are you kidding? I know that. It was obvious from the look on your face. Priceless." He grinned, and she relaxed a little.

"Miranda found out right before the show, but she didn't want to tell me because she was afraid I'd go off the deep end. Then the PR people and Amy and Cassie got involved and they thought it would be a great idea to surprise me onstage, and—"

"And it was a moment you'll never forget, witnessed by hundreds of people."

"Exactly."

If it had been up to her, they wouldn't have told her about the last-minute turn of events while she was onstage—but it hadn't been up to her. She was coming to find out that very little seemed to be up to her in this business, and she simply had to roll with it.

"I was so proud of the way you handled it, Destiny, and so was your mother."

"My mother! Where is she?"

"Oh, she's doing a meet-and-greet of her own somewhere. She's had her first taste of stage motherhood, and I'd say she likes it."

Destiny smiled fleetingly. "Seth, the thing is . . . about Pigeon Forge . . . I mean, we're not going to be able to spend that week together at Christmas, and—"

"Um, excuse me . . ."

Destiny turned to see an unfamiliar young woman standing behind them. "I'm so sorry to interrupt, but I just have to tell you that I love your voice."

"Thank you."

"Could I possibly get your autograph?"

Destiny blinked. "My autograph?" Seth gave her a gentle prod, and she nodded. "Uh . . . sure."

"Thanks so much! My name is Amber."

Destiny took the pen and paper the girl thrust at her and tried to think of something clever to write. At any moment she expected Cooper to jump out of a corner and announce that she had been punk'd.

But after she handed Amber the autograph, a few more people approached her, probably just holiday tourists who thought she was famous. Still, she couldn't keep from grinning, particularly as one woman said, "I just love your voice. You're my favorite new star."

Star?

"Thank you," Destiny replied warmly, and although she had gotten many compliments over the past few weeks, this one floored her.

Star.

And they'd asked for her autograph!

It just blew her away.

"Wow." Seth leaned over and said, "Your first autograph session. I bet next year you'll have a line at the CMA Music Fest."

"Yeah, right," Destiny scoffed, but experienced a shiver of excitement at the prospect.

"Don't feel self-conscious about your success. Think about how excited you've felt getting a smile or autograph from someone you admire."

"Still, it feels strange to be on the other side of it. I mean, I'm just *me*."

"And *you* are a star, and it's all part of the business."

"I know," Destiny said softly, but it was difficult not to feel a measure of guilt that tomorrow she would once again be leaving him.

"Listen, I was thinking Mike must need to be walked by now . . ."

"Mike! I forgot all about him!"

"It hasn't been that long. I'm sure he's—"

"No, I mean Pigeon Forge. What about Mike? Can I bring him with me, do you think?"

"Probably, but you don't need one more thing to worry about. Why don't you let him stay here with me? My place even allows pets."

"You'd do that for me?"

"I'd do anything for you. Don't you know that by now?"

"And I—" She broke off. She just couldn't say it. She couldn't tell him she'd do anything for him, because it wasn't true, and they both knew it. She wouldn't give up her career for him. He wouldn't ask her . . . but if he did . . .

But he wouldn't. And that's what counts.

"I really appreciate it, Seth," she said, swallowing a lump of emotion.

"No problem. Listen, I'll go back to my place now and take care of him and make us something to eat. How long do you think you have to stick around here?"

"Not long, I hope. Miranda wants me to do a couple of interviews, but all I want to do is get out of here so that I can be alone with you."

"Oh, you just can't wait to change into some sweats. Admit it."

She grinned. "That, too."

"Okay, but keep the glitter in your hair. It's sexy."

"Yeah? What about the false eyelashes?" She playfully batted her eyes at him.

"Those can go."

"I was hoping you'd say that. I just need Grace to help me take them off so I don't pull out all of my real eyelashes—which I thought were adequate, but apparently I was mistaken."

"You weren't mistaken. There isn't anything about you that isn't adequate."

"Gee, thanks."

Seth shook his head wryly. "Okay, that didn't sound as smooth coming out as it did in my head, but you know what I mean."

Destiny smiled. "You are such a guy."

"That's good, right?"

"Very good."

"Destiny?" Miranda called. "We need you over here."

She sighed. "I'm sorry."

"Don't be. Your public awaits," Seth said. "Just don't forget . . . your private will be awaiting, too."

"Don't you mean *your privates*?" She grinned naughtily, and he laughed.

"Destiny!"

She sighed and gave Seth a quick kiss. "I promise I won't be long."

"Something tells me it's not up to you."

Something told her he was right.

But at least they'd sleep in each other's arms, and maybe share a leisurely breakfast in the morning before she had to head out to Pigeon Forge.

She made her way over to Miranda, who was waiting with Grace and Cassie and Amy and several publicity people.

Miranda wasted no time in getting down to business. "Listen, Tammy Turner thinks you and the band need to arrive in Pigeon Forge in style. She's sending her tour bus for you first thing in the morning."

"And there just might be a camera crew out there capturing the whole thing on film," Cassie said.

"And press," Donna, one of the publicists, put in. "Local newspapers, radio, TV."

"What do you think?" Miranda asked.

Destiny swallowed hard and looked at Grace, who gave her a big thumbs-up.

"Riding on a superstar's tour bus? What do you *think* I think?" Destiny quipped. "I'm *there*."

She just hoped she wouldn't spend the holidays wishing she were *here*.

TWELVE

*A*fter two hectic weeks in Pigeon Forge, Destiny found herself back in Nashville—in the greenroom of *Country Music News*, the country music countdown show that aired live every Saturday on CMT. She'd been watching faithfully for years and now here she was, about to be interviewed by the host, Ronnie Lee.

"I hope I don't say anything stupid," she told Grace, who was hovering again over a long table laden with snacks and coffee service.

"Read over the questions again," Grace advised, pointing at the sheet of paper the producers had handed Destiny earlier.

"I've read them over about thirty times now," Destiny answered with a sigh. "About the same number of times you've picked up that doggone doughnut. Eat it or leave it alone."

Dropping the glazed doughnut back into the box, Grace retorted, "I happen to think that picking it up thirty times and not eating it shows that I have a tremendous amount of willpower."

"Really? I think it shows that you're nuts."

"I'll eat one if you do," Grace challenged.

Destiny groaned. "Are you kidding? My stomach is doing flip-flops as it is. One bite of something sticky-sweet and I'll be sick. I'm a nervous wreck."

"You'll do fine." Grace reached over and put a hand on Destiny's thigh. "You've done dozens of interviews over the past couple of weeks."

"Yeah, on the radio and most were taped. Grace, this is *live* television. Oh, why did I agree to do this?" She put a hand to her throat. "And why do I suddenly sound like Olive Oyl?"

Grace laughed. "You don't."

"I don't?" Destiny squeaked.

"Well, maybe a little."

Destiny paced, wishing she could at least call Seth for some extra reassurance. But cell phones weren't allowed in the greenroom, for some reason. She supposed they didn't want the guests getting distracted before their appearances.

I wouldn't be distracted. I'd be much more relaxed if I could just hear Seth's voice.

"Sit down, Destiny," Grace told her. "You're making me nervous."

She plopped on a couch and looked down at her black jeans and vest. "Am I too casual? Do I look like Johnny Cash? Not that I don't love him, but . . ."

"No, this look is part of your updated brand, remember?"

"Right. Country chic. Successful but approachable."

Grace nodded. She'd been working with the creative team on branding, going for a cross between Taylor Swift and Carrie Underwood.

"Anyway, the silver cuff bracelet and high-heeled sandals give you some sexy flair."

"You think?"

"I know. Just do what Miranda Shepherd told you to do. Relax and be yourself."

"Be *myself*? Sexy flair is not *myself*. *Myself* is . . . I don't even know what myself is anymore!"

"You're panicking. Close your eyes and breathe."

Destiny tried. "Please don't say anything stupid," she told herself, and fisted one hand to her forehead. "Or what if I laugh? You know how I giggle at inappropriate times when I get rattled?"

"When do you do that?"

"Remember at that potluck church dinner when Aunt Ada sat down in that folding chair and it collapsed? She quit giving me Christmas presents after that."

"Aunt Ada gave everybody homemade potholders that fell apart and Ronnie Lee's chair is not going to collapse and that was years ago so calm down because you really are making *me* nervous, and when *I'm* nervous, *I* eat."

She grabbed the doughnut again, and took a huge bite.

A young woman with a bright smile and a clipboard breezed into the room. "Five minutes," she announced. "Follow me, Ms. Hart."

Destiny turned, wide-eyed, to Grace.

"Break a leg," Grace said around a mouthful of doughnut.

"I don't think it's the right time to say that," Destiny answered as she stood up. Her knees felt as if they were made of jelly. Great, she was going to walk like Olive Oyl too.

"Well, good luck, then."

"Thanks." Destiny willed her knees not to knock as she followed the perky intern down the hallway.

Photos of famous country stars lined the walls and Destiny experienced a familiar surreal feeling.

Was this really *her* life?

Most days were such a flurry of activity that it had yet to sink in. She'd been pinching herself ever since she'd arrived in Pigeon Forge on the day after Thanksgiving to begin rehearsing for the Christmas show, which opened tonight.

"This way, Ms. Hart," the intern said and held open the door to the studio. "Have a seat on the sofa. We're on an extended commercial break, but we need to get you situated."

Destiny nodded and thought that the studio appeared much smaller than on television. Two cameras seemed almost hidden in the background, but the set was brightly lit and on a raised platform.

Ronnie Lee also seemed smaller in real life. He sat studying his notes in a wingback chair that thankfully looked very sturdy and in no danger of collapsing.

The intern made a quick introduction and he glanced up with a brief but friendly smile as Destiny sat down on the green velvet sofa. A small coffee table with a silk flower arrangement and a potted plant to the left was the extent of the surprisingly simple set. The lights felt hot but the air remained cool so at least she wouldn't sweat.

"Hi. I'm Dave," a shaggy-haired tech announced, coming up beside Destiny. "I need to attach your mike."

"Oh . . . okay." She tried to take it in stride as he leaned in close and told her to unbutton the top few buttons of her shirt, then fumbled around with the mike and her lapel.

"There. That should be good. Say something."

"What?"

"Anything . . . we just need to test the sound."

"Okay. Uh . . . testing, one, two, three," she said, feeling a bit foolish.

"Sounds good," a disembodied voice boomed.

"Two minutes," a cameraman warned Ronnie, who nodded and put his notes off to the side.

He smiled over at Destiny and leaned in to shake her hand. "Welcome to *Country Music News*. Are you nervous?"

"A little. Well, maybe a lot," she found herself admitting, and he grinned.

"Just relax and have some fun. I promise this will be painless. Don't look at the cameras or worry about them or the mike. Just focus on me and we'll have a conversation like we're old friends."

Destiny and Ronnie Lee, old friends. Yeah, right.

"If you draw a blank," he added, "I'll get you past it."

"Do I look that freaked out?"

Ronnie chuckled. "Yes. But let me assure you that there are lots of big stars who still get rattled doing live interviews, so you're in good company."

Destiny smiled with gratitude. "I wish it was just about

the music—not that I don't want to be here," she added quickly. "It's just . . . I'm not used to all this other stuff yet."

"Hey, I understand." Ronnie winked at her. "And guess what? In the end, it really *is* all about the music. Never lose sight of that, okay?"

"I won't."

Destiny smoothed her shirt, rubbed her glossed lips together, and fluffed her hair. Just when her heartbeat slowed to an almost normal pace, the cameraman said, "Three, two . . . one."

He pointed at Ronnie, who gave a toothy smile to the camera.

"Welcome back to *Country Music News*! Sitting here with me is Destiny Hart, a rising star whose upcoming single 'Restless Heart' will be the new theme song on CMT's top-rated reality show. *Cowgirl Up* airs every Thursday night and the new season begins in January. Meanwhile, Destiny will perform in a holiday concert series with the legendary Tammy Turner at her new arena in Pigeon Forge, Tennessee."

Destiny could only swallow and nod. The camera to her left moved closer. She tried to ignore it, but it loomed there like some sort of science fiction robot.

"You must be incredibly thrilled."

She nodded again. The other camera moved.

Uh-oh . . . the robots are coming to get me!

For some reason—nerves?—she found her silent observation hilarious and to her horror her lips twitched.

Oh . . . mercy.

A cold bead of sweat rolled between her shoulder blades, making her silk shirt stick to her back.

Ronnie, who had promised to save her if she drew a blank, seemed to be waiting for more of a response.

"I'll just be opening with a few songs," she managed to say, despite the laughter bubbling up in her throat, making her heart pound with the herculean effort not to let it out.

She took a deep breath, gripping the arm of the green velour so hard that she was sure she would leave the fingernails behind, and added, "I'm honored to share the same stage as Tammy Turner. I'll be starstruck, that's for sure."

The cameras were moving.

The robots are coming . . . the robots are coming . . .

"Well, from what I hear, you're quickly gathering fans of your very own, Destiny Hart."

As nonchalantly as she could, Destiny curved her hand up to her left temple to block out the sight of the cameras, which looked like something out of a Disney movie.

"I read a glowing review that said you have a distinctive voice . . ." He grabbed his notes and read, "'whiskey smooth but with a bit of a bite.' Another review here says you have 'depth and emotion but mass appeal, with a voice that's a combination of classic country with a hot new edge.' Sound right to you?"

"I, um, I suppose that's a pretty good description. I grew up singing at barn dances and in the church choir, and I fell in love with gospel, bluegrass, and classic country. My mother said I was an old soul, but I love the new country too." She shrugged. "What you see is pretty much what you get."

"Well, you must be doing something right, because you'll be releasing a CD and a music video to go along with 'Restless Heart's' debut on CMT's *Cowgirl Up*, and word has it you've written all the songs yourself."

She nodded, still not used to being showered with praise and then expected to toot her own horn in response.

"Word also has it"—Ronnie Lee leaned in closer— "that you and Brody Ballard are dating."

"*What*?" She'd met the guy—a fellow up-and-coming country musician—just once in her life: backstage after he performed at Tammy's theater last weekend. "We barely know each other!"

"Well, you sure looked cozy holding hands in that *Nashville Gab* photo."

Remembering that there were press photographers all over the place that night, Destiny couldn't help but laugh at that. "Shaking hands, maybe—but definitely not holding them."

"Is that so?" Ronnie Lee gave a knowing wink, and her amusement turned to annoyance as she thought about Seth, somewhere out there watching the interview.

She opened her mouth to further explain the situation, but it was too late.

"Destiny, I'm sure we'll be seeing you here on *Country Music News* again very soon. Congratulations and the best of luck to you."

"Thank you so much."

Ronnie smiled and then turned his attention to the camera. "You can get ticket information about the Tammy Turner Christmas tour on our Web site. But don't go away. Next up is a sneak peek of Keith Urban's hot new video." His smile remained frozen for a moment and then the cameraman gestured, and he turned to Destiny. "You did fine."

"I started to freak out when I couldn't ignore the

cameras." *And when you accused me of cheating on my boyfriend.*

"I figured." He chuckled. "But you recovered and that's the sign of a real pro." He stood up and shook her hand as Dave removed her mike. "Thanks for coming by, and the best of luck to you, Destiny."

"My pleasure." She hastily rebuttoned her shirt and made a beeline for the greenroom.

Grace was polishing off another doughnut—white frosted with red sprinkles.

Grace took one look at Destiny's expression and guiltily reached for a napkin. "Don't look at me like that. I saw the frosting and I caved."

Destiny shook her head. "What? How can you sit there noshing on a doughnut when I almost lost it there on the show!"

"Lost it?" Grace licked icing from her thumb. "Lost what?"

"My composure! I was doing fine and then the cameras started moving around like robots, and—"

"You wanted to laugh."

"You could tell?"

"No. I'm guessing, because I know you so well. I didn't even notice."

"Because you were stuffing your face with a doughnut!"

"That's not true. I didn't eat it until after you were finished. You know, those red sprinkles are delicious. Much better than the green ones."

"Red is a color, not a flavor."

"Bet I could tell in a blind taste test," Grace argued, obviously trying to keep Destiny's mind off the near fiasco on live television. "You should have one, too."

"Blind taste test?"

"No, emergency snack. You're shaking."

"Ya think? After that interview, and what he said about me and Brody Ballard—what the heck was he talking about?"

"I don't know, but if your name is out there in the gossip columns, Destiny, that's a great sign."

"What about Seth?"

"What about him? I'm sure he doesn't read *Nashville Gab*, and even if he does, he trusts you. Don't worry."

"I feel sick."

"It's just low blood sugar, and you'd better eat something healthy."

"Like doughnuts?"

"Actually, I was thinking that if we hurry, we can stop by Back in the Saddle and grab something to eat before we head back to Pigeon Forge. But we need to leave, like, *now*."

"Don't you think that's a little out of the way?"

"It's only a few miles."

"Yeah, but I'm starved, and there are plenty of places right here ..." Destiny couldn't resist saying, fully aware that her sister had ulterior motives.

Then again, she realized, she really was suddenly famished. In this business, food, she was finding out, was rarely consumed at traditional mealtimes.

"But none of those other places will have burgers as good as Back in the Saddle's."

"You mean bartenders."

Grace shrugged. "That, too. Here ..." She thrust a doughnut at Destiny. "This'll hold you over till we get there. And keep your mouth busy, too."

"Hey, listen, just because I know—heck, everyone

but Max knows—that you're crazy about him, and yet you're going out with Jesse Jansen instead."

"We had a date. So what?"

"More than one."

"Two."

"Three, at least."

"Just so you know, Destiny, I don't count going out to eat after rehearsals as dates, when you and the rest of the band are there, too."

"Why not? You and Jesse are in your own little world anyway."

"He's a friend."

"What is Max?"

"Max is not my type."

"Right, you go for jerks, not nice, hard-working good guys."

"Hey!"

"Truth hurts."

"Jesse's not a jerk. He's also not hundreds of miles away. Max is."

Destiny shrugged. "Well, you know what they say. Absence makes the heart grow fonder."

"You know what else they say—out of sight, out of mind," Grace shot back, and Destiny winced.

"Are you talking about you and Max? Because obviously, that's not the case."

"I'm talking in general terms. Not about me and Max, *or* you and Seth."

"I know that," Destiny said defensively. "Why would you be talking about me and Seth?"

"Because we were talking about long-distance relationships, and you're in one. And if you don't eat that doughnut, I will." Grace gave her a pointed look.

Destiny took a big, soft bite, trying to remember the last time she'd eaten anything. Between rehearsals and costume fittings and photo sessions last night, and the crack-of-dawn road trip this morning . . .

"Hey, you're finally smiling again. Is that a party in your mouth, or what?"

"I was just thinking how time keeps on flying by and I never get a chance to stop and sit and sort of take it all in, you know?"

Grace shrugged. "It seems like we've been at this forever."

"I know . . . but how can that be? It's been only a few weeks since we rode out of Wilmot on Tammy's tour bus."

"Guess you just get used to it. This is your life now."

"I know, but . . . looks like 'normal' has taken a permanent holiday, hasn't it?"

"Come on, Destiny. Our lives have never been normal. And anyway, normal is overrated, don't you think?"

"Not necessarily."

"Well, abnormal has always been as normal to us as normal is, so it's all good."

"I'm the only one who understands your twisted sense of logic, but yeah, Gracie, it's all good."

Well—*almost* all good.

She hadn't seen Seth since the morning after the Wilmot concert, and they hadn't even had a proper good-bye.

How could they? Tammy Turner's big, flashy purple bus pulled up on Main Street right outside of the town square. Destiny dearly wanted to say good-bye to her mother and especially Seth in private, but they were surrounded by security and swiftly ushered toward the bus, with camera crews filming the entire procession.

She called Seth from the bus to apologize. It seemed to be a new pattern.

"It's okay," he said, and she could hear Mike barking in the background. "I get it. *We* get it. Don't we, Mike?"

She could only smile through her homesick tears, wishing things could be different—even as she wouldn't change a thing.

There she was, riding on her idol's tour bus. She'd be crazy to long to be anywhere else.

Maybe I am *crazy,* she thought, thinking she'd give anything to be in Seth's arms right about now.

But that would have to wait until Christmas, when he was coming to see her show. He was going to bring Mike with him and spend the whole week—just as she was supposed to do in Wilmot. She'd be busy with the production, but at least he'd be close by.

And then he'll have to leave again, she thought glumly. *He'll always have to leave.*

*W*ho the hell is Brody Ballard?

Seth clenched the computer mouse hard, waiting for the search engine to generate the results after he'd typed in the name.

It took only a few seconds, but that was long enough for his brain to conjure an unwanted image of Destiny holding hands with some other guy.

Shaking hands—she said that's all it was, he reminded himself as the screen filled with a list of links pertaining to his rumored rival.

Apparently, Brody Ballard was a hot new country stud—according to his own Web page, anyway.

Staring at the photo of a blond, square-jawed, guitar-toting cowboy, Seth felt sick inside. Quickly, he added Destiny's name to Brody Ballard's on the search engine page. He hit Enter, and the results were instantaneous, topped by a link to *Nashville Gab*.

He clicked it, and there it was: a big close-up photograph of Destiny with Brody Ballard.

At a glance, they were, indeed, holding hands. But they were facing each other, and it was clear—to Seth, anyway—from her body language that there was nothing going on between them.

The caption read "Future Superstars Only Have Eyes for Each Other."

Yeah, right.

How could Seth have even believed, for a moment, that Destiny would get involved with someone else behind his back?

Relieved, he turned away from the computer and looked over at Mike, sound asleep on the rug.

"I'm an idiot," Seth told the sleeping dog. "I know her better than that."

And when the phone rang a minute later, he was so certain he'd hear Destiny's voice on the other end that he didn't bother to check caller ID. He picked it up with a heartfelt, "You were incredible!"

"Gee, thanks." It was Tracy Gilmore's voice that greeted him on the other end of the line. "But all I did was put you in touch with Tim. You did the rest yourself."

"Oh . . . yeah, I guess." Trying to shift gears, he grabbed the remote and put Keith Urban's so-called hot new video on mute.

"I heard you made an offer this morning."

"I did, but I haven't heard back." Having been awakened by the phone, Mike trotted over, panting the way he did whenever he had to go out.

"Oh, I'm sure you'll hear back," Tracy told him as he looked around for the pooper scooper, "and I'm also pretty sure you'll be opening a bottle of champagne before the day is over."

Champagne—that made him remember the day he and Destiny had celebrated her *Cowgirl Up* coup at Back in the Saddle. It seemed like a lifetime ago.

"Seth? It's a great house for you."

"Yeah. It is, isn't it?"

Brick, with an eat-in kitchen, three bedrooms, and a big wraparound porch.

"I'm so excited about this," Tracy said.

"Under these circumstances? Really?"

"Well, I'm upset about my brother's marriage and everything . . . but they were never really happy together in the first place, so . . ."

"They weren't?"

"No. Joyce gave up her career because he didn't want her to work after they had kids, and I guess she always resented it."

"Yeah . . . that happens." Seth opened the utility closet so hard the door banged the wall.

"Personally, I don't know what she was complaining about. If my husband wanted me to be a stay-at-home mom, I'd be more than happy to do it. Not that I don't love teaching, but . . . you know what I mean."

"Yeah," Seth told her, slamming the door closed again—no pooper scooper. "I know what you mean."

"So listen, after you get the phone call—which should be any second now—why don't you call me back and I'll come over with a bottle of champagne?"

"You don't have to do that."

"I *want* to, Seth. Unless you don't want me to?"

He hesitated. "It's not that. It's—"

He broke off, hearing a beep on the line.

"That's call-waiting," he said. "I have another call."

"I bet it's Tim. I'll hang up. Call me back."

He heard a click before he could respond.

He pressed the flash button. "Hello?"

"Seth, it's me."

"Destiny! I saw you on TV. You were great!"

"Before or after I almost burst out laughing in Randy Lee's face?"

"I must have missed that. What was so funny?"

"*You'll* understand. Grace didn't, but she doesn't get me the way you do. See, there were these cameras ..."

She kept talking, and he tried to make sense of what she was telling him, but all he could think was that she'd just been on live television in front of millions of people, and here he was, hunting for a pooper scooper.

"Isn't that crazy?" she asked.

"Yeah, crazy. So the cameras reminded you of robots?"

She hesitated. "Yes, but ... you know what? It's not important."

"Talk about crazy—what about that Brody Ballard thing? That was pretty crazy, too, huh?"

"Definitely. I mean, someone introduced us the other night, and I guess there's a picture on the Internet or something, so ... You know it's not true, right, Seth?"

"Are you kidding? Of course I know!"

"Good, because I didn't want you to think ... I mean, I know you wouldn't think—but the way Ronnie Lee said it, it was just—and I didn't even have a chance to explain."

"It's okay. I get it."

"I'm glad." The hollow tone to her voice sent warning signals through his brain. "Listen, I should probably—"

"Guess what," he blurted in an effort to keep her from hanging up. "I bought a house."

There was a pause—just a fraction of a pause, but it was there, and then she said, "Seriously?"

He hesitated. It wasn't exactly official yet, but . . .

Oh, who was he kidding? Tracy wanted to come over here with champagne. Not that he'd let that happen, but . . .

"Seriously," he told Destiny.

"Seth, that is just so . . . exciting!" she said brightly—too brightly. "Where is it?"

"Over by the high school. I can walk to work on nice days."

"Tell me all about it."

He did, trying not to sound like he wanted to sell *her* on it.

"Oh, I love those old brick houses. They have so much history and character. Does it have a front porch?"

"Yeah. A big wraparound porch."

"Oh, that's so awesome!" He knew her enthusiasm was totally forced. "You have to get a swing! Nothing is better than sipping a cold glass of tea on a front porch swing, just watchin' the world go by."

He tried—and failed—to imagine her doing just that.

"When are you moving in?"

"I don't have all the details yet, but as soon as possible, I hope. It's a fixer-upper."

"That's perfect. You're handy."

"Yeah, I love doing that kind of stuff. And between now and when baseball starts, it'll keep me busy and my mind off of—"

He broke off.

"Off of what?"

Off of you. What else?

But he couldn't admit that. It would sound pathetic. He sure as heck didn't think she was sitting around mooning over him.

No, she was flitting around on TV and onstage with Ronnie Lee and Tammy Turner and backstage with some hottie jerk in a cowboy hat . . .

"You know, I've been pretty stressed about the spring baseball season," he told her, "and about Chase's situation."

"Oh, Chase—how is he? Any new developments?"

"His mother wants him to move out there over the Christmas break."

"Is he going to?"

"He doesn't want to, but he might not have a choice."

"Oh no."

"Yeah. I'm doing everything I can to support the kid and convince his mother that he's got a real shot at an athletic scholarship if she leaves him here, but it's like talking to a brick wall."

"I'm sure it is," Destiny said, and he heard a voice in the background urging her to get off the phone. A female voice, he noted with some satisfaction.

"That's Grace," she told him. "She wants me to say hi."

"And get off the phone!" Grace shouted. "We have to go eat!"

"Okay, okay," Destiny said, and asked Seth, "Hey, one last thing—how's Mike doing?"

"He's okay. He misses you." He hesitated. "We both do."

"I miss you, too." She cleared her throat. "Listen, e-mail me some pictures of the house, will you? Do you have any?"

"Yeah. I only took about a million of them. I want to document the renovations."

"That will be fun. Be sure and send them to me."

He paused, then said, "I was hoping you'd be able to come and see for yourself."

"Well . . ."

"Hey, never mind. I don't know where that came from. I know you're too busy."

"Seth, it isn't that I don't want to come home."

"I know. Believe me. Forget I mentioned it," he answered, and bent down to pet Mike, who was still panting at his feet.

"I miss you," she said again.

"I miss you, too."

"Good-*bye*, Seth," Grace said pointedly in the background.

He hung up and looked at Mike.

"She's doing great," he told the dog.

Mike tilted his head.

"Yeah, I know. I'm glad to hear it, too," Seth said. "*Really* glad. What, you don't believe me?"

Mike just looked at him.

Seth sighed. "Come on, let's go out."

Max was behind the bar at Back in the Saddle, and glad to see them, giving Destiny a bear hug and Grace a shy once-over. The television overhead was tuned to

CMT, where Ronnie Lee's news program had given way to a Toby Keith video.

"We all watched," Max told Destiny. "You should'a heard the hoopin' and hollerin' when you came on-screen."

"What, was everyone laughing at me?" she asked with a wink, forcing herself to stop stressing—at least momentarily—about Seth and his new house.

"Nah, you were great. I was hoping you'd stop by before you headed back to Pigeon Forge." He was looking at Grace as he said it, and she smiled.

"We figured we could say hello and grab some burgers before we hit the road. We don't have much time, though. Destiny has to be back."

"Sit right down here at the bar and I'll take your order myself. Need menus?"

"I don't. I'll just have the usual," Destiny told him, and couldn't resist rolling her eyes when it took Max a moment to drag his eyes away from Grace.

"The usual?"

"Um, hello . . . ? Cheeseburger, extra pickle, mustard, no onion."

"Oh. Right. You want cheese on that?"

"On my cheeseburger? Sure, why not?"

"Okay, got it," Max said, oblivious to the irony in her tone.

Destiny chuckled, shaking her head as he painstakingly took Grace's order. She watched Grace discreetly follow Max's progress as he headed to the kitchen.

"If you ask me," Destiny said, "he makes I'm-all-that-and-a-bag-of-chips Jesse seem shallow and unworthy."

"I didn't ask you."

"But I'm right, and you know it."

Grace shrugged. "What does it matter? He's too shy to do anything about . . . anything."

"So? *You're* not shy."

Grace shrugged. "I'm also leaving town in about"— she checked her watch—"a half hour."

"You know . . . you don't *have* to go."

"What do you mean? You have to be back at Tammy's theater by—"

"No, I know *I* have to go. But you don't, Grace."

"I'm your personal assistant and you're opening in the biggest gig of your life. I wouldn't do you much good from here, now, would I?"

"Wow, you're one loyal personal assistant—and sister."

"Aren't I, though?"

Destiny smiled faintly, then toyed with the straw in her glass, poking at the slice of lemon floating on top.

"What are you suddenly brooding about, Destiny?"

"I'm not brooding."

"Sure you are. And I think I know. Seth, right?"

Destiny shrugged, watching the lemon twirl around in her glass.

"Just because he bought a house doesn't mean he's moving on without you, you know."

"I know."

"And it doesn't mean he expects you to settle down there with him."

"I know," Destiny said again, but less convincingly.

"Unless you want to."

"You know I don't want to settle down in Wilmot, Grace. And so does he."

So why the hell did he buy a house there? Is he trying to tell me he's moving on?

If so, message received, loud and clear.

"Look, Destiny, you've always known where you were going and what you wanted, unless you've changed your mind now that you and Seth—"

"I haven't."

"But the thing is ... who says you can't have your cake and eat it, too?"

"*Everyone* says. Anyway, what is this, cliché day? First absence makes the heart grow fonder, and now—"

"Hey, *you're* the one who said that. Not me. I said—"

"Yeah, I know. Forget it. Let's talk about something else."

"Like your hair? Because I was thinking you could try wearing it up later, sort of poufy and soft ..."

Destiny sighed, and was grateful when Max arrived a few minutes later with their food. "Here you go, ladies. Enjoy, and let me know if you need anything else."

Destiny lightly kicked Grace under the bar and waggled an eyebrow at her. Grace stuck out her tongue.

"You guys okay?" Max asked, watching them.

"*I* am," Grace told him, "but you know these showbiz types can be a little ... how do I put it delicately ... *nuts*."

Destiny kicked her again—for real this time.

"Hey, you're the one who thought the cameras were robots," Grace said, and told Max about Destiny's on-set experience.

"I guess you'll get used to it soon enough, Destiny— you know, cameras in your face all the time. Before you know it, you'll be on magazine covers and billboards ..."

"Yeah, right," she scoffed, and pointed to her face. "Who'd want to see this mug on a magazine?"

"You've got to be kidding." Max laughed and started singing, "She don't know she's beautiful . . ."

"Wow," Grace said, "Destiny was right. Max, you have an amazing voice! Deep and sexy. Kind of a cross between Jake Owen and Chris Young."

"Uh-oh, my friend—your talent has just been outed. Grace will not let this go without hounding you mercilessly to sing. The business is in her blood now, too."

"I was just joking around," Max protested, then arched an eyebrow at Grace. "But did you say sexy?"

"Sure did," Grace replied coyly. "And I didn't think you were joking. Destiny might be the star, but the diva role is still my department. In fact, I thought you were singing about me."

Max blushed. "I . . . uh . . ."

Grace burst out laughing. "Don't worry, Max. I happen to know I'm beautiful." She fluffed her hair.

She was teasing, Destiny knew, but judging by the look on Max's face, he was thinking just that.

When they were finished eating, Grace announced, "It's time to leave. Ready, Destiny?"

She took one last look around the bar room. "Not really," she said, feeling tears welling up in her throat. "I really miss this place."

Grace squeezed her hand and nodded. "This door is closing for you, but just think about the one that's opening."

"I know, I'm trying, but . . ." Destiny closed her eyes and swallowed hard. "I'm sorry, I don't know what came over me. I guess the past few months have been overwhelming."

"That's understandable," Grace told her, and Max, standing by, murmured in agreement.

"I feel sick—it's like joy, excitement, and fear all wrapped into one tight little bundle lodged somewhere in the pit of my stomach."

"Maybe you should just throw it up," Grace said, deadpan.

"Hey, when did you morph into me? That's something I would say—and get a warning look from Mom."

"I bet not anymore. Mom's a prime example that we can change the direction of our lives at any age. Remember what Granny used to say about strong-minded women?"

"She called them steel magnolias," Destiny recalled with a nod. "Delicate on the outside, but strong on the inside."

"Sounds like she was talking about both of you," Max said, and stepped closer to Grace, who sighed and looked again at her watch.

"We really do have to go, Destiny."

"I know, I know." She gave one last look around, then lifted her chin and took a deep breath, announcing, "I'm ready."

For anything, she added silently.

This was wrong, and Seth knew it.

So why didn't you stop it before it happened?

He knew why. He'd been so excited about the new house, and he wanted to share it with someone . . .

Not just *anyone.*

Destiny.

Destiny, who had just appeared on national television. By contrast, Seth buying his first house was obviously insignificant.

Not to Tracy Gilmore, though.

Here she sat on Seth's couch, sipping the champagne she'd brought over, and going on and on about how great the house was—how he could put a home gym in the basement and turn one of the bedrooms into a study, and refinish the built-in cabinets in the dining room, and how he'd made the right decision . . .

It was everything he wanted to hear.

But not from her.

"And if you want some help planting flowers this spring," she said, "I'm great in the garden."

"Great," he said, thinking about Destiny, who—he had no doubt—had never planted a garden in her life, and wouldn't be free to hang around in the spring to help him settle into the new house.

"Seth?"

"Hmm?"

"You're a million miles away."

He blinked.

Tracy tilted her head. "Who is she?"

"Who is who?"

"The woman you wish was sitting here instead of me."

She was so dead-on that Seth couldn't deny it. "It's . . . she's . . . you don't know her."

But that wasn't true. Everyone in town knew her, and pretty soon, everyone in the world would know her name.

Okay, maybe that was a slight exaggeration . . . but still . . .

"Destiny Hart," Tracy said. "Right?"

"I—uh, right. What are you, psychic?"

She smiled and shook her head. "Call it women's intuition. Or small-town gossip. Or a little of both."

"Oh."

"Look, Seth . . ." She laid a hand on his sleeve. "I just want to be your friend, okay? And nothing more . . . unless that's what *you* want. I'm here and she's not."

Seth looked at her. Yes, she was. Those words were an open invitation, and he knew it.

THIRTEEN

"I can't believe it's Christmas Eve already," Tammy Turner told Destiny as they sat in adjoining makeup chairs backstage at the big white-pillared music hall. "Seems like it was just Thanksgiving. Time sure does fly when you're having fun."

"Sure does," Destiny agreed, but to her, time seemed to be doing just the opposite. It wasn't that she hadn't been having fun—she loved getting up onstage and playing to sold-out crowds day in and day out.

But she'd also been counting down the hours until Seth arrived. Now there were only two more to go—and just three until curtain time. Hardly enough time in between for her and Seth to catch up on a month's worth of conversation and kisses, but there was always later—and tomorrow, and every day until New Year's.

Pure heaven.

"You're grinnin' from ear to ear," Tammy said, catching her eye in the big mirror that stretched across the wall in front of their makeup chairs. "What's that about?"

"I think I told you—my boyfriend is coming to spend the holidays here."

"Oh, that's right. Seth, isn't it?"

Destiny nodded, impressed and touched that she remembered his name. As busy—and spectacular—as she was, Tammy had a real down-to-earth side. She made it her business to get to know everyone involved in the production, from the backup musicians to the food service workers.

"So refresh my memory—what does Seth do?" Tammy asked, as the stylist teased her jet-black hair.

"He lives in my hometown—he's a teacher and a coach at our old high school."

"That so?"

"I know what you're thinking," Destiny said, and Tammy raised an amused eyebrow.

"Really? What am I thinking?"

"That it can't possibly work between us, because he's there, and I'm . . . here." She waved a hand at the bustling backstage scene surrounding them.

"I didn't say that."

She didn't have to. Destiny was well aware that her idol had been married—and messily divorced—three times. Her first two husbands had been fellow country singers—neither of whom were nearly as successful as Tammy.

The third husband was an "Average Joe"—the title of Tammy's Grammy-winning song written about heartache in the aftermath of a doomed marriage.

"You've been feeling a little overwhelmed, haven't you?" Tammy asked knowingly.

"Does it show?"

"No, sweetie. You carry yourself very well. But I can see it in your eyes. Let me explain something to you. Everyone is going to think you're living a charmed life, making piles of money. But as you'll find out, a hit record barely makes enough money to get your band on the road. It's a tough life and the sacrifice is huge."

"I thought you were going to pep me up," Destiny said with a small laugh.

"Destiny, I'm a straight shooter and I'm going to hit you right between the eyes the way I dearly wish someone had done with me. This is a hard, grueling lifestyle. In the end, toughness often wins out over talent." Tammy gave her a measuring look and said, "I believe you have both."

"So what keeps you going?" Destiny asked.

"The fans. Think about how much joy music has brought to your life. You"—Tammy gently tapped Destiny's shoulder—"are bringing that same joy to your very own fans. Music heals. Brings happiness. Marks a place and time in our memories. We play it at weddings and at funerals. Music touches our lives each and every single day in some way, shape, or form. Can you imagine even one day void of music?"

"No," Destiny replied.

"You have the gift of creating music and you need to share it. But you know all of this. You've been told this, I'm sure."

Destiny nodded.

"You feel an outpouring of love when you step onto that stage, don't you?"

"Yes. Definitely."

"Never lose sight of what your voice, your songs bring to others. No matter how hard it is to keep that in mind. The music business today moves at turbo speed. The Internet and the media can propel you so much faster now than years ago. Your picture is splashed everywhere . . ." She shook her head. "You have to be careful, or it can spiral out of control."

"So how do you keep balance in your life?"

Tammy laughed softly and shook her head. "That's an easy question. You don't."

Destiny raised her eyebrows.

"You'll see. Pretty soon, touring will become your lifestyle. You'll wake up in hotel rooms and not remember what city you're in or where you're heading next. You'll eat dinner at midnight and get up at the crack of dawn. You'll feel as if you're short-changing your friends and family. It's going to take a special man to deal with your success, your absence. Rumors. And you will be faced with temptation in ways you never dreamed of."

Destiny shook her head. "I would never—"

"Don't be so sure. Night after night, alone, far from home . . . you'd be surprised the possibilities that enter a woman's mind."

Destiny shook her head firmly. That would never happen to her. Not as long as she knew Seth was waiting for her back at home.

Home?

His home. His house—the house he had bought without first discussing it with her.

Not that he needed her permission, or even her blessing, but still . . .

When she'd first found out about it, all she could think was that he was moving on without her. But Grace convinced her she was wrong to assume anything.

"I mean, geez, look at that picture of you and Brody Ballard, Destiny. You know Seth must have seen it, and he didn't go and accuse you of moving on. Don't do that to him. It isn't fair."

No, it wasn't.

She just hated that she could feel so secure, suddenly, about her career, just as she found herself so insecure about her relationship with the man she loved. Talk about unfair . . .

"How does Seth feel about your career?" Tammy asked.

"He's is a strong believer in fate and that things will turn out the way they should be in the end."

"Is that what you believe?"

"I think you have to *make* things happen."

"It's been my experience that God helps those who help themselves. So in other words, you need a bit of both."

"That makes sense."

"So Seth is supportive?"

"Very."

"And so far, the career hasn't gotten in the way of your relationship?"

"That depends on what you mean by 'in the way,'" Destiny said with a rueful smile.

"I don't know about that man of yours, but you seem like you've got your head screwed on straight. It's a tough life for someone who wants to have a marriage, too. But I know plenty of people who've made it work.

I'm just not lucky enough to be one of them, and it's probably my own damned fault."

Destiny didn't know what to say to that. But Tammy almost seemed to be talking more to herself anyway.

"The first time, I married for money—hey, don't look so surprised." She shifted her gaze back to Destiny in the mirror. "I was a nobody back then, and he was up and coming. Then the tables turned, and he couldn't deal with my success. The second time, I married for companionship, because I hated feeling like I was alone even though I was always surrounded by people, know what I mean?"

"I'm starting to," Destiny said, as the makeup artist behind her own chair began brushing foundation over her skin.

"In the end, my husband turned out to be even more a stranger than the strangers who acted like they were my best friends—and this business is full of those, in case you haven't noticed."

"Oh, I have." Her suite and dressing room were full of gifts from people she didn't know: roses and chocolates and fruit baskets, even a hand-knit sweater from an elderly die-hard fan who had attended every performance.

It was touching—and disconcerting—to be the object of affection of so many strangers.

Tammy went on with her story. "So the third time, I figured I'd do things the right way and marry for love. I thought that one would have to last forever. Ha. In the end, it didn't turn out any differently than the others—but it sure as hell hurt a lot worse."

"I'm so sorry," Destiny said softly.

"Yeah. Me too." Tammy shrugged. "Why am I telling you all this?"

"I don't know . . . but I'm glad you did. I mean, in this business, it's not like you get to have many peers—not that I think you're my peer!" she added quickly, horrified at the implication that she considered herself anywhere near Tammy Turner's pedestal.

Tammy laughed. "I know exactly what you're sayin'. You start to leave your old friends behind, because they can't possibly understand what it's like to be in your shoes. And the few who do get it are usually hopin' you'll fall flat on your face, so don't let 'em kid you."

Destiny thought of Cindy Sue, and nodded knowingly.

"You're all set, Miss Turner." The woman who'd been working on Tammy's hair removed her drape with a sweep of her manicured fingers.

Tammy stood up and turned back to Destiny. "I want you to remember that it's a cutthroat business, darlin'. The higher your star shoots, the more likely that you can count your friends on one hand. But if you ever need advice from someone who's probably been there, done that, then you know where to come."

Touched, Destiny smiled—then closed her eyes and coughed as her own stylist aimed a can of hairspray at her and pulled the trigger.

When Destiny opened her eyes, Tammy had vanished, but her words lingered, more like a warning than an inspiration.

Clutching a bouquet of slightly wilted wildflowers that had traveled with him from Wilmot, Seth hesitated before knocking on Destiny's dressing room door. He could hear her in there, warming up her voice with scales, and he knew her mind must be on tonight's performance—of course it would be. It was sold out, and the parking lot behind the concert hall was already jam-packed, an hour before the show.

Seth had been forced to park in a municipal lot down the street, feeling like he was well out of his element even before he approached the theater and saw the marquee.

There was Destiny's name—right below Tammy Turner's, and in type that wasn't a whole lot smaller.

Seeing it up there in lights had left him speechless, driving home the reality of who and what she had become.

Feeling like an outsider in a world in which he did not belong, he'd gone around to the back entrance, as Destiny had instructed him, and showed the security guard the VIP backstage pass Grace had FedExed to him.

The guard was a strapping, good-looking guy, and Seth found himself unreasonably jealous that this person was so at home here, and he, Seth, needed a special pass just to get to his girlfriend.

"Go on in," the guard said amiably, after checking Seth's photo ID to make sure it matched.

"Thanks." Seth wished the guy would ask how he had come to have special access—just in case he had any ideas about Destiny and didn't realize she had a boyfriend.

But the guard didn't ask, and Seth told himself he was being ridiculously insecure all of a sudden.

Now, as he stood there trying to work up the nerve to

knock, he wondered if things would even be the same when he saw her.

"Seth!"

He spun around and saw Grace hurrying toward him. "I'm so glad you're here! Did you find the hotel okay?"

"Found it, checked in, and got Mike all settled."

"Did they give you the room adjoining Destiny's suite, like I told them to?"

He nodded, feeling slightly uncomfortable. They both knew he wouldn't be sleeping in his own room, but Grace had told him it would be a good idea for him and Mike to have a separate space.

"Too many people are in and out of Destiny's suite every day, Seth," she'd said. "It might get on your nerves."

He was pretty sure it wouldn't, but the implication was clear: He and Mike might be in the way.

Oh, well. He didn't care about the days, anyway. It was the nights that mattered.

His heartbeat quickened just thinking of later, having Destiny all to himself.

Grace eyed the bouquet in his hand. "Those are so pretty, Seth. Wildflowers in winter? Where did you find them?"

"Bobbi Callahan ordered them special." Bobbi ran Wilmot's only florist shop.

"Destiny's going to love them. I'll make sure they don't get lost in the shuffle after you give them to her," Grace promised. "Come on, let's let her know you're here."

Lost in the shuffle? It was such a strange thing to say.

But he understood the moment Grace opened the door with a "Destiny, guess who's here!"

Every surface of her dressing room was covered with flowers—dozens upon dozens of roses, in vases and exotic arrangements. Beside them, his limp little bouquet seemed almost . . . pathetic.

What was I thinking?

I should have brought roses.

Destiny broke off her scales and rushed toward him. "Seth!"

A wave of emotion crashed over him and he held her close, burying his face in her hair as Grace discreetly slipped out of the room.

"I've missed you so much," he murmured, inhaling her sweet herbal scent.

"Bet I've missed you more. Where's Mike?"

"Back at the hotel. Guess they don't make canine VIP passes."

"I can't believe you're really here. I kept thinking something was going to go wrong—like your car would break down or there would be a blizzard in the mountains—and you wouldn't be able to make it."

"Nothing could have kept me away, Destiny. I'd have walked here if I had to." He kissed her head, then chuckled.

"What's so funny?"

"I taste sparkles on my tongue."

"Sorry . . ." Her laughter rumbled against his shoulder and she splayed her hand across his chest. "Mmmm . . . you smell so good, all woodsy and spicy."

"As opposed to peach-scented?" he teased, remembering the night he'd taken a shower at her apartment back in Nashville.

"That seems like a lifetime ago, doesn't it?" she asked. "So much has happened to us since then."

That she'd said "us" instead of "me" was encouraging enough for him to hold out the flowers he'd brought. "These are for you."

"Oh, Seth—"

"Destiny, we need you to—oh, sorry."

Seth looked up to see a casually rugged stranger standing in the doorway. Obviously a stage tech, he wore jeans and boots, a flannel shirt, and a mouthpiece. Like the security guard, this guy inspired in Seth yet another flare-up of jealousy.

"Hey, Jack," Destiny said, glancing up from the wild-flower bouquet, "this is Seth. Seth, Jack."

They shook hands politely, and Seth wondered why Destiny hadn't introduced him as her boyfriend. Had it been a deliberate oversight?

Jack told her she was needed backstage right away.

She gave Seth a helpless, apologetic look.

"It's okay," he said quickly—and insincerely.

"Thank you for understanding. It's just always kind of crazy before a show."

"I get it. I'll see you afterward." He gave her a quick kiss, conscious of Jack hovering, waiting to escort her away.

Couldn't the guy see that they might want a moment of privacy here? Didn't he realize that it had been a month since they'd seen each other?

If he realized, he didn't care—in fact, for all Seth knew, Jack was trying to move in on Destiny and had manufactured a reason to whisk her away.

Part of him felt that it was a ridiculous notion; another part wasn't so sure.

"Oh . . ." Halfway out the door, Destiny stopped

short and looked down at the wildflowers in her hand.
"I . . . I need to find a vase."

"You don't have time for that, come on," Jack told
her.

"I'll take care of them," Seth told her. "Here, give
them to me."

"No, you don't have to—"

"I've got it."

"No, really—"

Suddenly, Jack reached out and plucked the bouquet
from Destiny's hand and thrust it at Seth. "Dude, here,
you deal with these."

What the . . . ?

Refusing to take the flowers, Seth balled his hands
into fists instead. "Who the hell do you think you are?"

"Me? I work here." Jack recklessly tossed the flowers
aside, snapping several fragile stems as they landed.
"Who the hell are *you*?"

I'm her boyfriend!

But he couldn't say it. It was so stupid, so cheesy,
so . . . high school. He wound up his fist, as infuriated
with himself for losing control as he was with this jerk
for making him.

"Come on, guys, cut it out!" Destiny grabbed Seth's
arm and hung on tight.

"Hey, I'm just doing my job," Jack said, so mildly that
if Destiny hadn't been holding him back, Seth would
have punched him for sure, "and that's to get you to
where you're supposed to be, so let's go."

She shook her head, looking in dismay at the ruined
bouquet. "I need to—"

"*Go.*" The word came out more sharply than Seth

had intended. He saw her eyebrows furrow. She hesitated for a split second, biting her bottom lip, before turning and following Jack away without a backward glance.

Seth looked down at the scattered, broken wildflowers, then at the dozens of roses surrounding him. With a curse, he gathered his pitiful offering and dumped the whole thing into the nearest trash can.

"Merry Christmas," Destiny told Grace, who trailed the band members out the door of her suite following an impromptu after-show party.

Destiny's original plan had been to come back here alone with Seth, but it was Christmas Eve, and no one else was in a hurry to get back to their own room.

"Merry Christmas to you, too. And you." Grace pointed a finger at Seth, who stood behind Destiny. "Make sure you get some sleep, or Santa won't come."

"What about me?" asked Jesse, who was standing in the hall.

"You're a lost cause." Grace shook her head as she stepped out after him. "Santa only visits good boys, and you're the opposite."

"In that case—want to come keep a naughty boy company?"

Grace pulled the door closed before Destiny heard her reply. She looked at Seth.

"Don't tell me Grace is seeing him."

Destiny shrugged. "I don't know what's going on, exactly. She knows I don't approve, so I'm not allowed to bring it up."

"What about Max?"

"As Grace put it, Max isn't here, and even if he were, he probably wouldn't get his act together enough to ask her out."

She wasn't entirely comfortable discussing the prospect of a long-distance relationship—even someone else's—with Seth. In fact, she wasn't entirely comfortable with him, period. Not after the scene in her dressing room.

Maybe that was why she hadn't protested when someone suggested gathering in her suite with eggnog and champagne after the show.

The moment Jack had interrupted them, she'd picked up on a distinctly disturbing vibe between him and Seth. Well, coming from Seth, anyway.

He'd obviously resented the interruption from the start, but she was stunned when she realized he was actually going to haul off and hit Jack over something so . . . silly.

And yet . . .

Maybe there was also a part of her that was secretly thrilled at the blatant display of masculine possessiveness.

Clearly Seth hadn't moved on. Clearly he was still crazy about her.

Anyway, she supposed she couldn't blame him for his reaction. Jack had been pretty blunt and obnoxious.

But preshow chaos and intrusions on her personal space went with the territory. She was used to it, and she figured Seth would get used to it eventually, too, after spending a week here with her. If not . . .

No. She wasn't going to worry about that now. Her time with Seth was so limited. He was here with her now and they were alone together at long last, and she didn't want to miss one minute thinking negative thoughts.

"I thought you said you were going to get a Christmas tree." Seth gestured at the living room of the suite. A couple of gilt-sprayed poinsettias were the only hint of holiday decoration.

"I wanted to get one," she told him, "but I haven't had time."

"I'd have brought one if I had known."

"That's okay." She finally dared to ask the question that had been on her mind. "Where are my beautiful wildflowers?"

"What? Oh . . . I guess they're back in your dressing room." He busied himself picking lint off his red sweater.

Watching him, she felt another prickle of discomfort. She started to open her mouth to ask him whether he'd found a vase, but he spoke first, indicating Mike, who was curled up asleep on a chair.

"Looks like someone's settled down for a long winter's nap."

Destiny couldn't help but yawn, looking at him. "Oops, sorry."

"Are you ready to call it a night, too?"

"Are you kidding? Not yet. We haven't even had a chance to talk. How about if I go change my clothes and we go outside and sit under the stars?"

"Under the stars with a star—sounds good to me."

Destiny rolled her eyes and gave him a poke, but she was glad that he felt comfortable enough to tease her.

"I'll wait for you out on the fire escape—I mean, balcony," he amended with a grin, heading for the French doors.

Destiny slipped into the adjoining bedroom, humming "Have Yourself a Merry Little Christmas" while she tugged off her shoes and then found her favorite baggy sweatpants and matching hoodie.

After scooting her feet into some fuzzy slippers, she located a Nessie-rejected stadium blanket sporting the top half only of Elvis's head.

She found Seth out on the balcony, leaning against the railing and looking up at the night sky.

For a moment he didn't realize she was there, and she took the opportunity to simply gaze at his handsome profile.

When Seth spotted Destiny, he gave her a slow Southern smile that turned her insides into a molten puddle.

"Wow," Destiny breathed. "That sexy smile of yours has the power to turn me inside out."

Seth's smile slid into something more sensual and he held out his hand, stepping toward a chaise lounge. "Come on, let's cuddle."

"Wait, did you just say *cuddle*?"

Seth chuckled softly. "Yeah, guess I did. Destiny, you bring out something soft in me that I never knew existed."

She walked over and hooked her arm through his. "I like it."

"Me too, but keep it to yourself." Seth arched one eyebrow and then kissed the tip of her nose. "I have my tough coach image to uphold."

"Your softie side secret is safe with me," she told him, and wondered whether she should bring up what had happened in her dressing room. Talk about a tough coach image . . .

But she didn't want to get into that now. This was supposed to be a nice, romantic evening.

They settled on the chaise. Destiny snuggled close to Seth and looked up into the star-filled sky.

"You must be exhausted." Seth leaned over and kissed the top of her head.

"I don't want to be. Now that you're finally here, the last thing I want to do is fall asleep."

"You can't stay up for five days straight, Destiny."

She started to laugh, then pulled back to look at him. "Five days? I thought you were staying through New Year's."

"I was planning to, but—didn't you get the e-mail?"

"Which e-mail?"

"The one I sent last night when I found out I have to be back in Wilmot by the thirtieth to meet with Chase and his stepmother and their lawyer."

"I'm so sorry to hear that, and no, I didn't know." She shook her head. "My e-mail address got out to the public through one of Tammy's fan sites, and the in-box has been jammed ever since. I haven't had a chance to weed through it. Why didn't you just call to tell me?"

He shrugged. "Because I knew you'd be onstage right then, and by the time your show was over, I was planning to be asleep. I figured it would be easier to just e-mail."

"Oh." She didn't like the way he wasn't quite looking her in the eye. Something told her he hadn't been very anxious to tell her he'd have to cut short the visit. "Well, sorry I didn't get it."

"Me, too. Next time I'll call . . . unless you don't check your voice mail, either? Because I doubt I'd actually get you on the phone, so . . ."

"Come on, Seth, that's not—"

"Sorry," he said. "I was just kidding."

"It's okay," she lied. "Why does the meeting have to be done over the holidays? Can't it wait?"

Seth shook his head. "I told you, Chase needs me."

But I need you, too, she thought unreasonably—hating herself for resenting a kid in trouble. It wasn't the words that stung as much as the way Seth said them—as though it went without saying that Chase was his priority.

"I know you told me, but—"

"I thought maybe you'd forgotten. His mother wants him out in Alaska to start school there after the break, remember?"

"I remember," she said sharply—too sharply—bristling at the inference that she wasn't interested in the things he told her.

"And he doesn't want to go, and I don't blame him. It would be crazy. But I'm worried that nothing I do or say is going to help, and the kid is going to be shipped out by New Year's."

"I hope that doesn't happen. I just ... I mean, we both knew that we weren't going to have much time together as it is," she heard herself say, and hated that she couldn't hold back the plaintive reproach. "Now we're losing two whole days."

"I know, but look at it this way—we're not really losing two whole days. More like a few hours here and there between shows."

That was probably meant to soothe her, but it only made her angry. She pulled herself from his arms and stood to face him. "You knew what you were getting into when you came here. You knew I couldn't just ... just take off to hang around."

"Of course I know that. I don't expect you to." He,

too, was on his feet. "I understand that you've got a huge responsibility here, and I know you don't have time for me. I get it."

"Don't say it that way! That's not true!"

"So you *do* have time for me? Then come back to Wilmot with me, and we'll spend New Year's together."

"You know I can't do that, Seth!"

"Just like I can't stay here indefinitely."

"I don't expect you to stay indefinitely, just until—"

"I know, but I can't. We both have other responsibilities. I don't expect you to shirk yours, and I know you don't want me to do that, either, right?"

"Right." Destiny's throat ached with misery. "I just thought . . ."

She couldn't bring herself to say it. Not even when he prompted, "You just thought what?"

"I thought things were going to be different."

"You mean for the holidays?"

No. Different forever. Different from the way it turned out for everyone else—her own parents, even, and Tammy Turner and her three husbands.

That was what she'd been thinking.

But she and Seth weren't married, and he didn't owe her anything, and anyway, he'd bought a damned house back in Wilmot. That, more than anything else he'd done—or even said—told her how he felt about their prospects for a future together.

"Destiny . . . ?"

"Yes," she said quietly. "I thought it was going to be different for the holidays."

There was a long moment of silence.

"Well, I guess that's how it goes," Seth told her at last.

"Sometimes things don't turn out the way anyone's planned."

The words sounded almost casual. Seth, however, looked anything but. She could see the hurt in his eyes, could see the tension in his jaw and the slightest tremble in his hands.

She, too, was trembling. With fear, and with anger, too, as something snapped inside of her. "So that's it, then? That's all you have to say? 'That's how it goes'?"

"What else do you want me to say, Destiny? What do you want me to do?"

"Don't put it that way. Don't put it all on me. What do *you* want to do? It's not about what I want. It's about what—"

"It's not about what *you* want?" he cut in, and she saw that she wasn't the only one who was angry here. "Really? I thought that was the whole point."

"What are you talking about?"

"What *you* want, Destiny. This—" He waved a hand around. "Being here in Pigeon Forge, and in Nashville, and on the road . . . this is all about *what you want*. What you've always wanted."

"If you're trying to make me feel selfish—"

"I'm not. Believe me, I'm not trying to *make you* feel anything that you don't feel. All I asked you was what you wanted me to do."

"Nothing, Seth. Okay? I don't want you to do anything."

He looked at her, then shrugged and looked away.

She swallowed hard. "I really am exhausted—and I think, since you have a room of your own, that you should sleep there tonight."

He turned back to meet her gaze again, and the sorrowful expression in his eyes told her everything she didn't want to hear him say out loud, and couldn't say herself.

"I'll head back in the morning," he told her.

"Back?"

"Home. To Wilmot."

"But—"

"Look, I think it would be best, don't you?"

She nodded miserably.

"I'll take Mike with me."

"You don't have to."

"How are you going to take care of him here?"

She didn't reply. He was right. It wouldn't be fair to Mike. He deserved loving attention, and outdoor space.

"He'll be fine with me, for as long as you want him to stay. Pets are allowed—and in the new house, too," Seth added with a hollow attempt at humor that fell hard and flat between them.

"As soon as I'm settled back in Nashville," she said tautly, "I'll take him back."

"Are you sure about that?"

"He's my dog, Seth," she reminded him.

"I know that. I meant are you sure about the 'settled' part? Because I'm betting things are going to be crazier than ever with *Cowgirl Up* coming on the air, and your single coming out."

He was right. She knew that.

"I'll call my parents and arrange for them to keep Mike for a while," she told him, deciding on the spur of the moment.

"Why?"

"Because I know you're busy with Chase, and your new house, and—"

"Your father will never go for a dog in the house."

"You don't know that," she pointed out, hating that he would say that, rather than assure her that he did have time for Mike—and for her.

"He never let you have one before."

"So? People change, Seth."

"What's that supposed to mean? Do you expect me to change for you? Because I—"

"We were talking about my father," she reminded him curtly—though that wasn't entirely true, and they both knew it.

"Okay," Seth said quietly, "I'll drop Mike with your parents when I get back to Wilmot."

"Thank you."

They walked back into the suite. Hearing them, Mike stirred, looked up, yawned, and gave a happy little bark.

"Come on, fella," Seth said, "let's go."

"Wait . . ." Destiny scooped her dog into her arms and hugged him close. "Mike, I'll be seeing you soon, okay? Remember . . . I love you."

Seth stood by in silence. She couldn't even look at him, burying her face in Mike's soft fur for a long time.

"See you, Mike," she said at last, straightening and turning away, a painful ache in her throat.

She hated that this was happening, and yet she couldn't figure out how to stop it.

"C'mon, Mike," Seth said, and the dog obediently trotted toward him, tags jangling.

"Good night," Seth told Destiny's back.

"Good night."

Who were they kidding? This wasn't good night; it was good-bye.

Seth went into his room.

Destiny locked the adjoining door behind him and went into her bedroom.

Numb, she sat shakily on the edge of the bed.

How could things have gone so wrong, so fast?

Just minutes ago, their relationship had seemed so full of promise, and now . . .

Haunted by Tammy's earlier warning, Destiny let the tears fall at last.

FOURTEEN

"Destiny? They're ready for you in hair and makeup," Grace said, sticking her blond head into the dressing room two days later.

"Tell them I'll be there in a second," Destiny said glumly. "I have a phone call to make."

"Seth again?" Grace, who knew the whole story, shook her head.

She nodded, pulling out her cell phone and hitting redial.

After a restless sleep on Christmas Eve, her first thought upon waking was that the falling-out with Seth must have been a bad dream. But the skin around her eyes was so tender from salty tears that she realized it had really happened.

Hurrying to the door that connected Seth's room to

her suite, she knocked. She had a fleeting moment o
hope when it opened, but found herself face-to-fac
with a hotel maid who informed her that the guest ha
checked out first thing.

She'd been trying to reach him for more than twenty
four hours, to no avail. Now, as her call went straight t
voice mail, her heart sank all over again. "Hey, Seth, giv
me a call. Please . . . I need to talk to you."

She hung up and turned to Grace. "I think he turne
off his phone."

"Maybe he just didn't hear it ring."

"He always has his phone on him, Grace."

"Well, maybe—"

"He left yesterday without so much as a good-bye
He obviously doesn't want to talk to me."

"Tell him he doesn't have to talk. He just has t
listen."

"How am I going to do that if he won't even retur
my calls?"

Grace fisted her hands in the pockets of her low-cu
jeans. "You're not going to like what I have to say."

"Since when has that stopped you?" Destiny tried t
laugh, but it sounded more like a sob.

"Never," Grace answered with a small smile, and pat
ted her arm. "Destiny, you know how I love Seth like a
brother . . ."

"I know."

"And I want nothing more than to see the two o
you live happily ever after. But maybe you were righ
after all."

"About . . . ?"

"I hate to admit this, but maybe it really was pretty
significant that he went and bought a house just as

you're this close to releasing 'Restless Heart.'" She put her thumb and index finger an inch apart.

"Maybe?" Destiny echoed, shaking her head. "I got the message, Grace. Loud and clear."

"The thing is, I know you don't want to lose him, but—"

"It's pretty tough to lose something you don't have."

Grace angled her head. "But you *could* have him. You just aren't willing to do what it takes."

"You mean give up my career right now, just when it's starting to take off?" Destiny asked incredulously. "Because there's no way I'm going to—"

"Wow, maybe you've got more in common with Daddy than you knew," Grace cut in. "That stubborn Hart pride—"

"Bull!" Destiny responded fiercely, but a tear slipped out of the corner of her eye.

"Destiny, you don't have to give up your career. It doesn't have to be all or nothing, you know."

"In this industry, you have to give a hundred percent, and you know it as well as I do."

"Still . . . maybe you can compromise a little and admit to Seth—and to yourself—that you might just need more than music in your life once you've established your career and have some breathing room."

"But that wouldn't change anything *now*. And it wouldn't be fair to ask him to put his own life on hold and wait for me while I go off to do my thing. That's what Mother did for Daddy, and look how that turned out."

"So what are you saying?"

"That you have to love yourself before you can love somebody else," Destiny told her with a bit of a sad smile. "And that Seth deserves to have someone to come home to."

"Like Daddy did?"

Destiny sucked her bottom lip between her teeth. "How can I do to Seth what Daddy did to Mom?"

"I get it. And if you don't pursue this with all you've got, then you'll regret it someday, and you might blame Seth."

"But will I regret losing a chance with Seth even more?"

*S*tanding on the familiar doorstep of the Harts' home with Mike in one arm and a bagful of toys and dog food in the other, Seth fought the urge to do an about-face.

Losing Mike meant losing another part of Destiny. But he knew it had to be done. He'd received an e-mail from Destiny this morning.

It said only: *You can drop off Mike with my mom this afternoon. She knows and she'll be home. Let me know that you got this e-mail. Destiny.*

That was it. Not a word about what had happened between them, nor an acknowledgment of the messages she'd left on his voice mail.

Yesterday, Christmas Day, as he drove home through mountain snow with Mike restless in the backseat and tears blurring his vision the whole way, his cell phone rang regularly.

Destiny, he knew. He saw her number on the Missed Calls file.

As soon as he got home, he turned off the phone, and hadn't turned it on yet.

He had no idea what she wanted to tell him, and it was better that way.

Nothing either of them could possibly say—or do—would change the reality that they were headed in opposite directions.

In response to her e-mail this morning, he'd typed out a three-word reply: *Got it. Done.*

He wondered if she'd even received it, after what she'd said about her in-box being overrun with fan mail from strangers.

Staring glumly at the Harts' front door, with its festive boxwood wreath, Seth pressed the bell and waited.

"This isn't my idea," he told Mike bleakly. "Just so you know. I'd be happy to have you live with me, but . . ."

The door opened and Sara Hart stood there.

He'd seen Destiny's mother a few times in the last month, but he still wasn't accustomed to her transformation.

He could tell by the nervous look on her face that she wasn't quite comfortable in her new skin, so he carefully kept too much surprise from showing in his expression.

She wore a frothy green dress that flared out just above her knees and shoes with a little heel. Instead of conservative pearls or something gold or silver, she had on a chunky beaded bracelet and necklace that added a funky vibe to her outfit. Shiny green hoop earrings peeked out from the feathered haircut that framed her face.

She looked fresh and vibrant and ready to take on the world.

"You look real pretty, Mrs. Hart," Seth said, causing her to blush.

"Why, thank you, Seth. You are ever the gentleman."

"I'm only speaking the truth." John Hart, Seth thought to himself, was totally missing the boat.

And so am I, with his daughter—but it's not my choice.

"I know Destiny told you I'd be bringing Mike over, so . . ."

"She did." Sara shook her head. "What happened between the two of you, Seth?"

"She didn't say?"

"No. But I could hear in her voice that something was wrong. When I asked, she said she was in a hurry and didn't have time to talk."

"That was probably the truth." He tried to keep the hint of bitterness from his tone, but wasn't entirely successful.

"If I've learned anything from my daughter, it's that you get one shot at this life," Sara said, "and you'd better make the most of it. She's doing what she has to do."

"I know that. And so am I."

"As you should. Congratulations on the new house. Destiny told me."

"Thank you."

"When are you moving in?"

"As soon as possible. In fact, I'm headed over there right now to take some measurements." He cleared his throat and looked down at Mike. "Listen, if the dog is too much trouble for you, or if Colonel Hart isn't happy about having him in the house—"

"It's not too much trouble, and Colonel Hart doesn't know about it because Colonel Hart isn't here. He left last night to go fishing."

"He left on Christmas?"

She shrugged. "It was quiet around here without the girls—not much of a holiday this year."

"Yeah . . . I know what you mean."

Seth gave Mike one last pat and handed him over, along with his belongings. "I've got a crate in the car for him, too. I'll get it."

"Seth?" Mrs. Hart called, as he started away.

He turned.

"Don't think that just because the timing isn't right now, it won't be right someday."

"A lot can happen between now and someday, Mrs. Hart."

⟶

$\mathcal{D}$estiny sat gloomily staring at herself in the mirror as a makeup artist scrambled to find something to cover the circles and raw, red skin around her eyes.

"My goodness, what's wrong?"

She looked up to see that Tammy had settled into the chair beside hers. "Oh . . . nothing. I'm great."

"I'm not buying what you're selling, girlfriend." Tammy lifted her chin as a stylist draped a protective sheet beneath it. "You look like you've been crying your heart out."

"Maybe that's because . . . I have."

"Let me guess—it's about Seth?"

Destiny nodded.

"So tell me, sugar, what's going on?"

"I realized on Christmas Eve that it would be better to just . . . ." She stopped and put her hand over her mouth.

"Let him go?"

"He's a high school teacher . . . and I'm doing this!" Destiny waved her hand in an arc. "How in the world can this possibly work?"

"Your love for each other has to rise above it. Instead

of being together every day, you have to treasure the time you do have together."

"That's so much easier said than done."

"Ah, sweetie. Like I said, it isn't easy, but as long as he's supportive—"

"You mean *was*."

"Uh-oh."

"We had an argument, and he left, and I've been calling, but I can't get through to him."

"You left him a message?"

"Yes."

"Then the ball's in his court."

Destiny sighed. "I keep thinking about how hectic things were when he got here, and after the show—I was pulled in every direction . . ."

"So what else is new?"

"But with Seth here, I felt so guilty every time something took me away from him."

"Erase that word from your vocabulary. Guilt is toxic."

"I'll try." She sighed. "I think he's realizing this might be too much to handle."

"Well, if he can't deal with it early on, then he surely won't be able to later in the game." Tammy put her hand on Destiny's shoulder and squeezed. "I told you I'm a straight shooter. I know it's not what you wanted to hear, but . . ."

Destiny swallowed hard. "But maybe I needed to hear it."

"Hey, what are you doing here?" Tracy Gilmore asked as her brother Tim escorted Seth into the living room. She was sprawled on the floor near the Christmas tree playing a board game with her nieces, who also looked up with interest.

"He's taking some measurements to see if he can get his king-sized bed up the stairs," Tim answered for Seth.

"No . . ." Tracy shook her head. "I meant, what are you doing in Wilmot, Seth? I thought you were in Pigeon Forge."

"I was. I'm back," he said simply.

She just looked at him . . . with women's intuition, it seemed.

"Aunt Tracy"—one of the girls tapped her arm—"it's your turn."

"Okay, sorry." She gave a little nod at Seth, and turned back to the game.

"I'll get a tape measure," her brother said.

"It's okay. I brought one."

Together they walked up the stairs. Seth felt distinctly uncomfortable when he saw, through the open door of the small guest room, that the twin bed had been slept in.

He thought of Destiny's parents, who—last he knew—were also no longer sharing a bed.

He swallowed and stopped to measure the turn in the hallway.

"Think it'll fit?"

"I hope so. It belonged to my parents. I'd hate to have to get rid of it."

"If it turns out that you can't get it in here," Tim said, "we could always leave this one."

"Thanks," Seth said, taking a floor-to-ceiling measurement, "but I think mine will fit."

And even if it wouldn't . . . he didn't necessarily want

to start his new life in a new house in a bed whose former occupants had gone their separate ways.

He swallowed hard again, noting the familiar lump that had risen in his throat.

Beside him, Tim Gilmore sighed heavily.

Seth looked up at him. "Are you okay?"

"Not really. I guess I never in a million years thought it would come to this . . . and I don't know why I didn't. Blinded by love, I guess."

"I'm so sorry, Tim."

"Me, too. And so is Joyce. And the worst part is, we still have feelings for each other. But that's not enough. I guess it never is."

"No," Seth said quietly, "I guess not."

FIFTEEN

"There she is!"

Met with applause, whistles, and cheers as she stepped out of the car in front of Back in the Saddle, Destiny saw that a fairly large crowd had gathered at the entrance. "Holy cow . . ." She put a hand to her chest and looked at Grace with wide, questioning eyes. "How did they know where to find me?"

"What can I say? You have lots of followers, especially locally. Oh, I might have Twittered just a little while ago that you were going to do an impromptu appearance here tonight," Grace continued with a shrug and a lift of her palms.

"Grace!" She shook her head in dismay.

She hadn't performed here in ages—not since "Restless Heart" had made its debut on CMT's *Cowgirl Up*.

She'd been looking forward to a nice, normal evening back where it all began, but obviously, things had changed drastically.

"Destiny Hart! Can I have your autograph?"

"Will you sign my CD?"

"Love your music!"

"Destiny, look this way!" someone shouted, and when Destiny did as requested, cameras flashed.

"You're amazing, Destiny!" Cameras and cell phones were held in the air snapping photos and blinking like strobe lights. Destiny smiled, waved, and then signed magazines and slips of paper with a black Sharpie that Grace handed to her.

She paused when asked to autograph someone's arm but then laughed and did it with a flourish. More people passing by joined in the crowd and Destiny wanted to shout, "Hey, I know I have big sparkly hair and a single on the radio, but it's just little ol' me!"

Destiny graciously signed everything shoved her way and posed for lots of photos.

"Destiny, we love you!"

"'Restless Heart' is my ringtone!"

"Hey, Destiny, are you and Brody Ballard gonna get married?"

That question nearly stopped her in her tracks, but she remembered what the label publicists had told her to say. "We're just good friends."

At least it was true. But she was supposed to say it coyly, so that no one would think so.

The label had arranged for her and Brody to be conveniently photographed together several times in the last month or so. She had no choice but to play along with it, both for Brody's sake and for her own.

Well, maybe she did have a choice—but refusing the guaranteed publicity might derail her own career, according to Miranda.

"Sundial needs you to do this, Destiny. You don't have to date the man. It's just a couple of pictures, just damage control to offset the rumors about Brody."

Destiny wasn't sure, exactly, which rumors Miranda was talking about, and she didn't want to know. She herself had heard a few: that Brody'd had a fling with his manager's wife, that he'd left a pregnant girlfriend back in his Arkansas hometown, that he was gay.

They couldn't all be true. Probably none of them were.

All she knew was that a hinted romance between two of the label's up-and-comers generated lots of buzz, and in this business, it was all about the buzz.

Anyway, there were worse things people could be saying about her than that she might be romantically involved with country's newest heartthrob. What did she have to lose?

Not Seth. I've already lost him.

"Destiny, can I have my picture taken with you?"

"Destiny, I love you!"

"Destiny!"

"Destiny . . ."

And look what I've gained. Adoration from hundreds of people who don't know me.

But they knew—and loved—her music. That was what she'd wanted all along, and now she had it.

"Hey, there, Wilmot, Kentucky! Thanks for tuning in to WKCX, Kicks Country!" Rex Miller shouted through

Seth's radio speakers. "How y'all doin' on this chilly Valentine's Day?"

With a grimace Seth reached over and turned down the volume as he braked for a stop sign a block from his house.

It had been a long day at school, marked by red paper hearts and furtive envelope exchanges and a gut-wrenching conversation with Chase, whose custody issues had been resolved last month in favor of his stepmother. But Chase felt guilty, and his mother made damn sure of that.

"She e-mailed me last night and told me she's not going to be able to get here for my graduation after all," Chase told Seth this afternoon, with tears in his eyes.

"Well, your stepmom will be there, and so will I," Seth promised, resenting Chase's mother and the ugly dynamic in his broken home.

To cap off the school day, Seth had had an initially awkward encounter with Tracy Gilmore.

They'd been politely sidestepping each other since the holidays. He was well aware that she was still available, but she hadn't brought it up—until today, when they ran into each other in the faculty break room.

She looked pretty, as usual, in a red sweater with silver hearts dangling from her ears.

"Hey," she said, "happy Valentine's Day."

"Same to you."

"Got big plans for tonight?"

"Painting the front hall," he said with a shrug.

"Need a hand? Because as hard as it is to believe, I'm dateless on Valentine's Day—not that helping you paint would be a date. I know you're taken."

"Actually," he heard himself admit, "I'm not."

Tracy broke into a smile. "In that case . . . what time do you want me to come over?"

He hesitated. *Did* he want her to come over?

Yes, he realized. He did. Maybe not wholeheartedly, but it was time he got on with his life.

After all, Destiny hadn't called him since Christmas, and though he'd picked up the phone several times, he hadn't gotten in touch with her, either.

He couldn't resist plugging her name daily into the Internet search engine, though, keeping track of her from afar.

One thing was certain: She wasn't sitting around pining away for him between gigs. She was spending an awful lot of time with Brody Ballard. He remembered what she'd told him the first time she'd been photographed with the guy—that it was all a publicity stunt—but now he wasn't so sure.

Anyway, she was free to see whomever she wanted.

And so was he.

"How about seven?" he'd asked Tracy.

"Seven it is. Can't wait to see what you've done with the house."

"I've only been there a few weeks," he pointed out—though already, it felt like home. He loved having his own house on an established, tree-lined street. The neighbors were a mix of young families, single moms, and older couples, creating a friendly, low-key atmosphere.

He had been working on the house nonstop in an effort to keep his mind off missing Destiny. And even though the weather was wintry, he sat on the front porch swing every night wishing she were there with him.

"We've got ten in a row here for ya here on WKCX."

Even with the volume down, Rex Miller's voice jarred Seth from his thoughts as he pulled into his driveway.

He parked and was about to turn the radio off, but Rex's next words froze his hand on the dial.

"Boy oh boy, do I have a treat for y'all tonight and quite a hometown story to go with it. If you watch the popular reality show *Cowgirl Up*, then you're already familiar with the next song I'm about to play, and I'll just bet you hum it all day long."

Seth's breath caught in his throat and his heart began to pound.

He'd known this day was coming, but now that it was here, he was swept with emotion.

"But that's not the whole story," Rex was saying. "The artist just happens to be Wilmot's very own Destiny Hart. So now crank it up and give a listen to 'Restless Heart,' the first single off her new album."

Seth leaned back against the headrest and allowed Destiny's voice to wash over him. The recorded version was beautiful and without flaw, but in his mind's eye he was back on her fire escape and she was singing directly to him.

The night breeze was gently lifting her hair from her shoulders and darned if he couldn't almost smell the sweet scent of her floral perfume.

"You did it, Destiny," he whispered with his eyes closed. "You really did it."

John sat in a white wicker rocking chair on the back porch of his cabin and cradled his warm coffee mug in his hands. Steam curled upward in the chill late-afternoon air as he absently took a sip and looked out over the pristine lake. The calm water appeared like glass and all was silent except for the occasional chirp of birds flying overhead and the rustle of dry winter leaves.

John usually savored his coffee and enjoyed the peaceful close of another day at the fishing camp, but today he felt restless and edgy.

With a groan of pure frustration John raised his legs, crossed his ankles on the porch railing, and tried to relax. But he couldn't seem to ignore Sara's empty matching wicker chair beside his—the chair that he had once complained was too girly for a fishing camp. All he could think about was how much he missed his wife and his daughters.

A big fish jumped up from the lake and splashed back into the water, as if to remind him why he was here. But for some reason, he couldn't seem to get excited about the prospect of fishing again tomorrow morning, or anything else.

He pinched the bridge of his nose with his thumb and index finger, trying to ward off the beginning of yet another headache. Lack of sleep coupled with poor eating habits was beginning to take a toll.

This morning he couldn't even muster up the energy to run, and without the endorphins to keep him going, he felt completely drained. He took another sip of coffee and grimaced when he noticed cobwebs between the railing posts and a pile of dried leaves and dust swept into a corner by the breeze.

Sara would have had that clean and tidy.

Ah . . . and when he'd come back in the late afternoon with a mess of fish—like he had today—she would bread and fry the fillets to a crisp golden brown, toss a green salad, and make some of her melt-in-your-mouth hush puppies.

John groaned and his stomach growled in protest at the mere thought of Sara's down-home cooking—one more thing he had taken for granted and now sorely missed.

With a shake of his head, he stared down at his mug and thought that not even the coffee tasted as good as hers—or perhaps it was because she wasn't here to drink it with him. He raked his fingers through his hair that was usually cropped short but had grown to curl over his ears and collar simply from lack of caring. Three-day stubble shadowed his jaw, but he couldn't muster up the energy to shave.

"This is just plain stupid," John muttered, and made an abrupt decision.

$\mathcal{S}$ara sat curled up on her sofa listening to Destiny on the radio, though what she really wanted to do was run outside and shout, "Hey, everybody, that's my daughter, you know!"

No—what she really wanted more than anything was to have John at her side for yet another amazing moment he was missing.

Sara whacked the cushion so hard that a plump pillow flopped to the floor. Of course, if John's sorry butt walked through the door right this minute she just might have to thump him the same way. Valentine's Day, and he'd spent most of it in the garage tinkering on his car before driving off in it.

When the song ended, Sara leaned sideways and rested her wet cheek against the cushion. Even if Destiny weren't her daughter, "Restless Heart" would have moved her to tears. Of course, lately she had been crying at greeting card commercials, she thought with a tired sigh.

Sleep had been eluding her and she suddenly felt happy for Destiny but emotionally and physically drained. With a yawn she decided to close her eyes for just a few minutes.

Feeling hollow inside, Destiny waved and smiled at the throng as Grace pulled her along toward the front entrance, but didn't realize that she was trembling until she was safely in the employee dressing room and alone with her sister.

"Wow," she said, exhaling at last. "Grace, I can't believe all those people."

"They aren't just *people*, Destiny," Grace reminded her. She leaned forward and put her hand on Destiny's shoulder. "Those were your *fans*. You're allowed to call them that, you know."

"It just seems . . . crazy."

"Why? Destiny, your single is on the radio, you've been on every station doing promos, Sundial Records has a big banner bragging about you outside of their studio, for goodness' sake, and your pretty face is plastered on the side of metro buses."

"I know, I know . . . it's all crazy." She looked down.

"What is it?" Grace asked gently.

Destiny shrugged. "It's just . . . the crowd just blew me away."

"No, it isn't."

She looked up at her sister in surprise.

"It's Valentine's Day, and you haven't heard from Seth in over six weeks. That's what it is."

Destiny shrugged. "I guess maybe I thought he'd send me a card, or call, or . . . something."

"You didn't do anything about it, either."

"But the ball's in his court, remember? It's up to him to get in touch."

"I didn't realize there was a rule book."

"Grace—"

She broke off, hearing a knock on the door.

"Come in," she called, expecting Amy or Miranda, but it was Ralph Weston who walked into the room.

"I'm going to run out and say hello to Max," Grace said quickly, and disappeared.

Destiny's eyes widened when Ralph presented her with a dozen deep red roses.

"Why, thank you—that's so sweet of you!"

"Yeah, well . . . everyone knows I'm a sweet guy." Ralph winked at her. "I just wanted to thank you so much, Destiny. I wasn't always fair to you." His bushy eyebrows came together and he rubbed his beard. "I let my ego get in the way of my good sense and yet you never batted an eye."

"Oh . . . don't be so sure about that," she teased.

"You taught this old dog a lesson and I have to say that I've missed you around here something fierce." He chuckled and added, "I don't just mean the loss in customers, although that certainly sucks, but I miss your energy, your smile, and most of all the pleasure of listening to your amazing voice. And I have to admit that I even miss that little chatterbox sister of yours, too. The best of luck to you both."

"Thanks. It means a lot."

"You know, I've been around this town a long time and my gut tells me you're going to go far in this business. You've already taken off like a rocket and the crowd eats you up, Destiny. You're gonna have to send an eight-by-ten glossy for my wall of fame."

Destiny smiled. "I'm flattered."

"Remember to stop by and have a burger once in a while—ya hear me? And forgive me for not recognizing what I had in you earlier."

"Hey," she offered softly, "no hard feelings. Cindy Sue was a manipulator. Forget about all of that."

"That's no excuse. I should have owned up to my behavior a long time ago. Ahhh, I'm just an old fool."

Destiny was floored when Ralph's eyes misted over. She'd always assumed he didn't have a sentimental bone in his body, but now the tip of his nose turned pink and he had to clear his throat repeatedly.

"None of us are without fault, Mr. Weston. But hey, the fact remains that you gave me my first real start. Thank you."

"You betcha. Well, I'd better get out of your hair so you can get out there onstage." He grinned. "Now don't you go forgettin' about us little folks when you're on top, okay?"

"First I have to make it to the top," Destiny replied with a chuckle and gave him a quick hug. "But don't you worry. I will *never* forget who my true friends are. Besides, you have the best burgers on the planet. It's what brought Nick Novell here, so you had a hand in my career in more ways than one."

"You know it! But all luck aside, your talent is what got you here, and they sure are excited out there. If I let one more person in, I'll have the fire department all over me. Now get on out there and rock the house!" he tried to say in his regular Ralph tone but couldn't quite pull it off.

After he left, Destiny opened her locker for what she knew was the last time at Back in the Saddle, and was hit with an unexpected pull of emotion.

This had been her home away from home for well over four years and she realized that in an odd way she was going to miss it.

Destiny took a deep breath and peered at her reflection. Her hair was big but her curls were tamed into temporary submission with glitter-infused hair spray. Drama was added with liquid eyeliner and false eyelashes that she had been talked into and now prayed would stay on. Tonight her jeans and button-up shirt were black. Silver glinted at her wrists and earlobes, and strappy high-heeled sandals revealed her shiny red-polished toenails.

Struck by an odd shot of fear at the realization that she didn't look like herself, she put a hand to her chest. She still felt like the girl in cutoffs and a T-shirt sitting on the back fire escape strumming her Gibson guitar while scribbling down lyrics. Now that the dream was becoming a reality, she didn't want to lose that girl.

But maybe she already had.

She took her cell phone from her pocket and tucked it into her locker, then closed the door and headed out to give her fans what they were waiting for.

Seth held the phone poised in his hand just as he had countless times since Christmas—only this time, he was determined to follow through.

Holding his breath, he dialed the familiar number.

The phone rang ... and rang ... and rang ...

"Hi. You've reached Destiny. Leave me a message!"

No ... he couldn't do that.

He didn't even know what he wanted to say to her exactly—but he did know that he couldn't say it into a voice mailbox.

Shaking his head, Seth hung up the phone.

After a long pause, he made up his mind and placed another call. This one was answered immediately, almost breathlessly.

"Hi, Tracy. I ..."

He was going to tell her he'd changed his mind about tonight. That was why he'd called.

But he was having trouble finding the words, suddenly unable to ignore the image of Destiny that had popped into his head. Destiny in Nashville, surrounded by fans and photographers, laughing with Brody Ballard ...

Destiny, with a single on the radio and a career that was about to take off ...

"Tracy ... about tonight ..."

"I'm really looking forward to it!" she said as he fumbled for the right way to phrase it.

"I ... I am too, but ... I just ... you know I'm, uh ..."

"Taken? Because I thought you said—"

"No, I did, but ... it's just ..."

"Hey, it doesn't have to be a date, you know. We can just ... paint."

"Tracy, if you come over here tonight, it won't just be about painting," he told her honestly. "I like you a lot, but ..."

"But not that way?"

"Yes, that way."

"Really?" She sounded shocked ... and hopeful. "What about ... ?"

"She and I are ... we're still ... we're not ..." Oh, hell, he didn't know what was going on with Destiny.

Oh, yes, you do.

Nothing. Nothing is going on. You can't even get her on the phone; you haven't spoken to her in weeks.

"Never mind," he told Tracy. "I'll see you at seven."

"Sara?"

"Mmmm?" Sara snuggled deeper into the pillow. "Yes?" She loved it when John whispered into her ear. In a minute he'd put his arm around her and snuggle closer and then maybe kiss her neck ...

Sara sighed.

"Sara?"

Wait a minute. "What?" Still thinking she was in bed, Sara sat up quickly and put her hand sideways for support but came up with air instead of mattress and tumbled to the floor with a yelp, followed by a solid thump.

"Ouch! That's gonna leave a mark," she grumbled, and covered her face with her forearm as Mike came barking and running.

"Sara!" John shouted and knelt down beside her. "Sweetheart, are you okay?" He pulled her arm back to get a better look at her flaming face, and Mike licked her cheeks.

"Sweetheart?" she said in a low tone. "You've got to be kidding me." She glared up at him, doing her best not to soften when she saw the real concern on his face— and the bouquet of red roses in his hand.

"It's okay, Mike," she told the dog. "I'm okay. Go lie down."

The dog trotted away obediently.

"I'm fine," she answered tightly but couldn't quite keep a bit of breathlessness out of her voice.

"Are you sure? You don't sound fine." A lock of dark hair fell over John's forehead. The dark stubble shadowing his cheeks made him look so much like the bad boy she had once loved that she had a difficult time not grabbing him and pulling him down for a passionate kiss.

"I just got the wind knocked out of me when you made me fall," she told him.

"I didn't *make* you fall," he said defensively. He set aside the roses and offered his hand, but she nudged it away. Mike lifted his head, watching warily.

"You made me fall when you snuck up on me."

"I said your name twice. You never even responded."

"I was *asleep*."

"Here," he said softly and extended his hand again. "I'm really sorry."

Sara answered with another glare, but John slid his hands beneath her and scooped her up into his arms.

"Put me—" she cried, but her protest was smothered with a long, hot kiss. The kind of kiss she had been craving . . . dreaming about for months.

"What are you doing?" she asked when he broke off.

"Kissing my valentine."

He dipped his mouth again, and his beard felt rough and masculine against her soft cheek. In spite of herself, she reached up and threaded her fingers through his hair. It hadn't been this long since high school.

John responded with a groan and deepened the sweet but oh-so-sexy kiss that curled her bare toes. Desire for her husband uncurled in her stomach and spread like warm honey in her veins, dissolving the last shred of her resistance.

When John finally came up for air, his amazing blue eyes were filled with unshed tears. "Ah, Sara, you're so beautiful."

He looked as if he was about to tell her something else, but then lowered his gaze.

"What?" she gently prodded, and ran a fingertip down his cheek.

His dark brows came together, but he didn't look up. "If I admit something to you, will you promise not to get angry? Or laugh?"

"I'll try . . ." she offered, but in her experience anything prefaced with either of those requests resulted in failure. Still, he seemed so serious that Sara gave him a reassuring nod to continue, praying she could hold her emotions in check—which, unfortunately, was not her strong suit.

John cleared his throat and closed his eyes, shaking his head.

"We've been married a long time, John. It's safe to say that you can tell me anything."

"I know." He inhaled a deep breath. "It's just . . . I was always so afraid when I was gone for months on end that someone would swoop down and take my place." He paused before admitting, "I asked you to dress like a military wife, but in truth my goal was to have you play down your looks."

"Oh, John . . . how could you think that I would ever even glance at another man?"

"I saw it happen to my friends all too often. The military divorce rate was higher than the national average for good reason."

She nodded. She knew all that. Long absences, injury, and the ever-present fear of the worst hit families hard. But they had weathered all that. It wasn't until it was over that they'd run into trouble.

"I loved serving my country, but being separated from you and the girls used to tear me up." He opened his eyes and finally looked at her. "Still does."

"But you have the power to change that now."

"How? What do you want me to do?"

"Allow Destiny, Grace, and me to be ourselves. Love us for who we are and not who you want us to be," Sara told him.

"I'm trying to do that—God help me, Sara, I am. I love you so much."

For a moment his declaration made her melt.

Then he added, "I feel like you just don't understand me anymore."

"*I* don't understand *you*?" She wiggled to a standing position.

"If you could just try to see why I feel the way I do—"

"Right back atcha, John. Maybe you can try to see why I feel the way I do, too."

"I *am* trying. It's all we ever talk about, Sara. You tell me how you're feeling, and why it's the right way to feel, and why how I'm feeling is the wrong way to feel. And you won't admit that you're having a—"

"Don't you dare say it, John."

She couldn't stand hearing, once again, she was merely having a midlife crisis that would soon pass.

"Fine. I won't." He shook his head.

"And, anyway, maybe you're the one who's having one."

"Me? I'm fine. I'm the same as I've always been, Sara. You're the one who's gone off the deep end."

He turned on his heel and left the room.

"Hells bells, that man is stubborn!" Sara mumbled to herself, shaking her head.

*W*ell over an hour after the show had ended, Destiny had done interviews with both the local news and *Nashville Now* magazine, and was still being hounded for pictures and autographs.

At last Miranda and Grace stepped in, her manager politely dealing with the lingering fans as her sister whisked her off to a dim corner of the bar.

"Need something to drink?" Max asked promptly.

"Mountain Dew if you have it. I'm drained," she admitted.

"You must be. That was some performance," Grace told her.

Max slid the soft drink across the bar. "It's all part of the business and this is still just the beginning. If you don't mind my asking, Destiny, do you think you're going to be able to handle all of this?"

"What, are you kidding?" She smiled and took a sip of the soda, and saw Max and Grace exchange a glance.

"What?" she asked.

"Nothing," they said in unison.

"Grace."

"Your phone rang after you left to go onstage, and I heard it. I checked to see who it was, thinking it might be . . . I don't know, someone important."

"Grace!" Destiny said again, this time with a frown.

Sometimes her sister crossed the line between personal assistant and nosy sister.

"It was Seth," Grace blurted.

Destiny nearly choked on her Mountain Dew.

"Did you answer it?" she asked in a strangled voice.

"No! Of course not! Destiny, I would never intrude on your personal business," Grace said indignantly.

Destiny rolled her eyes, already off the bar stool and making a beeline for the employee room.

Her heart pounded as she reached into her locker for the phone. She opened the Missed Calls file and sure enough, there it was: Seth's name and number.

With trembling fingers, she dialed her voice mail access number and held her breath in anticipation of hearing his voice at last.

"You ... have ... no ... new ... messages," the automated operator informed her, and her heart sank.

What now?

Should I call him back?

No.

The ball, she reminded herself stubbornly, and not for the first time, was in Seth's court.

He'd called once. Chances were, he'd call again. She'd just have to wait.

*T*he rest of Valentine's Day passed without another call from Seth, as did the next day, and the next ...

Weeks went by, and suddenly it was March, and Destiny stopped jumping in anticipation every time her phone rang.

And then, one gusty gray morning, she got a call she'd been waiting for, hoping for, praying for ...

But it wasn't from Seth.

"Destiny, are you sitting down?" Miranda asked.

She was ... but she instinctively jumped to her feet, sensing what was about to come.

"'Restless Heart' just entered the Billboard Country Singles charts at number fifty with a bullet!"

SIXTEEN

"Destiny, do you know who I just saw out there?" Grace squealed, bursting wide-eyed into the dressing room. "I just saw—"

"Don't tell me!" Destiny shook her head, but it was too late. Grace was already ticking off on her fingers some of the biggest names in country music.

"Well, what did you expect?" Miranda asked with a smile, looking up from her clipboard. "This *is* the Grand Ole Opry."

"Did you have to remind me?" Destiny strummed her guitar, trying to ignore the commotion beyond the relative seclusion of the dressing room. The halls backstage were filled with discord and harmony as artists rehearsed, bands tuned up their instruments, and technicians and stagehands rushed around doing their thing.

Out in the auditorium, more than four thousand people—including her mother, Nessie, Max, Cooper, and Annie—were about to witness Destiny's Opry debut.

Her father wasn't among them.

Nor, she knew, was Seth.

He'd never called back.

So that was that.

Or so she'd been trying to convince herself.

There was a knock on the door. "Destiny? It's time."

She took a deep breath.

*L*adies and gentlemen, our next performer is making her Grand Ole Opry debut. 'Restless Heart,' her first single, was a hotshot debut at number fifty on the Billboard Country Singles charts before skyrocketing to number fifteen! Because of the success of 'Restless Heart,' Sundial Records has moved up the release of her debut album, and Nielsen Soundscan Building Chart is indicating that the self-titled CD will debut on the weekly Hot Two Hundred albums—an amazing feat for a brand-new artist! Please give a warm welcome to Destiny Hart!"

Amid thunderous applause, sitting alone in the far reaches of the vast auditorium, Seth wiped tears from his eyes.

*E*ven now, a few hours after Destiny's Opry performance, Sara's body was still pulsing with energy—and her heart was still tinged with regret that John hadn't been there to see it.

She'd done everything in her power to convince him to go, and a few times, she'd almost thought he was about to agree to it. But something held him back.

Something?

Pride.

It's his loss, Sara reminded herself, and smiled across the restaurant table at her daughter, feeling blessed to have been able to share this incredible evening.

"Destiny, I know I've already said it countless times tonight, but I just have to say it again. You were wonderful. I'm still bursting with pride!"

"Thanks, Mom. Aren't you going to eat your potato skins?"

Sara looked down at her plate. She usually stayed away from such indulgences, but tonight was special.

"Sure she is," Nessie piped up. "We were chatting before the show and your mom's new motto is going to be 'Loosen up and live a little.' Right, Sara?"

"Nope." She shook her head, then laughed at their expressions. "It's 'Loosen up and live a lot!'" To prove it, she picked up a loaded potato skin, added a dollop of sour cream for good measure, and took a big bite.

"Yeah, you two sure were having a good time," Grace told her and Nessie. "I can only imagine what you were chattering about when you had your heads bent together."

"Just girl talk." Nessie winked at Sara, who wiped her mouth daintily with a paper napkin.

"Really?" Destiny arched an eyebrow and eyed them both.

"We were discussing how men are idiots," Sara announced.

"Hey, as the only man at this table, I resent that."

Cooper reached for a nacho chip piled with toppings but lost half of it down his shirt.

"You mean 'resemble'?" Annie asked slyly, and they all laughed.

"Geez, Mom—*idiots*?" Grace shook her head. "Don't hold back or anything."

"One thing's for sure—that big fella sure has eyes for you, sugar," Nessie told Grace.

Grace looked around. "Which big fella?"

"Max." He'd left them all after the concert, heading back to work the late shift at the bar.

"Oh . . . we're just friends and he's a little protective," Grace explained with a wave of her hand, but Sara noticed that she shot a look at Destiny, who raised an eyebrow at her.

"He seems like a good guy, Gracie," Sara told her. "Not your usual type."

"Oh, really?" Nibbling a chicken wing, Nessie eyed Grace with interest.

"My sister tends to go for the bad boys," Destiny said.

"Well, the apple doesn't fall far from the tree." Grace shot Sara a look. "Right, Mom?"

"Way to go, Mrs. H." Cooper offered her a fist bump.

"That was a long time ago . . . but yes, John certainly was a bad boy back when I first laid eyes on him," she admitted, suddenly missing him so much that the potato skins no longer seemed appealing.

She looked down at the food and sighed.

"Mom, are you okay?" Destiny asked.

"I'm fine. I hate to break up this party, but I do believe I'm about ready to head back to my hotel. I can't remember the last time I was out this late!"

"I should get going, too. I have to work at the hospital

bright and early," Annie said with a little pucker of her lips.

"Guess that means I'm leaving, too. We can drop you on the way, Mrs. Hart," Cooper offered, getting to his feet and politely extending his hand to help her from her chair.

"Oh, that's just silly, Cooper," interrupted Nessie. "My car's parked right here and I'm ready to get going myself. I'll drop Sara at the hotel. What about you girls?"

Destiny and Grace looked at each other.

"I was thinking maybe we could go for a nightcap over at Back in the Saddle," Grace suggested—undoubtedly with an ulterior motive, Sara thought.

So, apparently, did Destiny, because she smiled and shook her head. "You go ahead, Grace. I think I'll just head home."

"But it's your big night."

"Exactly, and I'm exhausted from it."

As they stood and said their good-byes, Destiny asked, "When are you heading back to Wilmot, Mom? Can you stay a few days?"

"Maybe. The only thing I have to get back to, really, is Mike, and your father promised to take care of him—and, would you believe, to get my garden beds ready for planting."

"You're kidding. Really?"

"Yes, and I was just as surprised, believe me. The man has never picked up a hoe in his life—"

"Well, *that*'s good news."

Sara threw her head back and laughed. "I've missed your humor so much, Destiny."

"Really? Then why was I always in trouble for it?"

"Because I'm your mother. I had to keep you in line.

It was my job. That didn't mean that I didn't secretly find you entertaining. And in truth, I could have loosened up more and realized that everyone should be allowed to be themselves. Shoving square pegs into round holes never works. Oh, why do we learn things way too late?"

"You were doing what you thought best." Destiny gently squeezed her arm.

"And so is your father. Don't get me wrong—I believe he should be supporting you in all that you do. But I also realize that his reasoning, however misguided and stubborn, comes from the love he has for you. I know for a fact that he misses you dearly."

Destiny swallowed hard and said only, "I do hope you and Daddy can work things out."

"So do I. And you and Daddy. You and Seth, too."

Destiny's eyebrows shot up, but she said nothing.

"I want you to remember something, Destiny. Life is a journey, not a destination. There will be times when you fail. But, honey, let me ask you this: Would you rather fail at something or never try and always wonder what might have been?"

"Are you talking about my career?"

"I'm talking about life. Standing up there onstage tonight at the Grand Ole Opry . . . you made that happen. You've always made things happen. Don't ever forget it."

Her mother's words lingered in Destiny's ears long after she slid into bed that night.

You've always made things happen . . .

Maybe in my career, Destiny thought. *But what about in my relationship with Seth?*

All this time, she—who had never believed in leaving things up to fate—had been telling herself that it was up to him to call her.

Why?

Because she was afraid to put herself out there, afraid of rejection, afraid of failure.

If she'd handled her career that way, where would she be now?

Not here in Nashville with a hit record and an album about to be released, that was for sure.

Shaking her head, Destiny got out of bed and padded barefoot across the floor to the phone, before she lost her nerve.

*W*alking into the house, Seth dropped his car keys on the table and shook off his jacket.

It was late, and he had an early day tomorrow. Baseball season was about to begin again, and he had to be on the field with the boys by seven. He was going to be dragging.

Still, he wouldn't have missed Destiny's Grand Ole Opry debut tonight for anything in the world.

He'd found out about the appearance via her Web site, which had launched right around the time he'd started hearing her single on the radio . . .

Which was right around the time he'd hung up on her voice mail and started dating Tracy.

It didn't mean he'd stopped following Destiny on the Internet. But every time he went to her Web site, his heart sank when he saw the ever-expanding photo gallery that had undoubtedly been assembled by Grace and the label's PR reps. There were countless photos of

Destiny—onstage, and surrounded by adoring fans, and quite a few with Brody Ballard, and even more with her guitar player, Jesse. In every single picture, she looked positively radiant.

Some part of Seth had been hoping to find that she was as lonely and miserable without him as he was without her, but that clearly wasn't the case.

I'm happy for her, he'd told himself, over and over again—until he actually believed it.

She was fine. He didn't have to worry about her.

On the surface, he was fine, too. He'd gone out with Tracy a few times, as often as their busy teaching and coaching schedules would permit. They'd shared some laughs, and yes, some affection. She was a terrific woman, and he enjoyed her company, but . . .

She isn't Destiny.

He didn't expect her to be. And he wasn't leading her on. She knew he still had unresolved feelings for Destiny. She felt the same way about her former boyfriend.

"This doesn't have to be serious," she told Seth, time and time again. "We'll just have some fun, and see where it leads."

Maybe, the more time that passed, the more inclined he would be to give his budding relationship with Tracy the chance it deserved.

But that didn't mean he couldn't lose himself in the Nashville crowd to watch Destiny's performance this evening.

He'd been worried, walking into the auditorium, that someone from home would spot him. He was on the lookout for Sara and Grace, Cooper and Annie, Nessie and Max. Indeed, he spotted them all, from afar, and it gave him a hollow ache to feel, once again, like an outsider.

That's what you are, though. Face it.

With a sigh, he started toward the stairs, anxious to get some sleep—and not certain he'd be able to.

Just as he put his foot on the bottom step, the shrill ringing of the telephone startled him.

It was midnight. His thoughts flew to his parents down in Florida, and to Chase, whose stepmother was now seriously dating a man who wasn't crazy about him—and vice versa.

"Maybe it would be better for everyone if I just took off and went to Alaska after all," the boy had said to Seth just this afternoon.

"You can't do that, Chase."

"Why not?"

"Because it would be throwing away everything you've worked for. You're going to get into a good college, and you're going to play baseball, like you always wanted. Just stick it out."

Chase just shrugged, and for the first time, Seth worried that he might not have gotten through to him.

Now he hurried to answer the phone with a sick feeling in his stomach.

"Hello?"

For a moment, there was silence.

Wrong number, he thought in relief, and waited for the click.

Instead, he heard a familiar voice softly saying his name, and his heart stopped.

"Destiny?" he breathed. "Is that you?"

"It's me. I know it's late. Sorry. I just wanted to say hi. It's been so long . . ."

With a gulp, Seth asked, "How are you?"

As if he didn't know.

"I'm good," she said. "Been busy."

"Yeah? I'll bet."

He waited for her to tell him about the concert tonight, but she said, instead, "It's nuts, Seth. Half the time I don't know if I'm comin' or goin'. I've waited so long for this to happen and now it seems like I'm moving at the speed of light. I fall into bed every night exhausted—not that I'm complaining! And Grace has been amazing. I don't know what I'd do without her."

"I'm so glad that she's there with you."

"Yeah, me too."

There was a moment of silence.

"Hey . . ." he said, pressing the phone hard against his ear, "I heard you on the radio a bunch of times."

"Yeah?"

"Yeah. You sound great."

"Thanks. I'm still trying to get used to the idea. To tell you the truth, I don't know if I ever will."

"I heard 'Restless Heart' did really well on the charts."

"Crazy, huh? It was totally unexpected, but being the theme song for *Cowgirl Up* really helped. Sundial is really pleased. My schedule has been insane, though. It changes just about every day without notice. They just give me this sheet with an agenda on it and then parade me around."

"I don't suppose they're parading you back here to Wilmot anytime soon?"

"I wish, but I'm getting ready to launch the album, so . . ."

"Yeah. I hope it's a hit."

"Thanks, Seth. How are things with you?"

"Oh, you know . . . the same. Not much changes around here."

"Is Chase okay?"

"Hanging in there. He's still here, but . . . it's complicated."

"I'm sure you've been there for him. He's lucky to have you." Was it his imagination, or was there a wistful note in her voice? "How's the new house, Seth?"

"It's . . ." *Lonely.* "It's really nice."

"I can't wait to see it," she said softly, surprising him.

"Well, then, don't be a stranger. Next time you're in town, be sure to come on over."

"I will," she promised. "I guess . . . I guess I should let you go. I hope I didn't wake you up."

"You didn't. Thanks for calling, Destiny. It was really good to hear your voice."

"Yours too."

Not wanting to be the one to disconnect the call, he waited to hang up until he'd heard a click on the other end.

Shaken, Destiny stood for a long time, holding the phone and thinking about what might have been, if only . . .

If only your dream hadn't come true?

No. That was silly.

But for the first time in months, she wondered if maybe there was a way to have it all.

Like Tammy said, some people did.

I just can't think of any offhand.

And, anyway, now wasn't the time for thinking. Not when her brain was as weary as her body.

Climbing back into bed, Destiny closed her eyes and thought again of Seth.

Hearing his voice had been as thrilling—if not more thrilling—than stepping out onto that legendary stage tonight.

That meant something, for sure ...

With a yawn, she told herself she'd figure it all out tomorrow.

SEVENTEEN

As the strains of "Pomp and Circumstance" filled the high school auditorium on a bright June morning, Seth was carried back over the years to his own graduation day. The world had been so full of promise then, the future bright with possibility. He'd still dreamed of a major-league baseball career . . .

And now, look at Chase, so handsome in his cap and gown, dreaming the same dream.

But for him, it looked like it might just come true. He was going to Gonzaga on a baseball scholarship. It wasn't Alaska, but almost as close as he could get, and Seth hoped that might open the door to a reconciliation with his mom.

She wasn't here today, but Chase's stepmother watched the ceremony proudly from her seat beside

Seth's, and a few times, he'd seen her dab her eyes with a tissue.

He'd been forced to do the same thing, though he'd been much more surreptitious about it. Chase wasn't his son, but he was as proud as if he were, and he was going to miss him when he left for the Pacific Northwest.

His life, it seemed, was all about good-byes lately.

Tracy Gilmore had accepted a teaching and coaching position in Lexington for the fall.

"It feels like the right thing to do," she'd told Seth. "There's a lot to keep me here—my family, my condo, my friends—but this job offer came out of left field, and I think I should grab it."

"So do I," Seth told her, filled with a curious blend of regret and relief.

He knew she deliberately hadn't named him as one of the things keeping her here in Wilmot, and he also knew she was wondering if he was going to amend that.

He didn't, because the more time that passed, the more certain he was that he and Tracy were just spinning their wheels—for now, anyway.

It wasn't out of the question that he might be tempted, down the road, to revisit his attraction to Tracy. The chances that a great girl like her would be indefinitely available were slim, and he knew it, but he couldn't lead her on now.

Not when a part of him was still pining away for Destiny.

After the ceremony, he waited for Chase in the crowded lobby. All around him, proud, emotional parents were embracing their children, most of whom didn't seem to grasp the milestone they'd just passed. They posed for pictures and poked fun at one another's mortarboards and made plans for parties later tonight.

They have no idea, Seth thought, *that nothing is ever going to be the same. Not in the way they think it is, anyway.*

It wasn't that they'd never see one another again—although that might be the case with some. But the rest—the ones who tried—would never see one another in quite the same way, now that shared daily perspective was falling by the wayside. That much was certain.

Look at himself and Destiny. Try as they might, they couldn't overcome the differences—and distance—between their grown-up lives.

"Coach!"

Seth turned and found himself caught up in a bear hug.

Chase had shot up and filled out over the past few months. Now he was taller than Seth, and stronger, too.

"Hey, Chase . . . congratulations! You did it!"

Chase shook his head so hard the tassel from his mortarboard slapped him in the nose. "No, Coach, you did it."

"No way. I didn't—"

"Okay, well, then, you *made* me do it. How's that?"

Seth shrugged. "That's still too much credit. You did it yourself, Chase. All I did was encourage you."

"You did a lot more than that, Coach. You made those scouts come see me play, you made me study, you made me fill out applications, you made me stay here . . . you made it happen."

Even as Chase said it, the echo of another voice—Destiny's voice—filled Seth's head.

You have to make things happen, Seth, not sit back and wait for them to happen.

Back then, he hadn't believed that.

Maybe he did now.

Yeah? So what are you going to do about it?

*S*itting in the studio at WKCX, Destiny adjusted her headphones and wondered why the heck she was so nervous. She'd done countless interviews in the three months since her album had been released, and this one wasn't even live. They were taping it to air later this afternoon, when the drive-time audience was listening.

Besides, Grace was sitting here with her, also wearing headphones and prepared to talk, and the interviewer was Rex Miller, whom she'd known forever. Well, since the beginning of her career, anyway.

Still . . .

"Okay, ladies, are you ready?" From the other side of the glass booth, Rex Miller's voice boomed through the speaker.

Glancing at Grace, and noting that for once she looked a little shell-shocked, Destiny answered for both of them.

"Okay," a sound technician said, and began the now-familiar act of counting down. "Three, two . . ."

He pointed a finger at Rex.

"Today, we have a little surprise for all of you listeners. Right here in the studio with me is Wilmot's very own Destiny Hart! Destiny and her sister, Grace—who also happens to be her personal assistant—are here to give hometown listeners the inside scoop, and I'm told they've got some exciting news to share for the first time ever here on WKCX, your one and only Kicks Country! Ladies, welcome."

"Thanks, Rex—it's great to be back here," Destiny said easily, her nerves slipping away.

"It sure is," Grace chimed in. "I mean, I've never been here before—well, I've *been* here, but—"

She broke off, catching a warning look from Rex.

"Destiny, your sensational single, 'Restless Heart,' rode to the top of the charts, and your new CD is a smash hit with great reviews. You must feel like all your dreams are coming true."

"Well, maybe not *all* of them," she quipped, "but, yes, it feels pretty good."

She glanced at Grace, sitting beside her. She could tell Grace was just itching to say something.

"As the story goes," Rex went on, "you were discovered almost a year ago by the legendary Nick Novell of Sundial Records while you were waitressing at Back in the Saddle Bar and Grille in Nashville, Tennessee. Is that right?"

"Sure is." Funny—now that her struggling days were behind her, she didn't mind announcing to her entire hometown that she'd been waiting tables for years.

"And now you certainly are a rising star . . . or maybe I should say shooting star! Are you ready to give your hometown the big news?"

"Well, actually, I'll let my sister, Grace, who just happens to be my amazing personal assistant, make the announcement."

"Fill us in, Grace," Rex requested.

"Well," Grace began in a much more flamboyant tone than Destiny's, "first I'd like to say that it's an honor to have a front row seat to my sister's success. As young girls moving from base to base, we were always close— weren't we, Destiny?"

"Definitely," she agreed, aware that Rex was growing impatient. "Go ahead, Grace—don't tease."

Grace's laughter tinkled through the studio. "Okay then, I'm just over the moon to announce that my sister, Destiny, is going to be launching a national concert tour this summer!"

"Get outta town!" Rex shouted, and Destiny winced at the volume in her ears.

"Actually, Rex, we're doing just the opposite," Grace cleverly improvised, "because Destiny is launching her tour with a special concert right here in Wilmot!"

"Well, speaking for the whole town of Wilmot, I can tell you that we're pleased and honored! We'll make it a day of celebration in your honor, Destiny."

"Thanks, Rex. We might have grown up all over the country, but Grace and I consider Wilmot our hometown. The honor is all mine."

*S*itting on the porch of his fishing cabin in the late-afternoon sunlight, John sipped sweet tea and thought about his wife.

Lord, he missed her. He'd spent the better part of the past few months up here, ever since they'd had a big blowup over his not going to see Destiny at the Grand Ole Opry.

Unable to stand the silence, he leaned over and turned on the ancient portable radio sitting on the small table wedged between the rocking chairs.

Toby Keith's song "She Never Cried in Front of Me" was playing on the local station.

"I sure don't need to hear that right now," John grumbled under his breath and reached over to turn the dial.

Channel surfing, he found a whole lot of static—but not as much as usual. Reception was never great out here in the woods, but on a clear day like today, he could sometimes bring in WKCX from back home.

Sure enough, there was disc jockey Rex Miller saying, "And that was a little bit of 'Big Dog Daddy' for ya on this gorgeous summer afternoon! Now I hope y'all can stick around after the commercial for an interview with Wilmot's very own Destiny Hart! Her sensational single, 'Restless Heart,' climbed the charts, and in just a few minutes Destiny's going to give us the inside scoop about her new CD. I'm told she's got some exciting news to share for the first time ever here on WKCX, your one and only Kicks Country!"

"What?" John jumped to his feet so fast that sweet tea sloshed over the rim of his glass.

He felt a hot flash of anger that he had to find out from the radio DJ that Destiny was in town.

She could have told me, he thought grouchily. But then, his daughter—no, both his daughters, now—had distanced themselves from him as deliberately as Sara had.

And whose fault is that?

He wanted to think it was Sara's, but for some reason, that wasn't as easy as it might once have been.

Could it possibly be his own damned fault that no one was speaking to him?

It could . . . and it was.

John reached over and cranked up the radio so he wouldn't miss a word. He was going to listen to his daughter's interview, and then he was going to hop into his truck and hightail it home to see his family before it was too late.

*　　*　　*

"*'d* like to thank you lovely ladies for dropping by," Rex Miller was saying. "And now, Destiny, let's cap off the interview by playing your smash hit single, 'Restless Heart'!"

Stung, Seth put the truck into park on his driveway and rested his head against the steering wheel as the opening notes of Destiny's song filled the speakers. A soft summer breeze blew in through the open window and afternoon sunlight settled over him like a blanket, yet brought little comfort.

That Destiny was right here in town—but hadn't even bothered to contact him—probably shouldn't have been so shocking, but it was.

She had promised she'd let him know when she was coming to Wilmot.

Well, obviously, she didn't mean it, now, did she?

But he could still hear her voice echoing in his head, with a note of sincerity he couldn't possibly have imagined . . . could he?

"Seth . . ."

Her voice sounded so real that it was as if she were almost here, Seth thought with a sigh.

"Hey . . . Seth?"

When a hand touched his shoulder Seth opened his eyes and sat up so swiftly that he bumped his knees on the steering wheel, blew the horn, and almost knocked his Mountain Dew out of the cup holder.

"Destiny!"

There she was, standing beside the car, looking as real as could be . . . and yet he couldn't quite grasp it. She had just been talking to Rex Miller over the radio.

He blinked, and she was still there. "Is that really you?"

"Last time I checked." She backed up so he could see her, tipped her cowboy hat up, and grinned. Then, in true Destiny form, she lifted her palms in the air and turned in a circle.

She was wearing worn, boot-cut jeans and a light blue V-neck sweater. Her hair fell in soft waves to her shoulders from beneath her hat. It was her smile that really got to him. For a long moment he simply stared.

"But you were just..." He pointed at the radio speakers. "Restless Heart" was still playing.

"Either I can be in two places at once, or we taped the interview this morning," she told him, and grinned, fisting her hands on her hips and angling her head. "Get yourself out of that truck, Seth Caldwell, and give a girl a hug!"

Seth scrambled for the door so quickly that he fumbled with the handle before figuring out that it was locked and the truck was still running. Attempting to open up and turn off everything all at once, he somehow managed to get out of the SUV in one piece.

"That was smooth," Destiny said with a grin, and he folded her into a fierce embrace.

"Why didn't you tell me you were going to be in town?" Seth pulled back to ask casually, though he watched her closely.

"I didn't know myself. They told me last night. That's pretty much how things work in this business, Seth."

He nodded, remembering the Tammy Turner announcement that had caught even Destiny off guard.

"Anyway, I heard it was graduation today, and I knew you'd probably be busy with that. How'd it go?"

"It was perfect. Chase made it." He quickly told her about the baseball scholarship.

"That's great. It sounds like everything is going to work out okay, then."

"Yeah." *For Chase, anyway.*

When he'd left the graduation luncheon a little while ago, he'd been filled with determination to do something about his situation with Destiny.

Hearing her on the radio—and realizing she hadn't told him she was in town—deflated his plans.

Now, however, he had hope again.

Fools rush in, he thought wryly, asking aloud, "Where's Grace?"

"She's at my parents' house. We drove separately since I wanted a little extra time to visit before going back out on the radio promo tour. I've been busy with the reps all day, doing press and scouting out locations for a video we're going to be shooting here. I was just finally on my way home to see my mother, but I wanted to drive by your new house and when I spotted your truck in the driveway, I just couldn't resist surprising you. I hope that's okay?"

"Of course it's okay. It's more than okay." He hesitated before asking, "What about . . . your father?"

She lifted her chin. "What about him?"

"You said you were just going to see your mother. Did he . . . move out?"

"Not officially. He's away fishing. What else is new?" A cloud passed over her face and she played with the rim of her hat. "I'm kind of glad about that. I'm not sure if I want to face him."

"I'm sorry about that, Destiny. I thought your success might change his way of thinking."

She pressed her lips together for a moment and then said, "You know, I've thought about that and it really shouldn't be about success or failure. Maybe I'm being just as stubborn as him, but I just can't help it."

Seth nodded. "You're absolutely right. And no matter what, he should have shown up to see you at the Grand Ole Opry."

She started to open her mouth as if to agree, then went absolutely still, staring at him. "How do you know he wasn't there?" she asked in a near whisper.

"Because . . . I *was*."

"You were . . . what?"

"There. I was there, Destiny. And you were incredible."

She shook her head in wonder, tears in her eyes. "Why didn't you tell me you were coming?"

"Because we hadn't spoken in so long, and—"

"And whose fault was that?" She was laughing and crying at the same time as she gave him a poke in the chest, and he could feel tears welling up in his own eyes.

She shook her head at him. "I was waiting for you to call back after Valentine's Day . . . but you never did."

"You knew I called?"

"Of course I knew."

He shrugged. "I wasn't even sure you checked your own phone anymore, now that . . . I mean, Destiny, your life is so different now."

"But I'm the same person."

Looking into her eyes, he somehow found that incredibly easy to believe.

"But what about . . ." He had to ask. "Brody Ballard? Are you and he . . . ?"

"Are you kidding? No. He's just a friend, Seth. And you have to believe that, because—"

"I do believe it, because I know you wouldn't lie to me," he said simply.

"No. Never."

A moment of silence passed and suddenly Seth just couldn't help himself. With a little groan he took a step closer and pulled Destiny into his embrace, kissing her hard. To his delight she melted against him, and her breathy sigh made his heart pound harder.

She tasted warm and sweet and when she wrapped her arms around his neck, Seth threaded his fingers through her thick hair and kissed her like there was no tomorrow. When he finally pulled back, he rested his forehead against hers and chuckled weakly.

"Now, that's more like it," Destiny said in Seth's ear.

"You got that right," he replied and hugged her even harder. "What was I thinkin'?"

She shook her head. "We're both to blame, Seth."

"And we've got a lot of lost time to make up for." He dipped his head and captured her mouth with his, then jumped as a car drove by and honked the horn. He looked up to see his elderly neighbor, Mr. Babcock, grinning and waving behind the wheel.

"Oops," he said. "I guess we're giving the neighbors something to talk about."

Destiny laughed with him. "Hey, this is Wilmot. They need something to talk about."

Seth raised his head and kissed her lightly on the tip of her nose. "True enough. But I'd better get you inside or we'll really be the talk of the town."

"Why's that?"

Seth gave her a slow grin and then reached down to pick up her hat. "Because kissing isn't all I feel like do-

ing," he admitted, then took her hand and gave it a playful tug.

Destiny tipped her head back and laughed, and her
hat fell to the ground. But her laughter trailed off when
Seth looked into her eyes . . . and he simply had to kiss
her yet again. Her eyes widened slightly and then fluttered shut.

At last, he pulled back, picked up her hat, and plopped
it back on her head.

"Follow me," he said, and led her to his house at last.

"Oh, Seth, I love this porch!" Destiny exclaimed as
they ascended the concrete steps. "And there's the
swing! I need to try it out!"

She let go of his hand and hurried over to plop down
on the cushioned seat. Swinging back and forth, she
smiled at him with such sincerity that it went straight to
Seth's heart.

He hoped that no matter how successful she became,
she would remember to enjoy the simple things in life
like a front porch swing.

"What?" Destiny asked and tipped her head to the
side.

"Nothing."

"Oh no you don't. Say what's on your mind," she requested softly.

"I was just thinking that you're a sight for sore eyes,"
he said in a lighter tone. "Come on, let me give you the
fifty-cent tour."

"Oh!" Destiny stood in Seth's foyer and put her
hands to her cheeks. To her left was a warm, inviting liv-

ing room that had a lovely fireplace as the focal point. A picture window overlooked the porch and the hardwood floors appeared recently polished. "Seth, I *love* it!"

"Thanks," he answered with a pleased smile. "It's a work in progress, but it keeps me occupied weekends and evenings."

"A labor of love, I'm sure," she answered and realized she had said the word *love* emphatically twice in the last minute—but not the way she wanted to.

"I mean, I can tell that you've put some hard work into the house already," she told Seth as she looked around, trying hard not to imagine him living in this house with someone else.

She was leaving tomorrow, and going on the road for months. What if some pretty little schoolteacher swept Seth off his feet and he forgot all about her?

"I've always wanted to live in an old house," she told him brightly, "because they have so much more character than a new home and we moved around so much. . . . When I'm in this house, it's fun to imagine how many memories were created over the years."

She was talking too much, too fast, but she couldn't seem to shut off the flow of words or emotion. Suddenly, all she wanted in the whole wide world was to be here with Seth, night after night, creating their own memories.

"I agree," Seth replied and the huskiness in his tone told Destiny that he was feeling much the same way.

"Wow, this is pretty." Directly in front of her was a steep staircase with a beautifully carved banister leading to the second story. "Guess you know what I want to do?" she asked with a grin.

"Probably the same thing I want to do, but I thought the bedroom would be the last stop on the tour."

"Seth!" She swatted his arm and shook her head. "That's not what I meant. I was talking about sliding down the banister."

Seth laughed. "I don't know . . . I just waxed it, so that might not be a great idea."

"That would make it even better!" She put one foot up on the stairs, but Seth reached out and took her hand.

"Come on. Before you risk your neck, at least let me show you the rest of the house."

He led her through the living room and into the connecting dining room. She could imagine lovely Thanksgiving and Christmas dinners served here in grand style.

"I had to peel away layers of wallpaper and then do some patching, but it's coming along."

"The built-in corner cabinets are fabulous." She squeezed his hand. "You have a real diamond in the rough here."

"I'm having fun with it," Seth admitted as they entered the kitchen. "This is really old-school," he commented with a wave of his hand. "I don't think this room has been touched since the 1950s. I've got my work cut out for me here."

"Well, obviously you can do what you want, but I think this is gorgeous just as it is."

"Wait, you *like* the fire-engine red cabinets?"

She nodded vigorously as she ran her hand over the shiny surface. "And the black-and-white-checkered floor."

He glanced down and then angled his head at her. "Are you joking?"

"Not at all. It's so retro. My mother always said I have an old soul." She put her hands on her hips while she looked around. "This kitchen just makes me smile. I feel right at home here," she added and then felt heat creep into her cheeks.

"Then I won't change a thing. Well, except sprucing it up a bit." Looking thoughtful, he ran his hand around the tarnished edge of the countertop.

She turned away so he couldn't see her expression, trying to sound gushy as she went on. "It would be fun shopping for retro stuff like a fifties Formica table and some old dishes and memorabilia."

"Hey," Seth said and slid his arms around her from behind, "there are so many things I wish we could be doing together, but it's not in the cards right now."

Destiny bent her head and nodded slowly.

"Come on, I'll show you the upstairs."

In silence, they returned to the front hall. This time, she wasn't even in the mood to joke about the banister.

She was about to head up the stairs when his voice stopped her in her tracks. "Destiny . . ."

She turned to see him looking serious. "What is it, Seth?"

He inhaled deeply but remained quiet for a long moment. Her heart was beating so hard she thought he must surely hear it.

Finally, he reached out, took her hat off, and hung it on the newel post, then cupped her cheeks with the palms of his hands.

"I love you," he said simply.

Her breath caught in her throat and her eyes fluttered shut when he leaned in and placed his mouth softly against hers. His lips were warm and firm and the

iss felt soft and tender, yet Destiny experienced a jolt
f heat that had her toes curling.

She threaded her fingers through his hair and kissed
im back the way she had dreamed of doing for a long
ime. Hot, wet, and deliciously sweet, the kiss went on
nd on. When she leaned against him and he wrapped
is arms around her tightly, she never wanted to let him
o, ever, ever.

Pulling back, Seth looked into her eyes and gently
ucked a wayward curl behind her ear. "I've wanted
o say that to you for a while now, but I didn't want
o interfere with your career." He placed his fingertip
eneath her chin and tilted her face up. "And I still
lon't."

"Seth . . . I love you, too." The words rushed out of
er on a tide of emotion, sweeter than any song she'd
ver sung.

He smiled tenderly. "Where do we go from here?"

"I don't know. I don't know how to handle the dis-
ance between us—and it's not going to change. Not for
long time, anyway."

He inhaled a deep breath and then blew it out. "I
robably shouldn't have even told you, if there's no
hance we can—"

Destiny silenced him with trembling fingertips.
"Knowing you love me will make my life better. Seth,
've loved you for so long, and I never dreamed you'd
e standing here telling me you feel the same way. I'll
emember this moment forever." She leaned her fore-
ead against his chest and he wrapped his arms around
er.

"But, Destiny—even without the physical distance
etween us—you have a recording contract with a ma-

jor label. You're headed for stardom and I'm a small town guy. I feel like you're living in another world."

"I am. And I need you now more than ever. Anyway you promised to keep me in line if I get too big for my britches, remember?"

"Ah, that's right. That seems like a long time ago doesn't it?"

She nodded. "We've wasted so much time . . ."

"But if we had gotten serious sooner, then maybe you wouldn't have pursued your dream. Maybe all of the pieces are falling into place now the way they were intended to all along."

"Fate?" she asked with a small smile and placed her palms against his chest.

"God's plan might be a better way of putting it."

"Seth, I wish I believed so strongly that everything will just work itself out, but this isn't going to be easy."

"Nothing worthwhile ever is." He leaned in and kissed her softly. "We knew from the start that this wasn't going to be easy, remember?"

"Yes, but the reality of it was like a being shocked with a cold splash of water. I've been up so many nights thinking about you and missing you . . ."

"Me, too. And there are going to be a lot more of those nights."

"I know." She squeezed his hands. "Seth, I know I'll be gone so doggone much and it's asking a lot. A big part of me longs to be home with you every night cooking dinner and living a simple life. But this is what I am destined to do."

"No one knows that better than I do."

She lowered her gaze and said softly, "I'll understand

ompletely if you want to find someone else to settle
own with in this house." She swallowed hard.

"Destiny, there's no one else for me. No one else be-
ongs here. Just you."

Destiny gave him a slow grin. "Good, because I was
otally lying. If you had said you wanted someone else, I
would have been banging on Grace's door crying my
eyes out."

Seth laughed and drew her into his arms. "Ah,
Destiny . . ." He lowered his head and kissed her tenderly. "This incredible journey of yours is just beginning.
And just so you know, you had me ever since you literally fell into my lap."

"I do believe there's a song just waiting to happen,"
she teased, but Seth's admission made Destiny feel
warm from the inside out.

"I can't imagine my life without you in it. Love will
just have to find a way."

"We'll *make* it happen."

"Ahh, Destiny, I won't lie. I'm going to hate it when
you're gone. But I'll tell you this . . . I will appreciate every single second we have together and count the days
until I see you again. And believe me, we won't waste
another minute. Ever."

"Ever," Destiny agreed, then looked at him with wide
eyes when a sudden thought hit her hard. "Oh my goodness."

"What is it?"

"Now I truly understand the anguish my mother must
have felt when my father left her for months on end.
Sure, Grace and I missed him, but it had to have been
torture for her. For him as well." She shook her head

hard. "And that's why *they* shouldn't waste another mo
ment either!"

"I agree." He looked at her, and she realized what h
was thinking.

She swallowed hard and had trouble getting the nex
words out. "Neither should I. I would get down on m
knees as a child and pray for Daddy's safe return. I re
member being so afraid I would never see him again—
and now . . . look at us. This estrangement is ridiculou:
isn't it?"

He nodded. "Reach out to him, Destiny. That's al
that you can do."

She squeezed her eyes shut and swallowed the ho
moisture pooling in her throat before she could speak.

"I'll call him right now. Can I borrow your phone?"

*D*riving down the highway toward home, John hear
his cell phone ring somewhere in the duffel bag besid
him on the seat. Keeping one hand on the wheel an
both eyes on the road, he fumbled for it, but was to
late.

The call had gone into voicemail.

Just as well. It wasn't going to be Sara—she neve
called him anymore when he was up at the cabin, just le
him be.

He drove on, thinking about her, wondering if sh
and the girls would forgive him.

It's about doggone time I came to my senses.

He only wished he didn't have so far to go to ge
home. What if it had been Sara trying to reach him
What if she wanted to tell him . . .

What? That the girls were in town?

Seized by impulse, John pulled off the road abruptly
d came to a stop in a gravel-spitting cloud of dust.

He dug out his cell phone and saw that the missed
ll hadn't come from Sara. He should have known.

He didn't recognize the number, but whoever it was
d left a message. He might as well dial in to listen to
now.

John was absently checking the gas gauge in the in-
ant before the message started playing, but the mo-
ent he heard her voice, he was riveted.

"Hi, Daddy, it's Destiny," she announced brightly but
ith a little catch in her voice that clutched at John's
art. "Um, I just wanted to let you know that I've popped
to town to do a radio interview and . . . well, if you get
is message, I'd like to get to visit with you before Grace
d I have to get back on the road tomorrow."

She hesitated and cleared her throat.

"Um, Daddy, I really would like to . . . see you . . ."
he paused so long that John thought she had hung up
e phone. "I miss you, Daddy," she finally said. "I know
u don't understand what I'm doing with my life, but I
pe you can find it in your heart to support me. I really
ed you to."

This time the tears in her voice were evident and it
re John apart.

She cleared her throat once more, then said in a much
rmer tone, "Oh, and by the way, if you don't make up
ith Mom, I'm personally going to kick your butt."

At her last unexpected statement, John opened his
yes and laughed up at the sky. "Oh, Destiny, you and I
re way too much alike."

*   *   *

*C*oming around the corner from the kitchen, Sa nearly crashed into John, who was just exiting the bath room, wrapped in a towel.

"Oh my goodness—" She pressed her hand again her wildly beating heart. "What are you doing home?"

"I live here."

"Yes, but . . . I thought you were up at the cabin for few days."

He shrugged. "I decided to come home and see n girls—all three of them," he added meaningfully. "Wl didn't you tell me they were coming home?"

"I didn't know it myself, and anyway, no one can g ahold of you way up in the middle of nowhere. And d you mind putting your clothes on?" She hated the shar tone coming out of her mouth, especially directed at h husband, but the sight of his bare chest did things to h libido that she didn't welcome.

"That's exactly what I'm doing. I just showered an I'm heading to *my* room to change," he replied wearil and tugged the towel tighter when it suddenly slippe low on his hips.

Sara noticed John had lost even more weight. It wa no wonder. He ran for miles every morning and some times again in the evening. They ate their meals sepa rately, but she knew he was surviving on nothing mor than cold cuts and cereal.

Guilt tugged at her already heavy heart, but sh squared her shoulders and brushed past him in the na row hallway. Her arm brushed against his damp ski He smelled shower-fresh clean, and she couldn't hel but notice the warmth of his skin beneath her fingertip

he quickly pulled away as if she'd gotten an electric
1ock.

This was, she realized with a heavy heart, a horrible
'ay to exist with the one you love. But she didn't know
hat to do to change anything other than give him the
old shoulder.

"Where are the girls?" John asked.

"Grace is taking a nap, and Destiny called from Seth's
arlier to say she'd stopped to see him."

She'd also said that they had a lot to talk about and
1at, Sara knew, was a positive sign. As positive as the
lmost giddy note she could hear in her daughter's
oice.

"I'll be there soon, Mom," she had promised. "And I
1ight bring Seth with me. He said it's been a while since
.e's seen y'all."

"When do you think she'll be home?" John asked,
ounding anxious.

"Any second now, I'd imagine. Why?"

"Because I want to talk to her." John disappeared
lown the hall, leaving Sara to stare after him in surprise.

Had John finally come to his senses?

Shaking her head, Sara slipped into the guest room,
vhere she was *sleeping single in a double bed*. The clas-
ic song started playing in her head and she sighed with
vry humor as she pulled down the fluffy comforter . . .

And screamed her ever-living head off.

Right there on the crisp white sheet was a mouse.

Sara tried to run, but her feet felt glued to the floor as
he stared at the rodent in her bed. She swore she saw it
nove, and her fight-or-flight instinct kicked in.

Opting for flight, Sara turned on her heel and ran

smack dab into John's bare chest. She prompt[
screamed again.

"Sara, what's wrong?" He grabbed her shoulders.

"Th-there's ... a ... a mouse in my bed!"

John frowned and looked over the top of her hea[
"Okay, I'll take care of it," he promised in a calm voice

"What if it bites you?"

"Trust me, it won't."

"You don't know that! It might have rabies!"

"Wow." He arched one dark eyebrow. "So you actu[
ally care? I was beginning to wonder."

Sara narrowed her eyes at him. "Of course I care [
you get bitten by a rat."

"It's only a mouse."

"Whatever!"

"Should I get my gun?"

"And shoot a hole in the mattress?"

"You can always come sleep in the other room," h[
said with a shrug.

"Really? You mean you wouldn't kick me out of *you[*
bed?"

"It's *our* bed," he pointed out, and it was her turn t[
shrug.

He looked again at the mouse. "Don't worry, I'll tak[
care of it without shooting a hole in the mattress."

"How are you going to get it out of here?"

He wiggled his fingers at her.

"Your bare hands? No, you won't, John Hart! Why d[
you always have to be so ... *manly*?"

"Hey, you're the one who screamed for me," he an[
swered with a grin that reminded her of the cocky teen[
ager she had fallen in love with.

"I didn't scream for you," she answered in the huff[

est voice she could muster. "I screamed because I was scared."

"Right ..." He drew out the word, making her want to shove him ... or maybe kiss him. "Oh and by the way, just why do *you* have to be so ... female?"

For a heart-pounding moment Sara thought John might actually lean down and kiss her.

Instead, he sighed and turned toward the bed.

"Stop!" Sara grabbed for his arm, but he marched right over to the mouse, reached right down, and snatched it up pretty as you please.

With her hand to her mouth, Sara stifled a scream. "Don't let it bite you!"

"I won't!"

When he made a show of wrestling with it like he was on the Discovery Channel, Sara's adrenaline kicked into high gear and she rushed forward, grabbing hold of the mouse's tail in an effort to save her husband from ...

"What? This mouse is rubber!" she shouted, and winged it hard at John, feeling some satisfaction when it hit him square in the middle of the forehead.

"Ouch!"

"I can't believe you would stoop to such a foolhardy stunt!"

John rubbed his forehead. "I didn't!"

"Right, and then just who did?" she demanded, and gave John a hard shove in the middle of his chest. He tumbled backward onto the mattress.

About to scold him, Sara saw his boyish grin and the mischief—and love—reflected in his gorgeous blue eyes.

She melted, her breath catching in her throat.

"Sara ... come here," John said gruffly and reached up, pulling her down onto the bed with him. He threaded his fingers through her hair and kissed her with such sweet, tender passion that Sara was helpless to resist.

"That was really brave of you to grab the mouse," he broke off to tell her.

"It was fake."

"But you didn't know that," he reminded her.

"No, I didn't ... but you did." She looked up at him with narrowed eyes.

"Of course not. I was going to save you with my bare hands!" he boasted, but couldn't keep a straight face.

"Yeah, right!" She gave his shoulder a shove but had to chuckle. "I have to admit that wrestling with it was genius. I just don't understand where it—oh! Mike must have put it there!"

"Who's—oh."

"The dog. You know that."

"I know, but for a second there, I thought—"

"What, that I had a secret boyfriend?" She shook her head. "Things might be bad between us, but not *that* bad."

"Sara." He closed his eyes and she could see a muscle jump in his jaw. "If you're planning on leaving me ... I need to know."

"Leaving you?" Her heart seemed to slide up and get lodged in her throat.

"Yes," he answered softly. The look he gave her was stark, scared, stripped of all pride. "You've been thinking about it lately. I can see it in your eyes. God help me, but I don't blame you."

Unable to deny it, because the thought had crossed her mind, she looked away.

"But, Sara, please." He paused, swallowed hard. "Don't. Please don't leave me."

The throbbing ache in her throat suddenly stopped and it felt as if her heart had slipped right back down to her chest, where it belonged. The weight of sadness that had been hanging over her like a wet cloak disappeared.

She finally got it. John's need for control and his un-yielding pride were really the shield that masked his fear.

"I'm not going anywhere, John. This is my home. Our home. The home we've always wanted. I love you. I've always loved you."

Forgiveness lifted her spirit and made her want to dance, or shout . . . sing, *something*. Anything.

As if reading her mind, John said, "I love you, Sara." He bent his head and kissed her softly, soundly, sweetly until her head was spinning once again, and looked down at her with such adoration that it took Sara's breath away.

"I'll never take you for granted again," he promised.

"You do, and I'll open up a can of whoop ass!"

Laughing in each other's arms, they kissed and rolled over—right off the bed. The lamp on the bedside table went over, too, shattering a bulb to plunge the room into darkness.

Mike came running, barking loudly, and Sara and John laughed harder and kissed—until suddenly, the overhead light flipped on.

"Mom, what's going on?" Destiny asked, framed in the doorway.

Grace came up behind her, wide-eyed. "Have y'all gone plumb crazy?"

"No, we were just—" Sara broke off and looked at John.

"Making up," he said with a firm nod, pulling her to her

feet. As they brushed themselves off, Sara knew what he was thinking and sent him a silent message that it was perfectly okay to lose control. She supposed old habits died hard because he seemed to wrestle with his emotions.

"Daddy?" Destiny asked softly, when at last he looked up at her as she stood petting Mike, who was thrilled to see her.

"Oh, Destiny . . . I'm sorry," he said gruffly.

"Me too, Daddy. Me too," Destiny said and Sara put a hand to her mouth when she saw John's shoulders moving up and down.

Colonel John Hart wasn't just crying. He was sobbing. With tears streaming down his face, he backed up and held his arms open. Destiny hurtled herself into them and they held each other, only to be joined by Sara and Grace for a group hug.

"Looks like we've got us another member of your fan club, Destiny," Grace said.

"It's about doggone time, Daddy!" Destiny commented, and gave her father's shoulder a playful nudge.

"You got that right." John had to swipe at his eyes with the heels of his hands. "You don't know how much I regret all that I've missed. I've been such a fool."

Destiny put a hand on his shoulder. "I was being just as stubborn as you. I haven't been the best of daughters over the past few years, either. But that's all in the past. We are who we are right here and now because of all we've been through, so no regrets."

"I agree," Sara chimed in. "No looking back. What's the point? We don't live in the past so why dwell on it? And, Destiny, I know you have a team of experts around you all the time—executives, managers, agents, and what have you."

"That's right."

"But we'll always be here for you. This is your rock to cling to." Sara turned one palm upward and waved her hand in an arc to encompass the family circle. "Always remember that, okay?"

Destiny's smile trembled. "I'll never forget it."

Seeing the pure joy in her daughter's eyes, Sara was reminded of something. "Where," she asked, "is Seth?"

"When we heard the commotion we weren't sure what was going on and I told Seth to stay outside until things, um, calmed down."

"You mean that boy's been outside all this time?" Sara asked as Miss Manners reared her Southern head. "Well, that will never do!"

"Mom, maybe he didn't want to intrude on our *Jerry Springer* moment."

"Grace! How could you say such a thing?" Sara held an offended hand to her chest. "*Jerry Springer* moment?"

Grace rolled her eyes. "I seem to recall overhearing you threatening to *open up a can of whoop ass*!"

John laughed. "She's got a point, Sara."

"It's just a figure of speech," she primly defended herself.

"Yeah, one that you've never used as long as I've known you. But I think it's kind of . . . *sexy*."

"Ew!" Destiny shook her head, then shouted over her shoulder, "Hey, Seth, the coast is clear. And no lamps are being thrown. You can come in now."

All eyes turned to the door as Seth entered, looking hesitant.

"Get over here," Destiny coaxed, and he crossed the room to wrap his arms around her as she rested her head contentedly on his shoulder.

Watching them, Sara said a silent prayer of thanks for another very special moment on this day of healing.

She knew there were going to be obstacles and disappointment in a journey as challenging as the one Destiny was embarking upon with Seth. Together, her family would give her strength and support to see her through, and would be prepared to catch her if she fell.

But for this is brief, shining moment . . . all was right with the world.

Moments like these, Sara thought, were what life should be made of.

EIGHTEEN

As the weatherman had promised, blue skies prevailed and the sunshine brightened the last official Sunday afternoon of the summer. Although the September breeze brought a hint of fall, the stately trees were just beginning to turn. The grass remained green and bountiful, and planters spilled over with late-summer blooms. The scent of crock-pot chili, pulled pork, and charcoal permeated the air, augmenting the sizzle of excitement buzzing beneath the surface.

As Seth headed toward the town square stage, he saw Destiny's parents in the front row of folded chairs reserved for friends and family. Sara had kept her hair a warm honey blond ever since her makeover. By the same token, John's hair was no longer military short and he was sporting a bit of a beard. Although there was still an air of command about the colonel, he had a more relaxed demeanor that suggested he was finally letting go and enjoying life.

This was to be the first time he'd ever seen Destiny perform, and having just come from her dressing room, Seth knew she was a bundle of nerves. If John felt the same way, he was hiding it very well.

After climbing the steps to the stage, Seth shook John Hart's hand and gave Sara a quick hug before sitting down.

"It's good to see you both," he said. "Excited about the show?"

Sara Hart's smile wavered, and she put her hand over her mouth. "Mrs. Hart, is everything okay?" Seth asked in alarm.

"Yeeh-ess . . ." She drew out the word in a squeaky Southern voice, dabbing at the corner of her eyes with a delicate hanky. Seth shot John Hart a worried look, but the colonel could only shake his head and sigh. "She's been doing this all day. First, when the big Welcome Home banner for Destiny was strung across Main Street . . ."

"Everyone stopped and cheered!" Sara protested with a sniff. "It was *such* a touching moment. Admit it, John."

"Okay, I admit that, but did you have to go and announce to everyone in the grocery store that Destiny was on the cover of *Women's Week Magazine*?"

"I knew the fine people of Wilmot would want to know. Seth, have you seen it yet? Destiny looks so lovely! Her hair was blowing back from her face and she has such a beaming smile!"

"I have seen it, Mrs. Hart," he said with a grin. "Seen it,

studied it—all but kissed it like an adolescent pining after a pinup.

But that was before the real thing—Destiny herself—blew into town last night, and . . .

And what happened when she got there wasn't something Seth particularly wanted to remember with her father sitting right beside him.

John's mouth twitched with amusement. "Sara hand-sold magazines to every sucker in the store, Seth."

Sara lifted her chin a notch. "I simply pointed out that a hometown girl was on the cover."

"And that her name was Destiny Hart and just happened to be your daughter and then handed them a copy," John added dryly. "Like everyone didn't already know that Destiny was your daughter . . ."

"Not *everyone* in the county knows us," Sara replied. "Grace said I'm a natural at marketing and I should go on the road with them and sell T-shirts at the merch table, I'll have you know." Sara leaned close to Seth and said, "Merch is the inside lingo for merchandise table at concerts."

"Does Destiny have merchandise?" he asked in surprise.

"No, but it's in the works. I'm really thinking about going on the road to sell it," Sara said, tossing a challenging but playful look at her husband.

"Fine, but then I'm coming with you."

Seth smiled. Whenever the two of them had popped up at his baseball games over the summer—and it had been surprisingly often—they were holding hands and beaming at each other.

"Now, there's a good answer if I ever heard one!" Sara's laughter sounded carefree and happy and she leaned over and gave John a peck on the cheek. He hoped Destiny still looked at him with adoring eyes so many years down the road.

Her parents had weathered some storms, but they seemed more solid than ever, and Seth guessed that their tough times had been the true test of undying love.

"Well, hey there!"

Seth turned to see little bitty Nessie coming down the center aisle. Sunshine glinted off of her bright pink sequined shirt and she hurried along, covering the uneven surface in platform heels without batting one of her false eyelashes.

"Did you save me a seat, hot stuff?" Nessie asked.

"Sure did," Seth replied and pointed to the chair right next to his.

"Well, hey there!" Nessie greeted Sara and John. "Is this excitin' or what?"

"Incredibly so!" Sara replied and then once more had to brush at a tear.

"Oh . . . *you*! Come on over here," she said to Sara and then gave her a big hug. "Congratulations! You must be proud as a peacock of both your girls!"

"We are," Sara admitted and then waved at Cooper and Annie, who were heading their way. "Oh, I'm so glad you two could make it!"

"Wouldn't miss it for the world!" Cooper said.

"The crowd is huge," Annie told them. "We had a hard time getting past the traffic and ended up having to park way down the street. There are people jammed beyond the square."

"Well, y'all best have a seat," Sara said and rubbed her hands together. "The show is about to begin!"

As if on cue, Rex Miller strode out onto the stage, grabbed the microphone, and waved to the cheering crowd. "Good afternoon, Wilmot, Kentucky! Welcome to this very special event. Trust me, you won't want to miss one minute of this concert and I've just been told that there will be an announcement immediately following the show, so don't run off!"

Again?

Seth looked over at Sara, who raised her eyebrows and shrugged her slim shoulders.

Destiny was already leaving on tour—what else could the announcement possibly be about?

As the Hart Rockers entered the stage and picked up their instruments, the crowd roared, but Rex quieted them with a raised hand. "In case you don't know the story, Destiny Hart began her career right here on a warm summer evening over five years ago. On a dare, Destiny participated in—and ended up winning—our Kentucky Idol contest when she wowed the audience with a stunning a cappella performance of 'America the Beautiful.' How many of you were here that night?" Rex asked and looked out over the audience for raised hands.

Seth looked around and wasn't surprised that many hands were up in the air.

Rex nodded. "Thought so! Okay, Destiny asked me to make Cooper Sparks stand up and take a bow. Cooper? Where are you?"

Seth looked over at Cooper, who had no problem standing up, turning to the crowd, and waving.

"Destiny also said that you are to open the concert by singing 'Free Bird,'" Rex added.

Seth had to laugh when Cooper stopped in midwave and whipped around with wide eyes to look at Rex.

"Gotcha, Coop," Destiny's voice rang out from backstage, and the audience erupted in laughter.

"Don't worry. You can sit down, Cooper," Rex said with a grin. "Getting back to Kentucky Idol, in spite of that hot, muggy night I got goose bumps listening to Destiny sing," Rex admitted and patted his chest. "Little did anyone know that Destiny had been composing songs all her life and decided to head off to Nashville to pursue a career as a singer-songwriter. A brave choice, if you ask me, but then bravery runs in her family. Her father, John Hart, is a retired air force colonel. Colonel Hart, would you and your lovely wife, Sara, please stand up?"

Seth watched John grasp Sara's hand and then rise to his feet.

"And Destiny has requested that all veterans and military families also rise and remain standing!" While the crowd roared in appreciation, Rex shouted, "And now allow me to introduce the one and only Destiny Hart!"

Just as Destiny appeared, a huge American flag unrolled from the ceiling to the stage floor. The audience erupted in wild applause, and Destiny stood at the microphone waiting for it to die down.

She didn't show it, but Seth knew how nervous she was and said a prayer that she could harness the jittery energy. He alone knew what she was about to do, and that it would be musically and emotionally difficult.

When the crowd finally fell silent, Destiny began to sing: "O beautiful for spacious skies . . ."

Her eyes closed and at first her voice held just a hint of a tremble but then gained strength and rang out pure and clear. The crowd remained so quiet that in the background the flapping of the flag could be heard through the microphone.

When Destiny sang the last bars of the a cappella performance, she raised her hands to the sky, bringing the entire crowd reverently to their feet.

Sunrays glinted off the silver at her wrists as she reached out, beckoning the audience to join in.

As the last note faded, Seth wondered if there could possibly be a dry eye in the town square. Sara had tears streaming down her face, and to Seth's surprise so did John. Seth had to clear his own clogged throat, and Nessie had her face buried in his shoulder. When Annie started to sniffle, Cooper put his arm around her waist and hugged her close.

Destiny paused for a long moment, and Seth realized that she, too, was overcome with emotion.

Finally she said, "I told myself not to cry, but I knew it was bound to happen!"

Seth saw John smile at Destiny's admission and squeeze Sara's hand, whispering, "I wonder where she gets that from?"

After inhaling a deep breath, Destiny smiled and said, "Good afternoon, Wilmot, Kentucky, and thank you for the warm homecoming!" When the cheers died down she continued. "I'm going to sing some songs from my new album and cover a few of my favorite country classics! I encourage you to sit back and relax and if you want to visit some of the vendors selling food, feel free! I understand the proceeds go to the local high school band, so go ahead and dig in.... Just save me some of that pulled pork barbeque!"

Nessie gave Seth a nudge with her elbow and said, "Destiny is a natural. To heck with the doggone barbeque—the crowd is eating *her* up with a spoon!"

Seth nodded with complete agreement.

Destiny had a way of connecting with the crowd on a human level. As she started singing "Kiss Me in the Moonlight," the real magic began. With her band backing her up, energy and excitement poured over the audience. And even though Jesse Jansen still rubbed him the wrong way, Seth had to admit that the guy was a talented musician.

With each song, Seth could tell she became more at ease. She joked with her band, had the audience laughing and line dancing in front of their chairs.

"Let's slow things down now with a little classic Patsy Cline." Destiny looked over at the row of seats that held her friends and family. "Oh, and, Cooper Sparks? Feel free to grab Annie and get up here and dance."

Seth grinned, knowing full well that the one thing Cooper dreaded was dancing. He was one of those guys who didn't have a lick of rhythm and had sense enough to know it. When Cooper shook his head firmly, Destiny grinned. After all, she was the one with the microphone.

"Hey, y'all, help me encourage 'Free Bird' Cooper to get his tush up and slow dance with his friend Annie." Of course, the crowd complied and shamed Cooper into pulling a somewhat reluctant Annie onto her feet.

Cooper mouthed, "I'll get you for this," but it was Annie's flushed cheeks that captured Seth's attention. He knew that look, that feeling ...

It came rushing back at him as Destiny started singing "Crazy." After the lineup of kick-butt songs, she closed her eyes and surprised the audience with the heartfelt rendition that had so moved Seth on that long-ago night beneath the stars.

"I think I'll close out my set with another slow one and a personal favorite."

When Destiny began singing "Restless Heart," Seth was amazed at how many people knew every word. Nessie sang her little ol' heart out and so did Cooper and Annie. Sara tried, but could only press her lips together and hold John's hand while they both beamed radiant smiles up at their daughter.

Destiny turned her head and her gaze locked with Seth's, and once again, just like that night under the stars, she was singing only to him.

Ending "Restless Heart" with a crescendo, Destiny closed her eyes briefly, then bowed her head, utterly spent.

"Thank you very much," she said breathlessly, and the town square erupted in wild applause.

She looked up, shooting a tremulous smile toward the wings, where Grace was beaming with pride and rightfully so ... Destiny wouldn't have come this far this fast without her. Beside her was Max, who would be joining them on tour—as Destiny's bodyguard, of all things.

Destiny had never really thought about any kind of danger associated with being a celebrity, not that she really thought of herself in that way. But this business was so much more complicated than what she'd ever envisioned.

She still hoped Max would one day return to Nashville and take the stage by storm, but he seemed content for now, just to be in the background—as long as Grace was near.

Destiny turned her gaze to the VIP section. Her father, applauding like a crazy person, put his thumb and pinkie to his lips for a shrill whistle, then leaned in and kissed her mother's tear-streaked cheek. Nessie was clapping so hard that her platinum-blond ringlets bounced like little springs. Cooper cupped his hands like commas to his mouth and gave her a loud "*woo-hoo*," and Annie watched him with adoring eyes before waving to Destiny.

And then there was Seth, smiling warmly and giving her two thumbs-up, here to share this extraordinary night with her.

Could life get any better than this? she wondered, fighting back tears.

"Ladies and gentlemen—" Back onstage, Rex Miller had to put up both hands to silence the audience. "Before Destiny leaves the stage to continue her first-ever national concert tour, we have an exciting announcement—and a very important guest here to make it."

He turned expectantly toward the wings.

Following his gaze, Destiny spotted the one-and-only Tammy Turner, and her heart started thudding like a Murphy Quinn drum solo. A stunned hush fell over the crowd, then gave way to wild applause as Tammy took the stage.

"Well, hello there, Wilmot, Kentucky—and hello, Destiny Hart!" Tammy smiled at the standing crowd, drawing a deafening cheer, and gave Destiny a big one-handed hug.

"Tammy, what are you doing here?"

"Well, you know how much I love your voice and I cannot *wait* to have you back on the stage of my beautiful new theater in Pigeon Forge, Tennessee, when you head out on tour!"

As the applause calmed down, she gave the audience a big Tammy Turner grin. "I want y'all to know I didn't come all this way just to give my music hall a shameless plug—even if it is bringing some of the best acts in country music to the Great Smoky Mountains!"

More applause. Destiny could scarcely breathe.

"Destiny, I am proud to announce that your single, 'Restless Heart,' has gone to number one on the Billboard Charts!" she shouted. "I'm certain it will be the first of many!"

"Oh my goodness!" Destiny blinked at Tammy. "Thank you!"

She avoided looking at her friends and family so that she wouldn't burst into hysterical tears.

Spotting cameras from local news crews in addition to her own team of videographers, Destiny realized she had to make some sort of speech. She inhaled deeply, trying to gather her wits.

"As if this day could get any better!" she said in a throaty voice, and paused to gather her emotions before continuing. "I want to thank my manager, Miranda Shepherd of Grandview Entertainment. She somehow knows how to organize everything even though it makes my head spin! Thanks to CML Publishing for getting behind my songs and, of course, to Nick Novell and Sundial Records. Oh, and let's see . . ." She began naming names, frantically hoping she wouldn't forget any of the people who'd had a hand in the single.

"And, of course, thanks to the fans who listen, download, and request my songs on the radio!" Destiny shouted.

She waited for the applause to die down before she said, more quietly, "And thanks to my friends, especially Nessie and Max and Cooper and Annie, and my family for their love and support . . . Mom and Dad . . . and my sister, Grace, who is the best PA in the business . . . or at least that's what she tells me!"

She had a difficult time containing her tears, but somehow she managed. There was only one more person to thank now.

As far as Destiny could see, people were cheering, clapping, and whistling. Cell phones were raised in the air taking pictures. A warm rush of excitement washed over Destiny and for the first time it settled firmly into her brain that this was no longer a pipe dream. This was her reality.

"And Seth . . . Seth, I couldn't have done any of this without you. You're my lifeline. My rock-steady. You told me, right before the first time I ever took this stage, that I didn't have to get up here and sing. Sugar . . . you were *so* wrong about that." She laughed along with the audience.

"But you were right about a lot of other things—even fate—I'll even give you that, because somehow, we found our way back to each other against all odds."

She was facing him now; his cheeks were wet with tears and his eyes full of love.

"Seth, this is the beginning of an incredible journey. I

might not be able to be by your side every step of the way, but I really will treasure each and every moment that I am, because I'd rather have snatches of time with you than a lifetime with anyone else." She swallowed hard, and grinned through her own tears, concluding, "Now, there's a country song title if I ever heard one. Let the adventure begin!"

Also available from

Wynonna Judd

The *New York Times* bestseller

Coming Home to Myself

From the heart of one of the world's most beloved
entertainers comes an engaging memoir of professional
triumph, private heartbreak, and personal victory. From
Wynonna Judd's beginnings as part of the celebrated,
multiple-award-winning, platinum-selling duo with her
mother Naomi to an equally triumphant solo career to the
dramatic turning point that forced the country music
superstar to reevaluate her life, her priorities, and her past,
this is a memoir as dynamic as the woman herself—
a story of survival, strength, family, and forgiveness.

Available wherever books are sold or at
penguin.com